Praise for *Sweet Thing*

"Sassy and sweet, *Sweet Thing* melts in your mouth and goes straight to your heart!"

—Katy Evans, *New York Times* bestselling author of *Real*

"5 stars!!!! This is what I've been craving . . . one of my absolute favorites this year, and just one of my plain old favorites altogether."

—Maryse's Book Blog

"I have a new book boyfriend and his name is Will Ryan. I'm in love . . . *Sweet Thing* was a sweet, heartbreaking and romantic story that kept me up reading all night! . . . A fabulous debut novel . . . I'll be watching out for more from Renée Carlino!"

—Aestas Book Blog

"What more can I say that hasn't been said already about this book? *Sweet Thing* was really a great read. I loved the characters, the story, and I loved watching them grow."

—The Autumn Review

"This is 5 HUGE stars—a soul-searing, beautifully written book that now owns a piece of my heart . . . this book has made my all-time FAV list. . . . I cannot wait to see what's next for Renée Carlino."

—Shh Mom's Reading

"Surprisingly, this is Renée's debut novel because she writes like a pro with words flowing effortlessly and beautifully, totally hooking me from the beginning. There was something intangibly real and special about this book, which kept me reading until I finished it . . . one of my favorite stories of the year."

—Vilma's Book Blog

"When Will and Mia's story of self-discovery unfolds, it will fill you with love, it will crush you, it will frustrate you, it will lift you up and bring you down. You will share every heartbreaking moment and you will live every warm, tender, angry and funny exchange. . . . You will read *the end* with that warm book glow . . . you know, the one that lets you know you've just hung out with some wonderful characters who burrowed their way into your heart."

—Totally Booked Blog

"*Sweet Thing* is such a great book that you are guaranteed a book hangover after you finish it! I am currently suffering from one. This story is sure to tug on your heart strings and touch your soul. It is unique, memorable, and breathtaking! Trust me, you want *Sweet Thing* to be a part of your personal library."

—A Bookish Escape

"Sometimes—out of all the books you read—you come across one that stands out amongst all the other titles. Sometimes, you read a book that completely overwhelms your mind, your heart, and your soul. An all-consuming read that totally captures your senses and puts them into overdrive—but in the *best* possible way. There's just nothing better than the completely sated feeling you get from reading it. For me, that book was Renée Carlino's *Sweet Thing*."

—Read This—Hear That

"*Sweet Thing,* with its sweeping love story, remarkable characters, and Will Ryan, is a love story that stands out from the rest."

—The Bookish Babe

ALSO BY RENÉE CARLINO

Sweet Thing

Sweet Little Thing

Nowhere but Here

A Novel

RENÉE CARLINO

ATRIA PAPERBACK

New York • London • Toronto • Sydney • New Delhi

ATRIA PAPERBACK

A Division of Simon & Schuster, Inc.
1230 Avenue of the Americas
New York, NY 10020

First Atria Paperback edition July 2014

ATRIA PAPERBACK and colophon are trademarks of Simon & Schuster, Inc.

For information about special discounts for bulk purchases, please contact Simon & Schuster Special Sales at 1-866-506-1949 or business@simonandschuster.com.

The Simon & Schuster Speakers Bureau can bring authors to your live event. For more information or to book an event contact the Simon & Schuster Speakers Bureau at 1-866-248-3049 or visit our website at www.simonspeakers.com.

Interior design by Dana Sloan
Cover design © Zoe Norvell
Cover photograph © Eduardo Joel Sosa Perez

Manufactured in the United States of America

10 9 8 7 6 5 4 3 2 1

Library of Congress Cataloging-in-Publication Data:

Carlino, Renée.
  Nowhere but here : a novel / Renée Carlino.
      pages cm
1. Women journalists—Fiction. 2. Chicago (Ill.)—Fiction. 3. Napa Valley (Calif.)—Fiction. 4. Love stories. I. Title
  PS3603.A75255N69 2014
  813'.6—dc23   2014018758

ISBN 978-1-4767-6396-5
ISBN 978-1-4767-6397-2 (ebook)

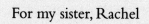

For my sister, Rachel

Game Changer

One morning in October, I woke up in my tiny Lincoln Park apartment at seven a.m., just like I always did. I got ready, ate a dry waffle, put on four layers of clothes, and walked to the L station at Fullerton and boarded the train at approximately eight fifteen, just like I always did. Nothing about that morning stood out, but it was a game-changer day—I just didn't know it yet. I walked through three train cars before I found him. I took a seat behind two of my fellow parishioners and prepared to take in the mass. This was our church every morning, and our pastor was Just Bob, or at least that's who he was to me. The first time I met him, I asked him his name and he said, "Bob." I waited for him to continue and then he said, "Just Bob," so that's what I called him.

Warning alarms of self-preservation should have gone off in my twenty-six-year-old head when a man named Just Bob began preaching on an elevated train full of innocent people seven months ago, but those warnings never occurred to me because the first time I had heard him speak, I was immediately hooked. He never brought up the Bible or religion or fire and brimstone—nothing like that. The first thing he had said that day was, "You're all you've got!"

AMEN.

He was an old, tired-looking man, probably seventy years old, at least. There were five gray hairs sprouting out of his round, bald head, and he wore the same Dockers and Pendleton every single day. His clothes were clean, or at least they looked clean, but he still had a very distinct odor. He smelled of old books, like the far-back recesses of the oldest library on earth. I imagined that he lived in a dinky apartment that was stacked ceiling-high with old hardbacks. He could barely stand, let alone walk, so it was a small miracle that he made it to that train like clockwork every day just to speak to his loyal followers. There were maybe ten of us. I didn't know the others at all—we kept to ourselves—but the faces had become easily recognizable to me over the last seven months.

Chicago has its share of totally insane people who like to get on the L and speak loudly to no one in particular. I've ridden that train my whole life, but Just Bob was different. He had a message to deliver, a message that I needed to hear. Every day was a different topic. Sometimes he would channel Suze Orman and talk personal finance; other days he would talk about pesticides and preservatives in food and how he thought they were making everyone taller. That day, I'm pretty sure he was channeling Gandhi with a thick Chicago accent. He was talking about being the change you want to see. He said, "Visualize to realize, that is what I'm telling you today, good folks. You must see it before it happens. You must be your own oracle. Visualize to realize the dream!"

As we approached my stop, I stood up and headed toward the door. Just Bob often sat at the front near the exit while he gave his sermon. As I passed, he stood on shaky legs and put his hand on my shoulder. This was very unusual. "Kate," he said—I didn't even know he knew my name—"It's a game-changer day for you. Visualize to realize it." And then, like he always said at the end of his speeches, "And remember . . ." Just Bob arched his eyebrows, waiting for me to finish the line.

"I'm all I've got," I said.

"Exactly."

It was kind of creepy, in retrospect, but it was exactly what I needed at the time. He let go of my shoulder, and I exited the train at State Street into the icy cold Chicago wind, with the weirdest feeling that my life would never be the same.

It's not like a little change would hurt. After my first chance meeting with Just Bob, I began searching for him every morning on the Brown Line, even though that route made me late for work. It started exactly one week after Rose died, when I first felt truly and completely alone. Rose was my mother's childhood friend and had raised me after my mom passed away from breast cancer when I was eight. My mother had me at the age of forty, after spending most of her life thinking it was impossible to become pregnant—until she met my father. Too bad he didn't stick around. I never even met him.

My mother was a wonderful person. She thought of me as a miracle, so she doted on me and tried to give me everything I needed. At the same time, she taught me to be an independent thinker. She was the type of person who always looked put-together until she got sick, yet I remember her telling me, *You're a beautiful girl, Kate, but don't ever rely on your looks.* She would tap her index finger on my temple and say, *It's what you do with this that matters.*

I remember she was affectionate but tough, like she was preparing me for the challenges of life. I always had the sense that she wouldn't be around for very long, and she wasn't, but at least I had Rose . . . until I didn't. She died from an infection after having textbook surgery to remove a gallstone. I didn't understand what kind of God would take away every person who cared about me. Then I realized, *There's no one to take care of me, no matter how many people surround me. I'm all I've got.* Those words became my mantra.

I chanted those words as I entered the lobby of the *Chicago Crier*, a well-known Chicago newspaper and blog, and my workplace for the last five years. I had been writing articles for the special interest section on topics like the dangers of trans fats, yoga vs. Pilates, the merits of red lipstick, and where to find inexpensive, quality wine. I was never given a serious assignment. Jerry, the editor, loved me, but from the time of Rose's death I had been producing subpar articles with zero enthusiasm. I had no expectation of moving up at the paper because my energy for life had withered, and frankly, I didn't deserve it. But somehow, when I walked through the doors that day, I had a new vision. I couldn't quite put my finger on it, but it was an image of me at a computer, writing with fervor and passion—something I hadn't done in eight long months.

When I reached my floor, I found Beth standing near my cubicle. She was a tall, mousy-haired, intimidating-looking woman, but she had a huge heart and a true talent for writing. She dressed like a teenage boy in basketball shorts, T-shirts, and sneakers every freakin' day, but it didn't matter because she was the head writer at the paper and damn well deserved it. She got all of the biggest assignments because she put her heart and soul into every single word she wrote. I admired her.

"Hey, kid."

"Hi Beth, how was your weekend?"

"Great. I knocked out ten thousand words."

Of course she did. Why couldn't I be more like that?

"What's this?" I pointed toward a stack of papers on my desk. The cover sheet was blank except for the bold words: R. J. LAWSON.

"Jerry is giving you that story," she said. I had no idea what it meant at first, but then I remembered hearing Jerry rant about R. J. Lawson. Jerry was obsessed with getting a story on him. I personally didn't know anything about him.

"Me? Why in the world would he give this to me?"

Beth just smiled her knowing smile. "I don't know, but he's gonna be over in a sec to talk to you about it. Boy, I wanted that story, Kate. No one has been able to get an interview with him since he disappeared from public life. I'm glad you got it, though—you need it."

I stared at her for several moments and then I mumbled, "Yeah, I know . . . might be a game changer."

Smiling, she said, "You got it, sister." Then she did a jump shot with a balled-up piece of paper, lofting it perfectly into the wastebasket behind me. "Swoosh, nothin' but net."

When she turned and walked away, I stared down at the neatly stacked papers and laughed to myself, thinking Jerry had truly lost his mind giving me a real assignment. I looked up to find him peering over the partition.

"You like? It's an exclusive," he said, arching his eyebrows.

"Why me?"

"Kate, what do you know about that guy?"

"Nothing except that you've been hounding his people for a story, and I can tell you that Beth would have easily sacrificed a limb for this assignment."

He nodded slowly and then looked up at the ceiling as if he was thinking. The large warehouse-like room was separated by about a hundred cubicle partitions. The huge space rattled and hummed with the sound of writers chatting and typing frantically at their computers. Jerry pumped different kinds of music through the overhead speakers, creating a cocoon of creativity, but I hadn't felt creative in a long time, and it was nobody's fault but my own. At that moment, a sad version of the song "Heartbeats" by José González was traveling through the airwaves. I watched Jerry as he continued to look up pensively.

He was forty years old and he looked exactly like Richard Dreyfuss circa *Close Encounters*. He wore his bifocals on the very last millimeter of his nose, which aged him, but he thought it gave him a look of credibility. He was in love with his wife and kids, a true family man, but he had no filter at all, so it didn't surprise me one bit when he finally looked back down and said, "You're a good writer, Kate. You have what it takes, and you have a nice ass, too."

"Jerry! What does that have to do with anything? I don't want you to give me a huge assignment because I have a nice ass."

"Yeah, yeah, that's not what I meant. I said you have what it takes. R.J. is a thirty-year-old bachelor. Looking the way you do can't hurt."

"Well gee, thank you," I said sarcastically.

"You don't want it?" He reached for the stack.

"No. I want it. I just can't believe . . ."

"It was a compliment, Kate."

"Okay, fine." He didn't mean any harm by it. Like I said, no filter. He was the most loyal man in the world, and he wasn't trying to objectify me. I think he thought that with R.J.'s history of turning down interviews—the only thing I did know about him, based on what Beth had told me—Beth's aggressive approach to getting a story wouldn't be a good fit.

"Fine?"

"I would love this opportunity, Jerry, thank you. Honestly though, I'm curious. Why in the world did he agree to give us an interview—and an exclusive one, at that? We're not exactly a nationally recognized newspaper."

"I just bugged the hell out of him," he said triumphantly. "I kept on sending requests until he finally replied. He said he was impressed by my persistence, and he felt our paper had more integrity than others. He most likely checked us out. He seems eager to spread the word about the winery's sustainability and their environmentally friendly practices, which sound pretty cutting-edge. The only thing is that his e-mail stressed how extremely private he is and how he would prefer the article to focus on the wine, not his personal life. But, Kate, a story like this could really launch the *Crier* into a whole new league, especially if you can get the dirt our readers want. That means finding out everything there is to know about R. J. Lawson."

I swiveled my chair out from my desk, crossed my legs, and leaned back. I was intrigued. "Tell me what you know about him."

"Hold on to your seat, this guy is truly a conundrum. In 1998, Ryan Lawson was a young MIT graduate, computer engineering prodigy, and cofounder of the largest technology company in Silicon Valley. He had the potential to be Steve Jobs and Steve Wozniak rolled into one—a savvy business mind and a technological genius."

"Wow."

"Yeah, he invented some computer server that's used in almost all government agencies, banks, and large corporations. It's impossible to hack."

"So you expect me to interview a tech mogul when I've been writing articles on lipstick and wine?"

"That's the thing, Kate. In 1999, he sold his share of J-Com technologies and fell off the radar. No one knew where he went or what he was doing with his three billion dollars. Rumors surfaced that he took the money to Africa and was building schools all across the continent with his own hands, but that was never confirmed."

"So how did you know where to find him . . . and what is he doing now?"

"I started hearing about him three years ago when it was leaked to a California newspaper that he had purchased a nine-hundred-acre ailing winery and outdated bed-and-breakfast in Napa Valley. He managed to keep things quiet until this year, when his wine started winning every award known to man."

The pieces were coming together slowly. "R. J. Lawson," I said. "Yes, that Pinot is fantastic!"

"Right? It's like everything this guy touches turns to gold."

"Why in the world would Beth want to interview a winemaker?"

"Because he's refused to grant interviews and hasn't been photographed in more than a decade. Imagine if Bill Gates or Steve Jobs had disappeared at the peak of their powers. It's a huge story."

"I still can't believe you're giving this to me."

"Well, I'm not gonna lie, Kate. You've been producing crap lately. Did I hear that you submitted a proposal to write a feature article on the myth that fruit gum gives you fresh breath?"

"It's true, though. Fruity gum does not give you fresh breath.

It gives you disgusting breath, and people need to know. Come on, that's what special interest is."

"Key word being *interest*. Our readers don't care about the worthlessness of fruity gum. They want interesting stories— stories that will make them feel. Even if you're writing a story about wine, you need to touch readers' hearts. There has to be an element of humanity in every piece you write."

"No, I know what you're saying. I just haven't been motivated since . . . Rose died."

He looked sympathetic for a millisecond. I got the feeling that excuse was wearing thin. "You'd have to leave for California tomorrow. He's agreed to do the interview in two parts. Tuesday and Thursday are the only days he has available, so you'll stay at the B&B there. It will be peaceful, and you can probably knock out half the article while you're there. Go home and talk to your boyfriend about it and let me know."

He won't care. He couldn't give a shit.

"I'm in, Jerry. I don't need to talk to Stephen about it. How long will I be out there?"

He paused with that profound look in his eyes again, and then in a low voice he said, "You've lost your spark, Kate. Don't come home until you find it. Bring back a great story."

Lonely but Not Alone

My boyfriend Stephen and I lived in the same apartment building. We met on a Monday two years ago in the basement laundry room and had done our laundry together every week since. I could barely call Stephen my boyfriend because, aside from our weekly laundry sessions and the occasional Friday night dinner, we rarely saw each other. He was a workaholic and moving his way up the ladder at a prestigious marketing firm. He called his firm a creative agency, but really, they were a moneymaking agency. He spent way too much time dreaming up ways to convince clients to sell out and change the look of their products so everyone could make more money. He was dedicated and had drive, but his work schedule left little time for a girlfriend. We had more sex in that basement laundry room bent over a washer than in an actual bed.

That day, I left the *Chicago Crier* early to begin packing for my trip. Stephen met me in the basement at six, our usual time. We would switch off picking up dinner for each other—that week he picked up Thai food.

"Hey, how was your day?" I said as I leaned in to kiss him.

11

Stephen was only a few inches taller than me, around five foot eight, but he had a much larger presence because of his confidence, which some people perceived as arrogance.

"Hi sweetie. My day was busy, and everybody is slamming their heads against the wall over the Copley account. I actually have to take a conference call in a few minutes," he said as he handed me a food container. "Yellow curry, right?"

"Uh-huh." He never asked me how my day went. I opened the lid and then immediately closed it. "Is this chicken?"

"Yeah, that's what you like." It wasn't a question.

"I'm a vegetarian, Stephen. I have been for ten years."

"Yeah, but I thought you ate chicken."

"Normally people don't call themselves vegetarians if they eat chicken."

"God, I'm sorry. I could have sworn I've seen you eat yellow curry before."

"With tofu."

"Well, I would offer you mine, but it has chicken in it, too," he said as he pulled his buzzing phone from his pocket.

"I'll just eat the rice."

He held his finger to his mouth to quiet me before answering his phone. "Stephen Brooks. Yeah, I'll take it. Hey, what's up, man? Oh, you're kidding, right? Two million. That's what I told her."

As Stephen continued his conversation, I wiped out the rice and began sorting the laundry. When I bent over, he moved behind me and pushed himself against me. I turned around to find him smirking.

I mouthed, *You're so dirty*.

You're so hot, he mouthed back.

Stephen was attractive in a clean-cut businessman kind of

way. He was always clean-shaven. He had a dark receding hair-line and dark brown eyes that looked almost black, and he wore only a suit or his gym clothes. He never dressed casually. I had on ripped jeans and a University of Illinois sweatshirt. We were mismatched in many ways, and although there was physical chemistry, I never felt like our relationship could grow beyond what it was. He had never introduced me to his family. On holidays he would go to his parents in the suburbs and I would go to Rose's. We rarely spent time in each other's apartments. After Rose died, I isolated myself even more, believing that I had to learn to be alone, so I never pushed things with Stephen. He never pushed for more, either. I stayed with Stephen because it was comfortable. I stayed with Stephen because he was nice and I thought he was all I had, but after two years, he was still bringing me yellow curry with chicken.

I jumped up to sit on the washer. When Stephen ended his call, he walked toward me but didn't put his phone away; his head was down, staring at the screen. I parted my legs so he could stand closer. Without looking up, he raised a finger and said, "Hold on, I just have to shoot this text off." It was amazing how lonely I could feel when I wasn't alone. Sometimes when I was with Stephen, I felt even worse about my situation. I really had resigned myself to the fact that our relationship was mainly physical. It was just a release for both of us. Stephen had never read a single article I'd written. His excuse was that he liked to read business journals and sports articles. He wouldn't even humor me.

"I'm going to California tomorrow for a story. It's a huge one that Jerry has been trying to land for months." He nodded, still staring at his phone. "Did you hear me? I'm going out of town tomorrow."

He looked up and then leaned in and planted a chaste kiss on my lips. "Have a safe trip. I gotta take this call, Kate. I'm sorry. Will you bring my stuff up when it's done? This is a really important call, a million-dollar account." He kissed me again. I nodded then forced a smile. "Thanks, sweetie," he said as he turned and headed for the basement door, taking his food with him.

Like I said, he wouldn't give a shit.

That night when I went to Stephen's apartment to drop off his clothes, he answered the door still wearing his suit. He had ditched the tie and rolled up his shirtsleeves, but the phone was still attached to his ear.

He mouthed, *Thank you. I'll text you.*

I handed over the basket full of his clothes and said, "You're welcome" very quietly.

He liked to text me. He thought it was sexy to send dirty messages back and forth, but the less we connected in real life, the more meaningless those texts became.

Sure enough, two hours later, while I was lying in bed, I got a text from him.

Stephen: U looked amazing 2night

I would have normally come back with something like *You weren't so bad yourself,* because at least Stephen was trying, and I felt like he meant well, but that night something became very clear to me. I began to visualize a relationship where I felt cherished. I couldn't make out the face of the person who would be that for me, but somehow I knew it wasn't Stephen.

I didn't respond to him for several minutes. Instead, I got on Google and typed in R. J. Lawson. I scoured endlessly boring articles about his early successes and the contributions his inventions had made toward technological advancements in communications and security. There was little, if anything at all, about his personal life. One article showcased a server prototype he had revealed at a science expo, with a picture of him standing next to the machine. He couldn't have been more than twelve years old, prepubescent with a mouth full of braces. I searched over and over for additional images, but every time his name was linked to an image, it was either of a computer gadget, the winery, or the logo for a charity organization he had formed. I would go into the interview knowing a lot about R. J. Lawson's accomplishments and philanthropic work but very little about the man.

Checking the time, I figured I had given Stephen enough of the silent treatment.

> *Kate:* If I looked so amazing 2night then y aren't u in my bed right now??
>
> *Stephen:* Early morning meeting. Have a safe trip. See you when you get back.

I didn't respond. I just fell asleep thinking, *I'm all I've got.*

Journalistic "License"

The next day I flew into San Francisco International Airport at two p.m. My first interview with R. J. Lawson was scheduled for five p.m., and I still had to get out of the city, over the heavily trafficked Golden Gate Bridge, and up to Napa Valley. I hoped that taxis were readily available once I got outside because I wouldn't have much time to dillydally. I didn't eat the plane food, so I was starving and starting to get a headache.

As I waited at the baggage carousel, I pulled out my travel itinerary from the coordinator at the *Chicago Crier*. Under the flight details it showed a reservation number for Avis Car Rental. I immediately dialed Jerry.

"Why is there a rental car reservation on my itinerary?"

"Well, hello to you, too. We got you a rental car because Napa is spread out. I thought you would want to go exploring while you're there. Plus . . . cab fare just one way would have been more money."

"I barely know how to drive, Jerry!"

"We have a driver's license on file for you."

"Yeah, I got my driver's license after my high school boy-

17

friend taught me how to drive in a mall parking lot. I haven't driven since."

"You press the gas to go, the brake to stop, and you steer with that giant wheel sitting in front of you. How hard could it be?"

"Fine, I just hope you have a big insurance policy. This is going to be a nightmare." I hung up and reached for my suitcase, which of course was the last one to appear on the conveyer belt.

At Avis, a young female clerk showed me to the car. "I need to do a quick visual inspection to mark any existing damage. I'll be real quick."

"Knock yourself out." I threw my bags in the trunk and then got into the driver's seat. It was a small Toyota sedan, nothing fancy, but it looked very new. I felt for the ignition and then realized the clerk hadn't given me the key yet.

She skipped around the car and then stood outside my door. Bending down to look at me through the window, she smiled really cute and said, "No damage, you're all set, but I think you might need this."

She held up a little black square. I opened the door. "What is that?"

"It's your key."

"How is that a key?"

She put her hand on her hip and cocked her head to the side. "You've never seen push-button ignition before?"

"No." *I'm so in for it.* Evidently cars had changed in the last ten years.

The clerk gave me a quick tutorial after I told her I hadn't driven in a very long time. I think she felt sorry for me.

"It's just like riding a bike, okay?"

"Yes, thank you, that is very good advice."

I typed the winery address into the GPS and then proceeded

to pull out of the rental company driveway. I screeched and slammed on the brakes every four feet until I got out onto the street. There was going to be a learning curve. The GPS lady successfully got me over the Golden Gate, but I didn't get to enjoy one minute of it. Paranoid that I was going to hit a pedestrian or a cyclist or launch myself off the massive bridge, I couldn't take my eyes off of the car in front of me. Once I was out of the city, I spotted a Wendy's and pulled off the highway. GPS lady started getting frantic.

"Recalculating. Head North on DuPont for 1.3 miles."

I did a quick U-turn to get to the other side of the freeway and into the loving arms of a chocolate frosty.

"Recalculating." *Shit. Shut up, lady.* I was frantically hitting buttons until I was able to finally silence her. I made a right turn and then another turn immediately into the Wendy's parking lot and into the drive-thru line. I glanced at the clock. It was three forty. I still had time. I pulled up to the speaker and shouted, "I'll take a regular French fry and a large chocolate frosty."

Just then, I heard a very loud, abbreviated siren sound. *Whoop.*

I looked into my rearview mirror and spotted the source. It was a police officer on a motorcycle. *What's he doing?* I sat there waiting for the Wendy's speaker to confirm my order, and then again, *Whoop.*

"Ma'am, please pull out of the drive-thru and off to the side." *What's going on?*

I quickly rolled the window all the way down, stuck my head out, and peered around until the policeman was in my view. "Are you talking to me?"

To my absolute horror, he used the speaker again. "Yes, ma'am, I am talking to you. Please pull out of the drive-thru." *Holy shit, I'm being pulled over in a Wendy's drive-thru.*

"Excuse me, Wendy's people? You need to scratch that last order."

A few seconds went by and then a young man's voice came over the speaker. "Yeah, we figured that," he said before bursting into laughter and cutting the speaker off.

The policeman was very friendly and seemed to find a little humor in the situation as well. Apparently I had made an illegal right turn at a red light just before I pulled into the parking lot. After completely and utterly humiliating me, he let me off with a warning, which was nice, but I still didn't have a frosty.

Pulling my old Chicago Cubs cap from my bag, I decided that nothing was going to get in the way of my beloved frosty. Going incognito, I made my way through the door. Apparently the cap was not enough because the Justin Timberlake–looking fellow behind the counter could not contain himself.

"Hi," I said.

"Hi, what can I get you?" he said, and then he clapped his hand over his mouth, struggling to hold back a huge amount of laughter and making gagging noises in the back of his throat in the process.

"Can I get an extra-large chocolate frosty please, and make it snappy."

"Do you still want the fries with that?" There was more laughter and then I heard laughter from the back as well.

"No, thank you." I paid, grabbed my cup, and hightailed it out of there.

Napa was beautiful in October. The sun was setting, the last long rays piercing through the large eucalyptus trees that lined the road to the winery. I pulled off and took a couple of photos and removed a few layers of clothes. At that point I was wearing very wrinkled black slacks and a blazer, unsuccessfully trying to pull off the sophisticated journalist look. It was warm in Napa compared to Chicago that time of year. I knew I was only a few minutes away, so I took some time to go over my interview questions and then I hopped in the car and drove toward the R. J. Lawson property.

GPS lady notified me that I was approaching my destination. When I got to a point where I needed to turn left into the winery, I stopped and waited for a car that was coming from the opposite direction to pass. That car passed, and then another popped up in the distance, and then another. Finally, I had to take my chances and turn quickly. I did just that, overcorrecting and running the car smack into a truck pulling out of the winery driveway. The airbag deployed rather rudely in my face at the very same moment that I heard crunching metal and felt the force of the collision. I started frantically pushing away the deflating airbag when I spotted a figure outside of the passenger window.

"Are you okay?!" he shouted.

I nodded and a few seconds later he opened my door for me.

I got out quickly and ran to the front of the car, then I looked over at the truck I had hit head-on. It was an old, classic Ford pickup. It didn't appear to have a scratch on it, yet the front of my rental car was completely smashed. What a day I was having. At that moment I wanted to call Jerry and tell him that the only way I was going to find my "spark" was if I lit myself on fire.

"Is that your truck?" I said, pointing. I was still shaken and confused.

I looked over at the guy. He began slowly walking toward me. He was tall with longish, sun-bleached hair. His deep green eyes looked concerned. I noticed that he was wearing a black T-shirt with the R. J. Lawson logo on it.

"Are you sure you're okay? You look like you might be in shock," he said. I started to sway. He braced me by putting his hands on the outside of my shoulders.

"Do you work here?"

"Yeah, I'm Jamie." He had a scruffy but defined jawline, and although he was thin, there was something ruggedly strong about him. He had on dark Levi's and black work boots. The skin on his face was completely flawless. He had darker skin than the typical Chicago white boy I was used to. He evidently spent a lot of time outside. When I looked at his hands, I could tell he used them for work. They looked strong and callused.

"I need to get your information, Jamie."

His pretty mouth turned up into a lazy smile. "I believe you hit me, so I'll need *your* information." God, he was handsome, and my embarrassment level was increasing by the second.

"Fine." I stood by the door and pulled a piece of scratch paper from my purse. I quickly scribbled out the information and reached behind me to where Jamie was standing. He took the paper from my hand. I didn't turn around but I heard a light chuckle from him.

I became even more peeved after realizing my car wasn't drivable and it was only five minutes until interview time. *Damn this world.* When I finally turned back toward Jamie, he was flashing a stupid, smug grin.

"What?" I said to him with as pointed a look as I could muster.

"You're Jerry Evans?"

"Yeah, so what."

"Well, when we spoke on the phone this morning your voice was quite a bit deeper."

"That's all the information you need, although it doesn't

look to me like your truck will need any repairs. I'm sorry I hit you, okay? I just don't drive very much and I'm running very, very late for my interview with R. J. Lawson."

"Oh, you're the reporter?"

"I'm the journalist, yes."

"Well, you better march your little tail up there. R.J. gets really pissy when people are late."

I huffed and then began pulling my suitcase out of the trunk. Jamie stayed firmly planted where he was, still wearing a silly grin.

"Hey, Jerry, do you want a ride? I don't think this car is going to get you too far." I leaned around his truck to take in the view of the very long treelined driveway up to the winery buildings. It was a twenty-minute walk at least.

"My name is Kate . . ." I fumbled for words and then in a shaky voice said, "and . . . yes."

"Yes to what, Katy?" He cocked his head to the side and arched his eyebrows. "You want me to give you a ride up the driveway? Is that how you ask nicely?"

"Again, my name is Kate, not Katy, and yes please, if you would be so kind to give me a ride, I would greatly appreciate it."

He paused, looked me up and down, and then looked up to the sky and began scratching his chin like he was making the decision of a lifetime.

"Hmm . . . okay, Katy, I think I will. Actually, it would be my pleasure to give you a ride up the driveway, even though you almost killed me today." I finally gave in and had to laugh at the situation.

Jamie managed to move my rental car off the road. I watched his arms flexing as he pushed. His right arm was completely covered in tribal tattoos. Not the typical kind you find on the walls of a tattoo parlor, but unique, almost jagged-looking, and some were a red-orange color. He was very attractive and seemed strong and capable. I wondered what he did at the winery, but my thoughts were interrupted. When I reached his truck to get in, I noticed a chocolate Lab sitting perfectly upright in the passenger seat, wearing a seat belt.

"That's Chelsea. You're gonna have to get in over here and sit in the middle 'cause that's her spot."

I walked around to the driver's side and smiled at him before hopping in. "She wears a seat belt?" I said, laughing.

"Yes, and it's a good thing she does, otherwise she would have gone flying right through that window when you slammed your car into us."

"I said I'm sorry." I sounded a bit whiny.

He got into the driver's seat, started the truck, and patted my leg. "I'm just teasing you."

I couldn't remember the last time someone touched my leg like that. Normally, that would have made me feel extremely uncomfortable. I was already sitting against him, a complete stranger whom I had just hit with my car, but there was something about his demeanor that made me feel at ease, aside from the fact that he smelled strongly of alcohol. There was an overwhelmingly potent scent of wine in the air. "Have you been drinking?"

He reached down and lifted his shirt to sniff it.

"Curious Katy, the reporter who's first on all the breaking news." He paused and shot me a self-satisfied smirk. "I work at a winery, cutie. I was cleaning the barrels today." He pointed his thumb out the back window of the truck. I turned and spotted three wooden wine barrels strapped into the bed of the truck.

I shook my head and rolled my eyes at myself. *Really, could I embarrass myself any more today*? I hadn't even met R. J. Lawson yet, but I was ready to throw in the towel.

"Where were you headed when I hit you?"

"Just a quick run into town for supplies."

"I thought people in California were more environmentally conscious. Aren't these old trucks gas hogs and horrible polluters?"

Looking straight out the window, he smiled. "I converted the engine. It runs on biofuel."

"What's that?"

"Donut grease. Zero pollution, and I get the fuel for free from the local bakery."

"You're kidding?"

He just shook his head.

Chelsea was staring out the front window. When I turned to look at her, she turned as well and looked me directly in the eye. "Hey," I said. I fully expected her to respond, but instead she nonchalantly looked away and continued gazing out the window.

"She's like a person."

"Yep, she's my girl."

I smiled at him and then he pinched my thigh.

"Hey!"

"Hey, yourself. We made it. I'll drop you here." He pointed out the window to a building. "There's R.J.'s office. Don't be too nervous, the guy's a douche to everyone."

I laughed. "Thanks." He helped me out of the truck and pulled my suitcase from the back. When I reached for it, he held on to the handle. My hand landed over his, but instead of pulling it away, for some reason I held it there. I ran my fingers over his callused knuckles and then I looked up at him. He was looking right at me, squinting slightly, like he was trying to read my expression. He moved closer and then leaned in farther, wearing a small, sincere smile. When he closed the gap between us, I could feel the heat radiating from both our bodies as he bent down toward my face. I thought he has going to kiss me—and then he did, just like that, though it was just a small peck on the cheek. His fingertips rested on my other cheek. His lips lingered there for a few seconds and then I heard him inhale deeply. He pulled away a few inches and then smiled. His eyes looked roused with curiosity and something else. Desire, maybe. "I told you, don't be nervous. It'll be okay." His voice was smooth.

I was completely frozen. I couldn't have pulled away if I wanted to. My hands were tingling. I was trembling while we stood there, staring at each other for several moments. I cleared my throat and then, just above a whisper, said, "I'm so sorry for hitting you."

He shook his head back and forth slowly, never taking his eyes off mine. "Don't worry about it. How long are you gonna be here for?"

"Oh." My heart started thumping like it was going to give out. *Is he going to ask me out? Holy crap.* "Um . . . I'll be here until Friday at least, but . . . I have a boyfriend."

"I was going to offer to show you around the winery in case R.J. doesn't have the time."

"Oh." *Yet another embarrassing moment to add to my apocalyptic day.* "Well, then yes, that would be great."

He smiled all the way to his eyes, "Okay, Katy the Reporter with a Boyfriend. I'll see you around." He turned to walk toward his truck.

"It's Kate, and I'm a journalist."

When he pulled away, he leaned out the window and waved.

"Good luck, beautiful girl. You'll do great." My knees buckled. I braced myself against the railing outside of the building. My nerves were in overdrive, but not because of my interview with Lawson. I was feeling something I'd never felt before. And I was feeling it for a guy I had just met.

Hyperbole

I took a moment to collect myself and take in my surroundings. All of the winery buildings were clustered at the top of the long treelined driveway. Each section looked as though it had been recently renovated. The Craftsman architecture gave the buildings a rustic, lodgelike feel. On the left, there was the bed-and-breakfast, a large three-story house with intricate stained-glass windows and a heavy oak door displaying a complex design of intertwining wooden vines. The sign outside read *Together We Bring the Warmth*. Even in the afternoon, with the sun blazing low in the sky, I could see an orange glow from the outdoor wall sconces and the mica path lights, which exuded a cozy friendliness. Situated to the right of the bed-and-breakfast was a smaller structure, similar in design, with a sign indicating that it housed the tasting room and restaurant. In the distance, behind the restaurant, I could see what looked like a large warehouse, which I assumed was where the wine was made, and next to it was a red barn that could have been taken right off of a Wyoming cattle ranch.

I stood in front of four small bungalows, one of which I assumed was R.J.'s office, the others more offices or staff buildings. From my vantage point I could tell there was much more to the property that I couldn't see. Surrounding the cluster of buildings, in every direction, were grapevines. They formed an endless ocean of identical rows, fading over the horizon. I couldn't see where the vines stopped; they repeated endlessly. The structures around me stood out against their uniformity, like little islands.

My phone buzzed once. I tapped the iMessage button and read:

> *Stephen:* I have a late work meeting. I'll call you in the morning, sweetie.

I didn't respond. He hadn't asked how my trip went, what Napa was like, or if I was even alive at all. It was just more of Stephen's rhetoric, the obligatory text, the obligatory "sweetie." They were just words—there were never any feelings or experiences to match those words. There was nothing to justify what we were doing. I closed my messages and realized it was ten after five. I was late. Just then I felt a hand on my shoulder. I jerked and turned quickly.

"Sorry I startled you. I'm Susan, the general manager here. You must be Kate?"

She looked to be in her fifties. She was on the plump side with a perfectly manicured and completely gray bob. She had on a black suit and white shirt and a pair of narrow, black-framed glasses.

"Yes, I'm here for the interview with R.J. Sorry I'm late, I had some car trouble. Jamie had to give me a ride up the hill."

She straightened and squared her shoulders. "Did he now?"

"Is that a problem?"

"Well, I had sent Jamie on an errand but I guess it's not unlike him to get sidetracked." She looked me up and down very slowly. *What the hell is that supposed to mean?*

"Oh?"

"It's nothing."

"I actually hit Jamie's truck with my car." She suddenly looked very concerned. "He's okay and he's running your errand. I just don't want him to get in trouble if he gets back late."

Her expression turned warm and then she chuckled. "Jamie's not in any trouble, sweetheart." She put her arm around my shoulder and pulled me toward the door. We left my suitcase lying on the porch. Susan leaned in and said quietly, "Come on, I'll introduce you to the big boss."

We walked through one small room with a desk and then headed toward an open doorway. I looked in to find R.J. leaning back in his chair, already sizing me up.

"R.J., this is Kate Corbin. Kate, this is R.J."

Susan immediately left the room. I approached him with my hand out but he didn't get up. He leaned forward over his desk, shook my hand, and sat back very quickly, making me instantly uncomfortable.

Regardless, I chose to speak confidently. "It's nice to meet you."

"I expected a blonde," he said with a smirk.

His comment stunned me. I was motionless. "Oh yeah, why is that?"

"I've just always associated the name Kate with blondes."

I supposed there was a very general resemblance between R.J. and the twelve-year-old boy I saw in the photograph the night before: white male with brownish hair and lighter eyes. Adult R.J. had no standout features at all. His braces were gone but so was his smile, which probably answered the mystery of why he was such a recluse—he clearly had poor social skills. He wore a really boring blue suit with a pin-striped shirt and tie. His big, nerdy-chic glasses and poor style choices made sense for a computer wiz who probably spent more time alone with gadgets than with other living, breathing people.

"I guess you've never heard of Kate Middleton or Katie Holmes?"

"Oh, you're quick."

"You're inappropriate."

He stood up immediately, clapped his hands once, and announced, "Well I guess that wraps things up, Kate."

"No, I'm sorry." I plopped down in the chair across from him. I was blowing it and knew I had to recover. "I apologize. You just threw me off. I didn't expect any comments about my hair color."

He sat down but still scrutinized me with his eyes. "Let's get on with it, then. You were late. I only have an hour and I still have to take you to the tasting room."

I fumbled with my things and pulled out a recorder. He stood up immediately.

"No. No recording devices and no pictures. Just notes. I was told Jerry was aware of this."

"I'm sorry, I just don't want to misquote you."

"Then don't screw up your notes."

Geez, this guy goes from inappropriate ass to stick-up-his-ass in two seconds.

Susan walked in and announced, "The tasting room is ready for you whenever you want to head over there."

"I haven't answered a single question yet." He wore a smug grin. She shook her head and walked out. I couldn't tell for sure if her gesture was directed toward me or R.J., but my guess would be the latter.

"Let's get started, shall we?"

He leaned forward, resting his face on his propped-up hands. "Shoot, Kate. We don't have all night unless you want to take this interview back to my room."

"No, thank you." *What was this guy's problem?* "So, I heard you spent some time in Africa building schools. Can you tell me a little bit about that?"

"I was told you were only going to ask questions about the winery, but if you must know, it's true. I have an organization that builds schools in Africa."

I glanced at his smooth, delicate hands with his perfectly manicured fingernails.

"So you weren't actually building the schools yourself, with your own hands?"

"Let's get to the winery questions, Kate." He smiled and arched his eyebrows.

"Right. Tell me about the winery. I'd like to know how you turned this place around and learn about your methods of production."

"Well, I put a pretty penny into this place, I'll tell you that. I think it's also about how you handle your employees, letting them know who's boss, you know?" I unintentionally snickered. "Do you disagree with that?"

"No . . . I guess I'm not surprised. And your method for production?"

"I don't know much about that. I let Guillermo handle that. I think it's pretty standard, though. He had worked for the previous owners since the eighties."

"So Susan is the general manager and Guillermo runs the wine production and distribution."

"That's right."

"What does Jamie do?"

He cocked his head to the side, "So you met Jamie?"

"Yes."

"What was he doing?"

"He was running an errand. He had some barrels he had cleaned in the back of his truck."

"Jamie does a little bit of everything around here. He works in the vineyard and also does maintenance. He sometimes works in the B&B and store when the need arises."

Interesting. A man who knows how to use his hands.

"What sets R. J. Lawson apart as a winery resort and wine producer?"

He glanced down at a notecard and began rapping off facts. "Our winery is almost one hundred percent self-sufficient. Our number one goal is to produce quality wines and a quality experience in a completely sustainable environment. We have a three-acre hydroponic and natural garden and a small ranch to feed our restaurant. Our animals are raised hormone free in the best conditions with the best feed available. We have nine hundred and fifty solar panels installed in various places across the property, which produce one hundred percent of the power we use, solely from the sun's clean energy. All of our vehicles are clean-energy-running or fuel-efficient—even the tractors and machines we use in the vineyard and ranch. We only use home-made, organic pesticides in the vineyard and gardens. The tradition of winemaking on this property has been handed down for years—we've just updated it. We added quality control measures and modern, environmentally sound methods to an old procedure. We take a really hands-on approach, and I believe that's the beauty of this craft." He finally glanced up at me with a faint look of trepidation. It was becoming apparent to me that this guy probably sat behind his comfy desk while he waved his giant wallet around and ran his equally giant mouth off at his staff. Why any staff would be loyal to a huge asshole like R. J. Lawson baffled me.

"That's amazing. I'm really impressed, but are you saying that *you* actually take a really hands-on approach?" I focused on his unmarked hands again. He stood up, leaned over his desk, and glared at me. "What's your play?"

"I don't have a play, I'm just trying to figure out who the elusive R. J. Lawson really is."

"Let's head to the tasting room, unless of course you want to skip that part, go straight to my room, and perhaps get a little more personal information on R. J. Lawson?"

"You've made three passes at me in the last twenty minutes. You do realize I'm writing an article about you that will be published worldwide?"

"I haven't made any passes at you. Don't flatter yourself— you're too uptight for me. Anyway, why don't you just stick to writing articles on lipstick and yoga? Isn't that what you female journalists are good at?"

"What's going to stop me from writing about what a misogynistic dickhead you are?"

"What's going to stop me from not approving your shit-ass article before publication?"

I looked at him and cocked my head to the side, completely bewildered. "What are you talking about?"

"Oh, I guess you didn't know about that clause in the agreement I made with Jerry?"

"No, I didn't. Why don't you enlighten me?"

He smirked with pure satisfaction. "Jerry agreed to my approval over the full article before publication. If it isn't to my liking, he'll toss it out. So, nosey little Kate, you still think I'm a dickhead?"

My heart was racing. I stood abruptly and leaned toward him, mere inches from his face. I balled my hands into fists and tried to contain the anger building in my chest. I took a deep breath, composed myself, and shot back, "The Verizon guy called. He wants his glasses back."

R.J. huffed and shook his head. "Time to go. I'll walk you over there, but I can't say I'll stay long. Somehow sharing wine with you lost its appeal the second I met you, and p.s., you have a mouse nose."

Prick.

What had come over me? I couldn't believe I was blowing the single most important assignment I had ever been given by trading juvenile insults with this asshole. His behavior was reprehensible, but so was mine, and I wondered how I would ever write an article that would do the winery, the paper, or myself any justice at all.

We headed toward the door, and to my surprise he actually held the door open for me. Susan stood from her desk in the first room and joined us as we headed out. Once outside, I looked down and saw that my suitcase was gone. In its place sat Chelsea. She was like a statue, looking out at the sun, which was slowly disappearing behind the horizon.

"Hi, Chelsea. What did you do with my suitcase?" She sat there stoically, a truly regal expression on her face. Then she turned, looked at me, then looked back, almost completely dismissing my presence.

Susan laughed. "Jamie took your bag up to the room. I can escort you over there when you're through in the tasting room." She smiled warmly at me and then put her arm around my shoulder. "Chelsea is going to be about as easy to win over as R.J. Don't sweat the interview. Just write the article about the winery and forget about him."

"Were you listening?"

"A little." She laughed and then I started laughing. R.J. was walking far enough in front of us that he couldn't hear our conversation.

"Is he always like that?"

She stopped and placed both hands on my shoulders, turning me toward her. She was about three inches shorter than me, a small woman but with a powerful presence. Her mouth was framed with thick frown lines. She had a naturally serious face, so when she smiled it almost looked condescending. "This winery is a really beautiful place and a fantastic operation. The people who work here have put their blood, sweat, and tears into making it what it is today."

"You didn't answer my question."

"Forget about R.J. The first thing you'll get to experience is our phenomenal wine, and we've picked only the best for you to sample."

"Thank you." I still couldn't understand the aloofness Susan showed toward R.J. and the frank disdain from Jamie. I smiled at her anyway and headed through the two large mahogany doors. The tasting room took my breath away. It was a large room with a high, beamed ceiling, Mission-style couches, and Arts and Crafts furniture everywhere. It felt like a cozy lodge, even though the ceiling was at least sixty feet high.

On one end of the room was a large, wooden, intricately carved mantel framing a grandiose fireplace, with river rock extending above it all the way to the ceiling. It would have been an intimidating room but there was some heavenly Miles Davis pumping through the speakers, and the warmth from the fireplace was so welcoming. There were a few patrons lounging in the chairs and couches situated near the fireplace, but most of the visitors were crowded around the large square bar in the center of the room where the tastings were happening. I walked toward the bar but stopped at a wooden hutch where some of the bottles were displayed, as well as some tapenades, jams, olive oils, and other artisanal goodies. Susan watched me patiently as I took it all in. R.J. just headed straight to the bar.

I looked up and stared at the ceiling for a few moments, at the art on the walls, at the old, early-century charm that was surely the prevailing theme. Large black-and-white photos of the winery's vineyards hung on the walls, clearly taken decades ago. The room was a tribute. It was as if I had traveled back in time to a better place, one where you could escape the modern hustle and bustle, have a glass of wine, listen to a jazz legend, and just be. I followed Susan to the bar, and as soon as I recognized the Miles Davis song, Jamie turned from the other side and came walking toward us. It was the song "Someday My Prince Will Come." Jamie never took his eyes off me.

He threw his arms up and smiled from ear to ear. "Katy, you made it!"

"I did."

"Good to see you again."

He reached a hand over to R.J. "R.J."

"Jamie. Everything running smoothly?"

"Always, R.J. Always."

Their exchange seemed strange, almost strained. I was getting the feeling that Jamie wasn't the most compliant employee, and clearly R.J. was not the best boss. I sat next to R.J. on stools at the bar. After Jamie set two wineglasses in front of us, Susan went behind the bar and Jamie followed her to the other side. He bent his tall, six-foot frame down toward her; I saw her whisper something in his ear. He looked at her cautiously and then she rubbed her hand up and down his back before he leaned over again and kissed her cheek. She patted his back and then left, waving to me as she walked away. There was something very maternal about her behavior toward Jamie. When he turned and headed back toward us, I took in his appearance more closely. He had cleaned up since our encounter on the road. He was wearing a black polo shirt with the R. J. Lawson logo on it and dark Levi's cuffed over a pair of new-looking Converse. His hair was slicked back. I noticed it was long enough for a little curl of hair to just barely stick out from behind his ears. It drew my eyes to that part of his neck. As he was pouring the first tasting, I glanced up and noticed his eyes were on me.

He shot me a crooked grin. "See something you like?" I shook my head nervously.

R.J.'s cell phone rang. "Put that thing away, man," Jamie said to R.J., scowling. Oh my god.

"I have to take this," R.J. said as he got up and walked toward the door.

"Wow, I can't believe you talk to him like that."

"He's kind of on my shit list right now. You know, no raise in a while." He smiled and then tilted his head toward the wine he had just poured. The small bit of growth on his face couldn't hide his subtle dimples when he grinned. He was undeniably handsome with his chiseled jawline, but there was also something really adorable about him. He still had a hint of baby face hidden in his rugged good looks.

I reached for the glass. "That's our 2009 Estate Pinot Noir, the big award winner." He watched me as I took a sip. When his gaze moved to my mouth, I noticed a tiny smirk play on his lips. "What do you think?"

"It's amazing, totally decadent and vibrant." He began nodding and smiling, seemingly thrilled at my satisfaction. "The acidity is perfectly balanced and it has such a full, earthy finish. It's really fantastic." He was watching my mouth again.

"I thought you would like it," he said softly.

The brief moment was intense. It seemed like it would have felt completely normal to lean over and kiss him as a way of thanking him for the wine. I had to do something quick.

"R.J. hit on me like twenty times during the interview. I wish I liked him more because this place is wonderful and this wine is absolutely divine." That definitely shattered the moment.

Jamie's eyes went wide and the muscle in his jaw flexed. "He hit on you?"

"Yeah, big time."

"You're kidding."

"Nope."

"God, what an ass."

"Yeah."

"Did you tell Susan?"

"I think she heard him, but anyway, what good would that do?"

"Well, she might be able to straighten him out." He was wearing a slightly penitent smile but I couldn't understand why. "I'm really sorry he treated you that way."

"Don't worry about it. It's not your fault."

He nodded slowly but seemed unconvinced. "What else did you talk about in the interview?" Jamie's eyebrows were pinched together and his lips were completely flat. I wasn't quite sure how to answer him. "Did he mention how hard we work here to make this place completely sustainable?"

"Yes, he did," I said immediately and smiled.

He nodded. "Good, that's good."

"He just didn't tell me much about his personal life. I was trying to find out about the organization in Africa."

"The organization is great. It's really grown over the last eight years, and it does a lot of good for people, especially children all over Africa."

"I guess R.J. might not be so bad after all." I reached for my glass and took the final sip of wine.

"Let's move on. What can I give you next—something deeper, more full-bodied?" Somehow I forgot that Jamie was talking about wine. He was leaning forward with his forearms resting on the bar. He looked me right in the eyes so intensely that it felt like he was looking inside of me.

"Huh?" Now I was watching his mouth. He smirked very slightly.

"What would you like to taste next, Katy?"

"Uh, what?" My voice got really high.

"The wine, Katy. The wine," he said, chuckling.

"Oh, right! Um, actually I'm famished, I think I really need to get to my room and settle in. I should get a bite before I have any more wine, otherwise you'll have to carry me out of this place."

"I wouldn't mind," he said. At that point R.J. had returned quietly and sat at the bar to finish his glass.

"Would you like me to walk you to your room? Or maybe you can use those investigative reporter skills to find it on your own?" He really was a smug bastard.

Before I could respond, Jamie chimed in, "Susan said she'd walk her up."

"Well then, I must be going. Kate, I guess we have to give

this another shot when I'm back in town on Thursday, although I don't think either one of us is too thrilled about that." He turned without addressing Jamie and headed toward the door.

I couldn't hold back, and once he was out of earshot, I let out the sigh I had been holding back. "What a total jackass."

Jamie nodded and then reached over and grabbed my hands in his. "Listen, forget about him—just write about the winery. We all love it here. He *was* being a jackass, but it's not a reflection of what we do. Susan and Guillermo and I will show you everything that we do here." There was urgency in his voice. "Listen, Katy, go up to your room and relax, I'll have the chef send up something special. I'm really sorry about R.J."

"Are you related to Susan?" I asked. He jerked his head back in surprise. "Well, I just saw the way you spoke to her, and it looked like she was comforting you."

"Oh yeah? Well, I guess I would say that Susan has been sort of like a mom to me. She got me this job."

"Huh, interesting." I stood slowly from my barstool. "I have a lot of questions." I said it softly, almost to myself, but I knew Jamie heard me.

"Let's pick up this conversation later. Do you have any food allergies, or is there anything you don't eat?"

"I'm a vegetarian."

"Okay." He smiled warmly at me. There was silence as we stared at each other. The connection was palpable. "Truffle mushroom risotto?"

I was in a daze, still staring into his eyes and he into mine. It felt like he was burrowing into the depths of my soul. He was captivating me, enchanting me with fancy names for rice dishes. I must have been very hungry.

"Is that hyperbole?"

"No." He laughed. "It's Chef Mark's signature dish."

"It sounds amazing."

He paused then whispered, "You're beautiful."

"I have a boyfriend." I whispered back.

"You mentioned that."

Right at that moment my knees buckled, but luckily Susan had suddenly appeared at my side and grabbed me from around the waist, hitching me up.

"You need to eat, young lady. You're a waif, and we don't want you passing out on us," she said.

I looked up at Jamie, who shrugged. "She's right. Up to your room, young lady."

Susan pulled me toward the door, and I turned and spoke over my shoulder. "Bye, Jamie. I'll see you tomorrow?"

"At least," he said, grinning.

Walking toward the inn, I took the opportunity to drill Susan.

"Does Jamie ride a motorcycle?"

"No."

"Is he in a band?"

"Not that I know of."

"What about rodeo. Does he rodeo?"

She laughed. "Jamie does a great many things around the R. J. Lawson property. He is our resident jack-of-all-trades—you'll see that for yourself over the next few days. And while I see you've picked up on some of his bad boy tendencies, he really is just a sweet, good ol' boy." Her smile flattened abruptly as she squared her small frame and looked me right in the eyes. "You should know that he's like a son to me. He's experienced great personal loss and betrayal by the people who were supposed to love him. He's found a home and a family in this place.

I hope you don't come in here looking for some kind of story in all of this. Or maybe you're looking for a fling? If so, you're looking in the wrong place," she said with a perfunctory smile.

"Whoa, Susan. Jamie seems like he can take care of himself," I said. She shrugged. "Anyway, I was just curious. I have a boyfriend, by the way."

"Who are you reminding of that fact?"

My eyes began to well up. She was putting me on the spot and embarrassing me, but I held back the tears. I was a professional.

"I'm looking for details for the article, that's it. I'm supposed to be writing an article on R. J. Lawson and, well . . . you know how that interview went." I said the last part with a huge lump in my throat.

"I'm sorry, Kate. He acted very inappropriately. That is not what we're about here, and I've asked that he complete the interview via e-mail so you don't have to go through that all over again on Thursday."

"What? No! My whole reason for being here is to conduct the interview in person. I won't get the answers I need if he can calculate all of his responses in an e-mail."

She tilted her head to the side and then huffed. "That man has a very small role in the operations here."

I pointed my finger up to the sky. "I knew it! It's just his big, fat, stupid wallet, isn't it? Everybody thinks he's like this genius, but he probably just throws his money at everything."

She took a deep breath. "I know where you're headed, Kate. Look, the staff will show you around and let you in on how we run the winery, restaurant, and inn. It's up to you what goes in that article, but I know by now you've heard that R.J. has veto power, so I hope you'll think twice about how you approach your commentary."

We entered the large, three-story bed-and-breakfast and went up a small flight of stairs to the first level. I held on to the fine, polished, wooden banister until we reached the landing. She handed me a key. "Your room is here. Your dinner should be up soon. I hope we can all start fresh tomorrow?"

"Yes. I'm looking forward to it," I said sincerely. *I'm going to get a story no matter what.*

She smiled and headed down the stairs, shouting back, "You'll get an itinerary under your door in the morning."

Wow, an itinerary? This was one carefully organized operation.

I shut the door and leaned against it, surveying the room, then slowly made my way around. It was finely decorated in the same Arts and Crafts style as the lobby. *Great taste.* It had a Mission-style four-poster bed next to double doors leading out to a small balcony housing two captain's chairs. The bathroom had a beautiful claw-foot tub, with gold fixtures and ornate tiles running along the walls, framing a porcelain pedestal sink. I collapsed into the feather bed covered in white fluffy pillows and an eyelet duvet and proceeded to type a text to Stephen.

> *Kate:* I'm okay, not that you care.

> *Stephen:* Do you realize how late it is here?

I'd really had a colossal mind-fuck of a day, but I was feeling feisty and decided to go for it.

> *Kate:* Do you love me?

My phone rang instantly.

"What's going on, sweetie?"

"Do you love me?"

"Of course."

"Do you know where I'm at and what I'm doing?"

"You're out of town on an assignment."

"I'm not in the fucking Secret Service, Stephen. I told you where I was going, but of course you weren't listening."

"You've been distant."

"Me?" I said in shock.

He sighed. "Ever since Rose died and you started having that dream, Kate—that bizarre fucking dream—and following that homeless dude around on the train like you worship him. I don't get what's going on with you. I wouldn't blame you for losing your mind for a little while, but this has been going on for months."

"I . . ."

"No, listen. We're different, Kate; we always have been. Things have felt wrong for a long time."

"Hold on. Are you beating me to the punch, you asshole?! You're trying to break up with me first?"

"Listen . . ."

"No, you listen, Stephen. God, how can you be so heartless? It's not a dream I keep having about Rose, it's a fucking nightmare, and sometimes I wake up from it and realize the nightmare is real. She's gone, just like my mother. She's never coming back, but her sad, lonely life still haunts me. I was all she had, and then when she was gone, it was like she never existed. I'm terrified I'll end up the same way, but at least I had you, though now I'm not sure I ever did . . . It doesn't matter now." I calmed down while Stephen remained silent. "It doesn't matter now because I don't want you. I'll tell you why I've been listening to Bob on the train. It's because he's right. I'm all I've got."

I began crying but made certain Stephen couldn't hear me.

Then he finally said in the calmest voice, "Well, I guess that's it then, Kate," indifference seeping through every syllable.

I swallowed. "Tell me the truth. Do you really think you love me?"

"I don't know."

"I think by now you should know." My voice cracked.

"I'm sorry," he said quietly.

"So that's your answer?"

Without waiting for him to respond, I hung up, feeling more stupefied than sad. The tears had stopped. I was shocked—not that I was losing Stephen, but that I had wasted two years of my life with someone who didn't love me. I guessed my reaction meant that I wasn't in love with him, either. Stunned, I stared at a tiny crack in the wall for several moments until I heard three rapid knocks. A shiver ran through me before I hopped off the bed and ran to the door, swinging it open dramatically. There was an older man carrying a tray. Had it been Jamie, I might have jumped into his arms. "Your dinner, ma'am." I stepped aside and let him set the tray on the small dining table in the corner of the room. "Truffle mushroom risotto and a bottle of our 2009 Pinot Noir, compliments of Chef Mark Struthers and R. J. Lawson."

"Oh, right!" I laughed maniacally, making a crazy cackling sound. The day had really gotten to me. The waiter gave me a frightened look as he opened the bottle of wine and proceeded to pour a glass.

"Enjoy, ma'am," he said and then hurried out the door. Once he was gone, I plopped onto the bed again as the tears began flowing once more. I thought about Stephen and tried to conjure up one truly happy memory with him besides him fucking me on the washer in the basement, which could hardly be deemed as happy. In retrospect, our time together was mediocre at best.

Rose never liked him; she had said he was cold fish. I thought about the dream Stephen referred to in our argument. Shortly after Rose died, I began questioning my life so deeply that it started to unnerve me. Not having any family or knowing where you come from can make you feel like you don't exist.

I would look in the mirror and not recognize myself. I would say, "Who am I?" over and over, and the feeling, the anxiety of not knowing the answer, would send me into a panic. I wished I'd asked every question I could think of before she died, but I didn't. There were just a few pictures and a tiny bit of information that I knew about my parents and grandparents, but it wasn't enough to imagine their lives. In my mind, if they didn't exist then I didn't exist, and it was when I started believing that to be true that the dreams began, those tiny whispers that sent me reeling.

Rose's funeral was closed casket, but in my dream it was open and she was lying there, looking nothing like herself. In my dream she wore white, a color she never wore and a dress she certainly did not own and one I definitely did not bury her in. It looked like a wedding dress with lace sleeves and a satin bodice, but Rose had never married—like my mother, she lived a solitary and mundane existence. I walked toward her and could feel someone else's presence next to me, but I didn't know who it was. I leaned over and stared at Rose, lying there lifeless and appearing much younger than she had been in reality when she died. She had long brownish-red locks that tumbled over her lace-clad shoulders in the most angelic way. Even though she appeared to be about twenty years old—much younger than I ever knew her—there was an obvious sense that the body lying there was my Rose.

When I turned to look at the figure standing next to me, something stopped me, an invisible force. It was one of those dreamlike moments when you try so hard to do something physically, but your body won't let you. I felt paralyzed. All I knew was that the figure gave off a peaceful and soothing presence. I wondered if it was my mother or my father or God. Looking back down into the coffin, I noticed a tiny movement, and then the motion became more pronounced. I leaned in closer. Rose's mouth was moving, but I could tell she was having trouble. I knew it was wired shut, the way a body is traditionally prepared for burial. Her eyes bolted open as wide as could be, and she was violently moving her lips, trying to open her mouth; it was horrifying. *She's alive! Help her,* I kept shouting, but my voice made no sound. She finally pried her lips apart. Her expression was urgent. She was desperately trying to give me a message, but I couldn't hear what she was saying. All I could hear was the sound of heartbeats, and that's the moment when I would always wake up.

Every time I had that dream, I would wish for one more second. I would replay the scene over and over, wanting so badly to decipher what she was trying to tell me. Her dead body lying there in a casket trying to speak to me was the most frightful vision. Still, I wished I could get an inch closer, just to hear her, because I knew it was a whisper. Even terrified, I knew it was a whisper that would change the course of my life forever, if only I understood what the message was.

Perhaps she was warning me about Stephen. Maybe it was her last plea for me to kick him to the curb. And maybe, just maybe, she had sent Bob down to remind me that I'm all I've got.

I composed myself, took a deep breath, walked over to the table, sat down, put the napkin across my lap, and began eating.

Table for one, and I was okay with it. I was going to concentrate on my job, write the article, hopefully impress everyone at the paper, and move on with my life.

One glass of that fine Pinot was not enough; I had two, then three. The risotto was divine. I ate every single bite and thought, *See, this is the life. Nobody gives a shit about me and that's okay, because I give a shit about me.*

It was dark out on the balcony, I could see every single star in the sky as I polished off my glass of wine. It made me feel as insignificant in the world as I knew I was. I walked in and called the front desk and told them they could collect the tray. I had drunk three quarters of a bottle of wine and was feeling numb when I heard the same three knocks. My plan was to apologize to the poor man for my wacky behavior earlier, but when I opened the door he wasn't there. In his place stood Jamie, in all his glorious beauty. He had a small box in one hand and something else behind his back in the other. I took a step back and let him enter the room.

"Hi."

"Hi. Don't you ever go home?" One corner of his mouth turned up, revealing the dimple. I realized my comment sounded rude. "I mean, do you work twenty-four hours a day?"

"I live on the property."

"Here?" I motioned around the room.

"No, I live in . . ." He laughed a little before speaking again. "I live in the barn."

"You live in the barn?" My eyes went wide.

"It's a really nice barn, okay?" he said in a low voice. There was something about the way he said it that made my fingers tingle, like he was promising me something—an invitation, perhaps.

For a few moments we were quiet and shy. I'd had a lot of wine.

"How was the risotto?" He glanced down at my mouth.

"Delicious."

"I like the way you say that word, like you really mean it."

"I do," I said, and then brazenly looked him up and down.

"I brought you something." He held out the small box and then set it on the long entry table, along with another bottle of Pinot. "In case you need backup. And that's just a little treat," he said, pointing to the box.

"I doubt I should be drinking any more wine."

He shrugged. "Well, just in case." He turned to walk out. At the door, he looked back at me. "It was nice to meet you, Kate. I hope you have a good night."

"Wait a minute."

He turned immediately, and there was something hopeful in the look on his face. "Yeah?"

"Well, I want to see what you brought me so I can thank you properly in person." I took the small box and opened it to find two of the most decadent-looking salted chocolate caramels seated on two tiny doilies. "Oh, my favorite. How'd you know?"

"Good guess, I suppose." He was still standing near the door, leaning against the wall with his hands in his pockets.

"And thank you for the wine, but really, I shouldn't have any more."

"We can share it if you want."

I smiled then took a chocolate from the box and bit into it, the caramel stringing out over my fingers. Taking a few steps toward him, I reached my hand out, holding the chocolate near his mouth. "We can share." I was drunk, but I didn't care.

He wrapped his hand around my wrist, pulling it closer. He never took his eyes off of mine when he slowly took the chocolate with his mouth and then sucked the caramel off my index finger. He leaned in next to my ear and spoke softly. "Does your boyfriend like to share?" Flushed from head to toe, I stood there, speechless. He stepped back and laughed a little.

"I'm just messing with you, Katy." He searched my face. I was shocked. "I'll be respectful, I promise."

I mock-punched him in the chest. "All right, open the wine then."

"Is that how you ask nicely?"

"Oh, you're pushing it." We both laughed. "Okay, please, let's have some wine."

He grabbed the bottle, bottle opener, and two glasses and then said, "Let's take a walk. We should be outside on a gorgeous night like this. I'll show you the pool."

Taking nothing but my room key, I followed him toward the door. I glanced in the mirror. I was still wearing my demure work clothes and matronly shoes. I had piled my hair on top of my head in a messy bun and had faint black mascara streaks under my eyes from crying. I was the picture of a man's worst date. *It's not a date*, I reminded myself, but I was also beginning to realize Jamie wasn't just any man. It didn't seem like he was turned off.

It was hard not to stare at him. There was something sweet but innately confident about the way he carried himself. When we got to the bottom of the stairs, he gave a chin nod to the man behind the front desk.

"Going to the pool, George."

"Okay buddy, I'll send some towels over."

I started to object. What on earth would we need towels for?

Jamie jutted an elbow out for me to loop my arm through, and then he shook his head.

"Don't worry about it, towels are good for sitting on."

"Right," I said assuredly.

We walked through the large great room, out to a huge veranda, and down several small sections of stone stairs to a gate. I read a sign on the fence that said the pool closed at ten.

"It's got to be after ten."

"I clean this pool. I can swim in it any time I want." He winked.

"I thought we weren't swimming? Wait a minute, you clean the pool, too? What don't you do around here?"

"I've worked every job on this property for at least a day. I even did housekeeping for a week."

"Why?"

"Curiosity, I guess. I wanted to know how to do each job, and Susan really loves me so she let me give it a go. Sometimes I just fill in for other people because I'm always here, you know?"

"Is R.J. always here?"

"He's here a lot."

The pool was gorgeous, with a stone waterfall on the opposite side from where we were standing near a table. While Jamie opened the wine, I pulled a chair out.

"Let's dip our feet in." He looked up at me eagerly. "Want to?"

"Isn't it cold?"

"It's heated."

"Okay."

I kicked my shoes off and rolled up my slacks, then followed him to the edge of the pool, where he set two towels down. He rolled up his jeans and sat gracefully before dunking his feet into the water. My fingers twitched with a desire to smooth back the disheveled hair that had fallen into his face. I watched intently as he reached up and ran his hand through it, displaying the flexing muscles in his arm. I couldn't take my eyes off him. When he handed my wine over, he noticed me staring.

"What?" he asked.

"Nothing. I just want to forget about everything for a little while."

"Really?" He looked excited. I nodded. "I have a great idea."

I dipped my feet in. The water was very warm, like bathwater. It was immediately calming my nerves.

"What's your idea?"

"Well, curious Katy, I'll show you."

He jumped up, ran to the gate, tinkered with something, and then all the lights went out—the lights in the pool, all around the patio area, even the waterfall. Everything was silent. I could see steam rising from the surface of the water. A million more stars became visible. I sipped my wine and then heard Will Ryan's soulful voice filtering softly through the outdoor speakers. Jamie appeared at my side.

"I love this guy. He's so good," I said.

"Yeah, he's awesome. He and his wife are playing at a little local bar on Saturday, if you want to check it out with me?"

"I'd love to, if I'm still here." I finally looked up and noticed that gorgeous Jamie was shirtless and undoing his belt buckle. Even in the dark, I could see the sinewy muscles of his arms and his defined abs and chest. He just smiled playfully at me. "What are you doing?" I whispered loudly.

"We're gonna take your mind off things with a little dip."

"*I'm* not taking a dip."

"Okay, fine." He yanked his jeans off and leaped into the

pool, wearing nothing but a pair of dark blue and gray plaid boxers.

When he surfaced, he held his boxers by a finger above his head and spun them around as if he were doing a striptease. He flung them toward me and they landed just to my left.

"Oh my god! I can't believe you just did that."

"What? You can't see me. Anyway, I know you have the crazy in you. You'll be in here in no time."

"How do you know that?"

"The pretty ones are always a little cray-cray."

"You think you're so smart, don't you?"

"You have no idea," he said with no trace of humor. "Just get in here, Katy. I promise I won't look."

At that point, it's fair to say that I was drunk, completely and utterly drunk from the wine, and Jamie's presence did nothing to sober me up. His long, wet hair left little glimmering droplets on his shoulders. I giggled. "Turn around, you better not peek!"

"I promise." He waded to one end of the pool and turned his back to me.

I quickly stripped down to my black bra and panties. Looking down, I thought it could easily pass for a swimsuit except that it was silk. *Oh well.*

As quietly as I could, I slipped into the pool on the opposite end of where Jamie stood. There were at least thirty yards between us. The pool felt amazing. I relaxed for a moment and then realized I was in a pool with a naked man I'd just met. A very attractive naked man.

"Okay, I'm in, Jamie, but keep your safe distance."

He turned around, grinned from ear to ear, and then disappeared under the water.

Good god, what is he doing?

I was suddenly very nervous. A small part of me was actually frightened. If it weren't for Will Ryan's sweet words pumping through the speakers, I would have been terrified. His hands on my hips didn't startle me at all because I could feel him getting closer. He rose out of the water, his warm hands gripping my waist. He wasn't smiling; he was searching my eyes. I looked around quickly and then back to his shoulders and pecs as he lifted his arms and slicked his hair back with both hands. I could see his tensing neck muscles. There was very little stopping me from licking the drops of water off his arms. I closed my eyes as he closed the gap between us. I felt his mouth brush my neck and then move toward my ear. "Baby, open your eyes."

"I . . ."

"I know. You have a boyfriend." One side of his mouth turned up. He moved back a few inches. "We can be friends though, right?"

"Yes," I sighed.

"You were crying earlier. Why?"

"I shook my head."

"Please tell me it wasn't because of how R.J. treated you?"

"No."

"Then what?"

"I just want to forget everything."

He nodded, looking away for a second. "Are you ticklish?"

"Don't you dare."

He laughed. "Well, there is one thing I know . . ."

"What's that, smart guy?"

He put his hands on my hips again and I let him, even though I knew it was crossing the line. It felt so good, like being enveloped in warmth and security.

His mouth turned up into a knowing smile, and then he

said, almost wistfully, "Just being your friend is going to be hard, but I'll try. It's just that . . . I like you. You're witty and sweet, and you happen to be the most infinitely beautiful woman I've ever met." I sucked in a startled breath. He paused, looking all drowsy with desire before opening his mouth to speak again.

"Don't," I murmured.

"It's not hyperbole, Katy. I promise."

Giggling nervously, I slowly sunk beneath the water, thinking Jamie was out of his mind. I never would have described myself the way he just did.

But then again, I had allowed Stephen to make me feel like I was barely worth coming home to.

Allegory

Slipping my clothes over my wet undergarments, I turned away from Jamie as he lifted himself out of the water from the side of the pool. He got dressed quickly, and when I turned back toward him, he was sweeping up his sopping boxers from the ground and wrapping them in a towel. *No qualms about commando. I like it!*

"I'll walk you back."

"Great, thank you, I'm dead-tired." I was feeling completely bashful after his poetic and sweet confession.

We headed toward the inn.

"I need to stop at my truck for a sec. Do you mind?" he asked.

"Not at all."

He opened the driver's side door and then blocked my view. I heard a zipper open and then he was shuffling with something. It was taking more than a second.

"What are you looking for?" I asked.

"Just one more minute, okay?"

Being the curious person that I am, I stood on my tippy-toes and leaned over to see what he was doing. He turned around abruptly, holding something behind his back.

"What is that?"

"Nothing, it's not a big deal," he said, nervously.

"Let me see." It was at least ten full seconds before he finally held his hand out, revealing some sort of syringe.

My mouth dropped to the ground. "Are you . . . are those drugs?"

"No. Well, yes, but not what you're thinking."

"What is it then?" We were both hesitant.

"It's insulin."

A breath rushed from my mouth. "You're diabetic?"

"Yes, type one."

"I'm so sorry."

He shook his head. "Don't be. I've been this way for a long time."

"Were you embarrassed to tell me?" I asked gently.

"No, I just didn't want to burden you with it, and I have to give myself this shot now. I didn't know if you'd be squeamish."

"Not at all." I started getting misty-eyed. "That would never be a burden to me, but thank you for the consideration." At the age of eight, I'd had to play nurse to my mother while she was dying, her body wracked with cancer. At twenty-five, I watched Rose, the only other person I've ever loved, get eaten alive by a plague-like bacteria she'd picked up in the hospital after her gallstone surgery. There were few things that could nauseate me.

He was still holding the syringe and looking into my eyes. "I'm gonna do this now, okay?" And then he smiled sweetly. I nodded. He took the needle cap off with his teeth, holding it in his mouth while he lifted his shirt on the left side. My eyes were drawn to his beltless jeans, hanging low on his waist. His stomach was thin and defined and angled in that way that encourages your eyes to continue looking downward. When I glanced up, I noticed his gaze was focused on the penlike syringe. He pressed something on the bottom and a tiny drop of insulin bubbled at the needle tip. The air was suddenly filled with a very potent, medicinal smell. And then, as if he had done it a million times, he pinched a chunk of his skin just above his hip and jabbed the needle into it. I caught a tiny wince flash across his face just as the needle hit the skin. He pushed the button on the bottom of the pen and then quickly pulled it out and replaced the cover using his mouth. He was still holding up his shirt.

"Shit," he mumbled.

"What?"

"I hit a blood vessel."

"Oh my god, what does that mean?" I said, suddenly frantic.

He chuckled. "Nothing, sweet girl, it's just a little blood." He was looking around for something. I looked down and noticed he was bleeding from the injection site. It was thinly streaming toward the top of his jeans. Spotting our wet towels on the hood of the truck, I quickly grabbed one and bent to carefully wipe away the blood.

"Whoa, what are you doing, Kate?" There was a touch of amusement in his voice.

"Wiping the blood away."

"I could have done that."

"Oh," I said. I stared at him for a few seconds, feeling mortified. I was trying to read his expression. "I'm sorry."

He smiled, but I think he was a little shocked, too.

"No, what I meant was that I wouldn't want to make anyone feel like they have to do something like that."

"I know. I told you, I'm not squeamish. I just wanted to help."

"Thank you." He held the towel to his waist for a moment and then let his shirt fall. "I should get you up to your room. You must be exhausted."

"Yes. It's been a long, strange day."

"Not all bad, I hope," he said quietly as we shuffled up the stairs.

"What?"

"You said it's been a long, strange day, but I hope it wasn't all bad."

"Definitely not all bad." When we got to my door, I turned around before unlocking it. "Actually, I should thank you. You turned a pretty awful day around for me, even after I hit you with my car."

He nodded. "Well thank *you* for sopping up my blood."

"No prob."

"My list is growing."

I crooked an eyebrow at him. "Oh yeah? What list is that?"

"All of the reasons why this is gonna be so hard." I tilted my head, encouraging him to elaborate. He smirked. "Now you've added compassionate and tender to the list." He leaned in and pecked me on the cheek. "Night, Katy, see you in the morning."

Oh, *that* list.

I was beginning to make a list of my own, and the promise of seeing him the next day made my heart bounce around inside my chest.

Stephen who? I thought to myself with a smile.

. . .

In the morning, just as promised, an itinerary was shoved under my door. At the top, under the emboldened word WEDNES-DAY, there was a list of breakfast items and the extension number to place my order. In the margin, someone had written, *I recommend the eggs Comtesse or the eggs Blackstone (minus the bacon, of course).*

Wow, this is amazing, I thought. *Personal recommendations—and they know I'm a vegetarian.*

Under the breakfast choices was a detailed schedule.

10:00 a.m.: Private educational tour of winery with Guillermo. Meet in lobby.

In small handwriting above "Guillermo," there was a little carrot arrow and the words *and Jamie* written rather messily. Well, I knew who the annotating culprit was now, and I couldn't stop smiling as I continued through the schedule.

12:00 p.m.: Private wine and food pairing experience with Chef Mark. And again, a little handwritten note with the words *and Jamie.*

2:00 p.m.: Facility tour with Susan. Instead of *and Jamie,* it said, *I have work to do, young lady* ☺.

There was a big space and then Jamie's writing again.

But, if you're willing, the staff at R. J. Lawson would like to take you on a sunset sail in the San Francisco Bay. Meet in lobby at 4 p.m.

Wow, really? They're going all out . . . or maybe Jamie is going all out . . .

After eating the best eggs Comtesse I've ever had, I searched my suitcase for something to wear. I had brought plenty of very reporter-looking clothes, not sure of what the weather would be like, but none of it was appropriate for impressing hot, rugged winery men. Spicing up the same black blazer was going to be a challenge, and then I remembered that I had brought a maroon camisole, something I would normally wear underneath a blouse. I went for it—my sexy silk camisole, the tightest jeans I owned, some heels, and the black blazer, for the sake of good form.

I decided I would tell Jamie as soon as I saw him that I had broken up with my boyfriend, but Susan's warning scared me, and I wondered if I really wanted a fling with a man who lived two thousand miles away. *Yes, with this one, I most definitely do,* I couldn't help thinking.

It was time to update Jerry, even though I had made no progress on the story. I dialed his number and it didn't even ring. "This is Jerry."

"I have a problem."

"Well, hello to you, too."

"I'm serious."

"Congratulations. You haven't been serious about anything in a very long time."

I often had these ridiculous back-and-forths with Jerry in which he would intentionally mock me or try to ruffle my feathers because he thought it inspired my writing. I was also ninety-nine percent sure that Jerry had undiagnosed ADD. Many days we ate lunch in the park together, sometimes Lincoln, sometimes Stanton. We'd eat our deli sandwiches and talk about life stuff. We would be having the most profound conversation about mortality or world hunger and Jerry would suddenly jerk his head around and say, "Oh man, look at that kite, it's shaped like a giant squid!" I would never even attempt to take him to Millennium Park—forget about it. I know he'd just sit there and stare, mesmerized at those giant sculptures. His brain would go into overload and he would probably chant, "Big metal object, big metal object," over and over. He did everything fast—he thought, ate, wrote, talked, even walked faster than the average person. His attention span didn't last longer than a few seconds. His deadlines were sometimes unreasonable, and his brain rarely allowed for small talk in conversations, which made him a straight shooter.

"Jerry, stop."

"Are you getting the dirt? That's all I really want to know."

"Yes, dirt is exactly what I'm getting. R.J. is kind of a dick."

"What do you mean 'kind of'?"

"Well, he *is* a dick. He kept hitting on me throughout the interview."

"Did you fuck him?"

"No."

"Good . . . Are you gonna fuck him?"

"No, Jesus Christ, Jerry, who do you think I am?"

"Well, it's great that he's a dick, just don't fuck him."

"*Okay!* And why is it great that he's a dick?"

"Because you need an angle, Kate. You always need an angle."

"But I love this place, and all of the people who work here are so nice, and the wine is phenomenal. Plus, I know he has veto power over the article."

In his typical superfast speech, he said, "Listen, there are always loopholes. If you would have told me that he was the most philanthropic, God-loving gift to all women and humankind, I would have said great to that, too. You just need an angle, okay? Don't stress so much, you're not fucking writing *The Jungle*. Just play up the facts. Get the dirt on how the staff feels about him. Find out why the wines are winning awards, etcetera, etcetera, etcetera."

"They're winning awards because the wine is that fucking good."

"Well, why? What are they doing that's different? That's what you need to find out." He suddenly paused and then continued. "By the way, I'm sorry to hear about Stephen."

"Oh . . . how'd you know?" I asked, somewhat alarmed.

"Beth saw him having breakfast this morning."

"So? What did he say to her?"

"Well, it wasn't so much what he said . . ."

"What do you mean?" And just like that, it hit me. "He was with a woman? This morning? Already? Fucking dog!"

"Yeah, and you know how Beth is. I guess she went up to him and said something like, 'While the cat's away, huh?' He blurted out that the two of you had broken up."

"What a fucker!"

There were several seconds of silence, which was rare for a phone conversation with Jerry. I wondered if he was rubbing his chin and staring at the ceiling. Then I could hear a smile in his voice.

"Yeah, you could say that again."

"Jerry!"

"No, I *am* really sorry, Kate. I just never really liked the guy."

Jerry wasn't alone in his feelings. Rose hadn't liked Stephen, and Beth couldn't stand him, though of course Beth couldn't stand most men. Still, even the superintendent of our building loathed him and would instantly scowl whenever Stephen would simply approach him.

"I'll call you later, Jer."

"'Kay. Don't think too much about Stephen. You deserve better. Focus on your job and get out there and knock 'em dead, kid."

"Yeah, because I'm so good at that," I said sarcastically.

"You stop it right now. I don't want to hear that kind of talk." His tone went serious and then turned right back around. "Oh, and don't fuck the genius."

"Bye, Jerry."

I had fifteen minutes before I needed to be in the lobby, so I plugged in my laptop and fiddled around for at least ten minutes, trying to log in to the Wi-Fi with no luck. They left me a code on the desk but it wasn't working, so I opened a Word document instead and began jotting down some notes.

```
R.J.: asshole, no sign of genius, brags
about his money, has girlish hands.
```

How I was going to get an article out of that little bit of information baffled me. Then I wrote:

```
Winery: sustainable, beautiful grounds,
rustic, old world charm, great wine.
```

And then, finally:

```
Jamie: vast knowledge and pride in
the winery, diabetic, sweet, genuine,
gorgeous, charming, warm hands, strong
hands, likes me . . .
```

And then I had to go.

On Three

Rushing from my room, I slammed the door and turned toward the stairway, running smack into Jamie's hard chest. I looked up. He was grinning, and then in the softest voice he said, "Hello, angel. You're gonna have to ditch those shoes. You know that, don't you? Did you bring anything else?" I took a step back and scanned him from head to toe. He was wearing grungy jeans, work boots, and a plain white T-shirt beneath a long-sleeved flannel shirt, unbuttoned. I looked down at my shoes.

"Okay. Give me one second." I turned and ran back to my room. Other than heels and flats, I only had a pair of gray and black old-school checkerboard Vans. They were my flying shoes because I could slip them on and off easily. Normally I wouldn't have been embarrassed to wear them, but when I looked in the mirror I noticed I was very mismatched. Shedding the blazer in a huff, I pulled on my dorky, heather-gray University of Illinois hoodie.

When I met Jamie again in the hallway, he looked down at my feet, smirked, and said, "Perfect. You're cute." And then he looked up and said, "Go Chiefs."

"Actually, it's Chief Illiniwek, and people have a huge problem with that. Did you go to college?"

"You're not convinced enough to say, 'Where did you go to college?'"

I laughed nervously. *Way to insult him.* He jogged down the staircase, motioning with his arm. "Come on, we have to meet Guillermo."

I followed him through the great room and out to the front of the building.

"I'm sorry, I didn't mean anything by that. Where did you go to college?"

He threw his arms out to his sides and gestured around us. "Everywhere. All over. Anywhere I could."

"So you didn't have a formal college education, per se?" I smiled kindly, trying to figure out what he was implying.

"I had that, too." One side of his mouth turned up. "But I've learned a lot more from the people in my life." He gestured toward a man walking in our direction and raised his voice. "Like Guillermo, for example. This guy has grown up on the vineyards, making wine and perfecting his craft."

Guillermo, a small man of maybe fifty, gave Jamie a guylike half-handshake, half-hug. "J, get your ass out there, it's still crush season."

Jamie laughed and then turned to face me. "Enjoy the tour, I'll catch up with you later." Still holding my gaze, he said to Guillermo, "This is Katy. Bring her back in one piece, okay man?" Guillermo chuckled.

When Jamie left, I said, "It's nice to meet you, Guillermo." He shook my hand. "And by the way, what is crush season?"

"It means we're still picking the grapes, *mija.* Let's go see how we make this stuff." We walked side by side into the vast sea of vines. "The first thing you need to know is that it's about the fruit, the grapes. These are not the grapes you're used to."

He stopped at a cluster of dull-looking grapes hanging from a vine.

"See, dear, these are Pinot Noir grapes. They have less color."

"They look bad."

He shook his head. "These are excellent grapes. It has taken us ten years to perfect the Pinot Noir grape on this property, something they have been doing in France for years." He pulled one from the bunch and handed it to me. I popped it into my mouth.

"Wow, that's not what I expected at all."

"Juicy, right? Juicier than the grapes you eat?"

"Yes, and very, very sweet, but it tastes nothing like Pinot Noir."

He chuckled. "Well, you see, much of that flavor is coming from the skin. The skin is a bit bitterer and much thicker than, say, a Thompson seedless grape, and that's why these grapes are not as enjoyable to eat. But they do make a magnificent wine, don't they?"

"I have to ask, if you've been here so long, why is it only now, since Lawson has taken over, that the wines have done so well?"

"He sent me to France." Pausing, he arched his eyebrows. "He paid for the whole thing. Let me spend a month there. I learned a lot, but mostly things I already knew and just needed to be reminded of. Lawson gave me the resources and space. Pinot Noir grapes have a low yield. When I got back, we focused on that specific wine here on the estate and set aside more acres to grow this grape."

"Why was Lawson so set on Pinot Noir?"

He popped his shoulders up into a shrug. "Hopeless romantic, I guess."

"I doubt that."

"No, truthfully, he said he wanted to make Pinot Noir because it's a sexy wine." He laughed loudly, like he thought that was ludicrous.

I instantly remembered a quote from a *Vanity Fair* article describing Pinot as *the most romantic of wines, with so voluptuous a perfume, so sweet an edge, and so powerful a punch that, like falling in love, they make the blood run hot and the soul wax embarrassingly poetic.*

"I guess that kind of makes sense because he's a"—*chauvinistic pig*, I thought—"Because he's trying to sell wine."

"Who knows. Let's move on, *mija*."

As we walked down a row of vines toward the big warehouse-looking structure, I decided to take the time to get to know Guillermo.

"Do you have family?"

"I do. We live down the road. My wife, Patricia, works here at the front desk in the lodge. I have two daughters. They're both in college—one at Berkeley and the other at the University of Arizona."

"Wow, and you can afford that on your pay here?" He turned toward me, looking affronted. "I didn't mean any offense, I'm sorry. You must work tirelessly here for R.J. Does he provide you with proper breaks and benefits?"

He hesitated and spoke in a quieter, more apprehensive voice. "Yes, I do . . . he does. He's putting both of my daughters through school. He's like a son to me, but he has taken care of me, too." I was shocked. R.J. was either a complete contradiction, acting like a douche while doing good things for the people around him, or he really did have it out for the media and his little tantrum was just to throw me off of his true personality.

We walked past a giant, red, tractorlike machine that was moving slowly down the row toward us. It was built to almost straddle the rows of vines. Guillermo gently grabbed my arm and pulled me into another row.

"Let's give the man some space."

Still looking back, I said, "What is that thing?"

"It's a mechanical harvester. We handpick a lot of our grapes, but we use a couple of those, too, to stay on schedule. Jamie made them more fuel-efficient."

"How do they work?"

"They vibrate the vine. It's sort of a delicate process for such a big, intimidating machine, but the vibration causes the cluster to drop from its stem and into a bin."

I spotted Jamie a couple of rows over. He had abandoned the flannel, and the reddish tattoos running down his left arm contrasted sharply against his white T-shirt. Even from that distance, I could see a gleam of sweat on his face and arms. He had added a plain black baseball cap and black sunglasses. *Bad boy, good boy. Ahh!*

I stuck my hand up and waved, getting his attention. In that moment another worker handed him something so his hands were full, but he tilted his head back and kissed the air in my direction. I smiled giddily and then looked over to find Guillermo grinning.

"Focus, *mija*."

I played it down by shrugging, like I had no idea what he was referring to.

"Is it okay for Jamie to work like that with his diabetes?"

"Oh yeah, of course. Exercise is good. It helps to naturally lower his blood sugar. That's why Jamie is so fit."

"Yeah. Jamie *is* fit . . ."

Guillermo raised one eyebrow. "I bet you want to see the grape crusher?"

I laughed. "You're damn right I do."

We walked into the quiet warehouse through a large, rolled-up metal door. Apparently the grapes that had been picked that day had not made it to the crusher yet because the warehouse was eerily quiet. Guillermo pointed to a stainless-steel square funnel with a large black machine attached to the bottom of it.

"That's it. One of the best. It's the most gentle of all large-scale grape crushers. We tested out a few others but weren't happy until we found this one."

Studying it, I walked around and took some mental notes, and then I thought about that episode of *I Love Lucy* when Lucy and the Italian woman stomp around the huge barrel, crushing the grapes with their bare feet.

"I was really hoping to have a Lucille Ball moment while I was here." I was half-joking, but I smiled to myself at the idea.

A voice coming from behind startled me. "I think we can arrange that." I turned to see Jamie, sweaty and gorgeous, leaning against the large doorway. Chelsea was sitting right at his heel, staring me down. He took off his hat and ran his fingers through his hair and then replaced his hat again. As I watched him move, it was like time stood still. His motions slowed down, as if someone had turned a dial or pressed a button on the remote.

"What do you mean, you can arrange that?"

"Give me ten minutes." And then he was gone. Guillermo looked down, shaking his head, trying to contain his laughter.

"I think that's it for me, *mija*. I have to get back to work. Do you have any questions?"

"Yes, I have a million questions," I said quickly.

"I think Jamie can help answer most of them, he really knows his way around here."

I nodded. "Okay, it was so nice to meet you. Thank you." I reached my hand out, and he shook it. "You're welcome, *mija*." He leaned in and kissed me on the cheek in a familial way that made my heart warm.

Jamie came in, rolling a barrel on its side. As he passed Guillermo, they nodded at each other. Chelsea plopped down in the corner on the cold concrete.

"Katy, are you ready for this? He turned the barrel upright and removed the lid. I leaned over and inhaled a mixture of aromas. It was sweet and sour, earthy and oaky—a pungent but natural smell. I could see the glimmer of grapes at the bottom as the light hit them.

He was watching me. "Well, shoes off." He grinned, grabbed a bucket, and turned it upside down so I could sit.

I removed my shoes and socks a bit reluctantly. "Am I going to ruin these grapes?"

He knelt in front of me and began rolling up my jeans from the bottom. Then he held one foot out and examined it. I was terribly self-conscious in that moment. *Jesus lord, is he checking for fungus?*

"I will personally drink every drop of wine made from these cute little feet." He wiped my feet off with a damp rag and then spread it on the floor for me to stand on. "You might want to take off your sweatshirt. You're probably going to get hot—it's hard work, grape-stomping."

Remembering that I was only wearing the camisole underneath, sans bra, I panicked. "Um . . ."

He flashed me the most self-satisfied smirk. "I've seen you in your underwear already."

"I have a tank top on," I huffed, and then removed my sweatshirt. The camisole fell an inch above the top of my jeans, exposing my midriff. It was fucking silk and I was braless. *Can you say zero class?*

Still grinning, he squinted his eyes as he scanned my attire. "I don't know if I would call that a tank top, Katy, but I like it. Let's get you into this barrel. Okay, put your hands on the top. On the count of three, you're gonna jump and I'll lift you in." He stood behind me, very closely, and put his hands on my hips. "One," he said in his normal voice. He smelled of cardamom and musk from working but his breath smelled fruity. "Two." He tightened his grip. This was taking way too long. My spine was tingling and my legs were losing all feeling. He leaned in, pressing himself against me. *Oh my.* His mouth hovered right over my ear. "Three." Chills shot through my entire body, my knees buckled, and I started to collapse. Holding me up, he chuckled. "You're supposed to jump, silly."

Fighting a smile, I turned around and faced him in mock anger. "Well, stop whispering in my ear like that."

"You liked it."

"You're making me shy, and I am not a shy person." I took a deep breath through my nose to steady myself.

"I promise, my goal is not to make you *shy*."

Turning back around, I jutted my ass out, forcing him back a few inches. He stepped back but still held a firm grip on my hips. "*I* will count," I said firmly.

"Okay, baby."

Goose bumps. Again. Just from the word "baby."

"One-two-three," I yelled in fast succession and then jumped. It was like floating; there was suddenly no gravity, and time slowed again. I closed my eyes and thought I would open them to find myself free-falling through a wild galaxy full of marshmallows and Sweet Tarts and chubby little cherubs playing tiny, heart-shaped lutes.

Back to reality, I bent my knees to clear the top of the barrel. Jamie lifted me effortlessly, as if I were a child. I stretched my legs, my feet touching the grapes. I squished my toes into them and giggled for at least twenty seconds while he watched me.

"Start crushing, lady." Jamie held the barrel steady while I stomped around, laughing. The grapes were tougher than I thought they would be, but still squishy enough that they tickled me a bit. I paused, took a deep breath, and wiped a bead of sweat from my brow with the back of my hand.

"Why are you so happy?" I said to a smiling Jamie.

"You really seem to be enjoying yourself."

"I am." I stomped around a bit more and then paused again. "You're right, this is a workout." I glanced down and noticed my silk camisole sticking to my body. Jamie followed my gaze and then looked back up at my eyes. I saw the movement in his neck from swallowing and then I watched his chest rise and fall on a deep breath. I felt my nipples harden against the material.

"Can you help me get out?"

"Sure." He stood behind me again. "Jump and pull up your knees to your chest."

When I jumped he grabbed my hips, lifting me high above the barrel, then set me down on the towel. He put the bucket behind me and I sat down.

Kneeling in front of me, he carefully cleaned every bit of grape from the bottoms and tops of my feet and between my toes. When he hit a ticklish spot, I jerked. "Ah, Kate Corbin, the always serious investigative reporter, first on all the breaking news, *is* ticklish!" He grinned impishly.

"No, no, no!" I shouted as he began a brutal assault on my feet, pulling me toward him off the bucket. I fell to the floor and began rolling around, tossing and turning like a freakin' animal. "Stop, please!" I began mock-crying. At this point I was lying on the concrete warehouse floor, flat on my back. He stopped immediately and leaned over me, a knee on either side of my hips, his hands planted on each side of my head. He was on top of me, essentially, and he was searching my eyes. There were tears in my eyes, but not sad tears.

"Are you seriously crying?"

"More like laugh-crying. I hate being tickled." He jumped up to his feet and held his hands out for me.

"You scared me, Katy. I thought I had hurt you."

"No, it's just a little embarrassing to be tickled by an almost-stranger."

"We're friends, remember? We decided last night."

"Oh right, friends," I said hesitantly.

His eyes were trained on my mouth. "Friends," he said again.

I nodded quickly and then looked away in embarrassment. I could feel red splotches appearing all over my face. My thoughts had gone way beyond friendship with Jamie, and I had only just met him.

Out of the corner of my eye, I saw him glance at his watch. He was wearing a plain black Luminox, the kind Navy SEALs wear.

"Are you a diver?"

He looked at his wrist again. "No, I got to hang out with the SEALs once and they were all wearing these watches. I thought it was cool, so I got myself one." He smiled a really boyish and innocent grin.

"Why were you hanging out with the SEALs?"

"It was one of those school field trip things a long time ago," he said quickly. "It's eleven thirty, I need to go get cleaned up before we meet Chef Mark. I'll meet you in the restaurant at noon?" I nodded. "Can you get back okay?"

"Yes, I'll see you over there."

Walking through the vineyard, I fantasized about what might've happened in those next few moments on that warehouse floor with Jamie as he hovered over my body. I would reach up and take his hat off, watching his hair fall to the sides of his cheeks. I would run my fingers through it, and then he would lean down to kiss me.

Just when his lips were about to touch mine, I was jolted from my daydream by the buzzing of my phone. It was a text.

> *Stephen:* I had the super open ur apartment so I could return some of ur stuff.

What the hell? I thought.

> *Kate:* STAY THE FUCK OUT OF MY APARTMENT AND LEAVE ME THE FUCK ALONE

The cursor rested just after the word "alone" before I hit SEND. Staring at it, I thought about my life in Chicago, and it made my stomach ache. I thought about Stephen with another woman. I thought about Rose and my mother and Just Bob, all alone, all their lives. I wondered what hurt more: the kind of loneliness you feel when no one is around, or the kind of loneliness you feel when the person who is supposed to love you doesn't care at all, not even enough to fight with you, let alone fight for you. Have you ever felt lonely in a crowded room? Have you ever felt alone when you are not? It hurts far more, and I didn't ask for that pain. I realized in that moment that Jamie made me feel that I could be, at the very least, at the bare minimum, worth coming home to.

I hit SEND. Almost immediately, he responded.

> *Stephen:* AREN'T YOU SUPPOSED TO BE A WRITER? IS THE F-BOMB THE BEST YOU CAN DO?

> *Kate:* GO FUCK YOURSELF, YOU PIECE OF SHIT.

Would Stephen fight for me?

> *Stephen:* HAVE A NICE LIFE.

Guess not.

Poetry

While visiting my room and cleaning up, I decided to go back to a blazer and flats instead of heels. Heels somehow seemed out of place here. I headed toward the restaurant and caught Jamie standing in the doorway of his truck. Hearing me come toward him, he turned. "I have to meter really quick before we eat." He was wearing a clean white T-shirt and black jeans with Converse. His hair was damp and slicked back. The growth on his face was thicker than the day before, and I wondered what it would feel like to brush my cheek against his.

I stood next to him and watched as he popped open a small container with test strips and then inserted one into the meter. He took a smaller device, a lancet, I assumed, and pricked his finger then smoothed the drop of blood over the strip extending from the meter.

"One hundred exactly. I'm good to go."

"What do you do when it's too high or too low?"

"Well, my ever-curious little kitten, I'll tell you all about that tonight when we go sailing. You'll need to know." He winked.

That little tidbit made me nervous. "Why will I need to know?"

He grabbed my hand and pulled me toward the restaurant, ignoring my question. "Come on, I'm starving."

The restaurant had a bar stretching around the open kitchen. Jamie explained that it was designed so guests could get an up-close experience with the chefs, who prepared their signature dishes and offered the guests wine pairings. The restaurant, called Beijar, was finely decorated and lit, with dark, rich booths and muted lighting against the stark light from the kitchen. The effect highlighted the clean, stainless-steel counters and drew my eyes to where the magic happened. I had no doubt Beijar was an experience as much as it was a meal.

We took our seats on the stools at the kitchen bar. Before Chef Mark came in, I swiveled toward Jamie. "Where did they get the name from?"

"It means 'kiss' in Portuguese." When I was with Jamie I forgot about everything else. Just the word "kiss" coming out of his mouth could freeze time.

"Oh."

"Food is like love, you know?"

"Yes," I said breathlessly.

"We need it to stay alive."

"Uh-huh."

"And wine is like poetry."

His words, his warmth, were like a stun gun to my brain. I was conscious of nothing but his words. "Oh?"

"If it's good wine." He revealed his dimple. "If not, then it's a tragedy."

I realized that he had dimples on both cheeks, but his smile was always just a little crooked so it only showed up one side. Adorable.

"Is it Portuguese food?"

"Not really. There's a little inspiration, but it's traditional American, farm to table."

Chef Mark entered. "Hi, Kate." He reached over and shook my hand.

"Nice to meet you, Chef." He wore the standard white chef's shirt and a black bandana across his hair, tied at the back of his neck. He was an average-looking guy of forty, at least, but his presence was strong. I imagined that he could command a busy kitchen of chefs and servers.

Jamie reached over, shook his hand as well, and said, "Chef."

"Hey, buddy." Clapping once, he suggested, "Why don't we start with a salad trio?"

"That sounds fabulous." Jamie got us glasses of water and opened a bottle of the Pinot while Chef Mark got to work. He poured me a glass but only poured himself a quarter of the amount.

"Why so little for you? Are you sick of the wine?"

"No, I love the wine, but I can't have too much because of the diabetes. I can taste it, though. I'd like to have some with you later, so I'm saving up." My heart did a somersault.

Chef Mark set a plate in front of me, describing each of the four salads as he pointed them out. "Heirloom tomatoes. Avocado and corn in a light vinaigrette. Quinoa with mango and red peppers. And, finally, beet and kale with goat cheese. Enjoy."

I took a bite of the avocado coated in dressing. Jamie watched my mouth as I chewed.

"What do you taste?" he asked.

"Shallots and lemon and avocado." I took a bite of the tomato. "That is perfection."

"We grow those in a hothouse on the estate. The big tomatoes are harder to grow outside in this region."

Chef Mark asked me how I was enjoying the salads. He mentioned that there weren't a ton of vegetarian dishes on the menu but that he would try his best to make accommodations.

"Well, I eat seafood, too." Jamie and Chef Mark both jerked their heads back.

Leaning in, Chef Mark spoke in the gentlest voice. "You are not a vegetarian, sweetie. You're a pescetarian."

"That sounds like a religion."

Jamie laughed and looked over at me with a pitying expression. It was funny how I had berated Stephen on the very topic of being a vegetarian, but here I was getting lectured myself.

"This opens up many possibilities for us. Halibut or salmon, which would you prefer?" Chef Mark asked.

"Surprise me."

"This opens up possibilities for me, too," Jamie said, turning his body toward me.

"How's that?"

He took my fork and stabbed the last piece of avocado off my plate and held it to my mouth. I opened for him. "I like feeding you. I want to take you into the city tomorrow night for dinner. Will you let me do that?" I had swallowed the avocado and now my mouth was hanging open. I must have looked like a moron. He shook his head and ran his thumb over my bottom lip. "There's no more. It's all gone, angel." I shut my mouth and shook my head, inhaling through my nose deeply to clear my head. I still couldn't believe his effect on me.

"So, will you let me take you to dinner tomorrow?"

"Okay." *Positively, undeniably, absolutely, emphatically, definitely, one hundred percent YES!*

We finished the lunch, which I could only describe as erotic, although I don't think Jamie was intentionally trying to make it that way. He fed me the last little bites off my plate, clearly a stickler about wasting food, but it was the attention that he gave me that lit my insides on fire. Never in my life had anyone given me that kind of attention. I sat there trying to commit each moment to memory so I could relive it later when I was . . . alone. Ahem.

Jamie was still a mystery to me. Even though it felt like I had known him forever, I hadn't asked him one real question about his life, his family—nothing. I made a mental note to do that and then I scolded myself for getting tongue-tied around him. I could not let that happen anymore. He practically hypnotized me with his looks alone. Add to that his words and his sweet mannerisms, and he fully entranced me. I thought about his thumb on my lip and how at ease I was with him. When we parted ways after lunch, I glanced at my phone and calculated the hours until I would see him again.

Susan and I met in her office for the facility tour. She basically took me through each of the buildings and explained the inspiration for the architecture and décor. She informed me that the inn and restaurant were legally on a separate piece of property from the winery itself. She said R.J. had gone to great lengths to make sure that the entire operation abided by all of the strict rules handed down by the Napa County Board. She said that he had paid more than the winery was worth, and it wasn't a matter of him throwing his money around so much as it was his passion to give the pleasure of this beautiful place to others. She referred to the winery as his escape. I couldn't see that at all. He seemed barely involved. When I tried to pry deeper into the dynamic between the employees and R.J., she skirted the issue.

"I just didn't see one redeeming quality in him, but I keep

hearing about all of the wonderful things he's done. Jamie called him a 'douche' on the first day and you said yourself to forget about him." She studied me intently as I spoke.

"Let's just say he was having an off day. I would recommend that you focus on the winery and operations, not whether or not R.J. is living up to his reputation. If he wants anonymity, what's wrong with that?"

"It's not in my nature to give anyone anonymity. I came here to get the story on him."

"I can see that. I left his e-mail address on a note in your room. You can send him any more questions you have, but I really believe you will get the best information here, on the grounds."

We left each other abruptly. I got the sense that Susan liked me but was perhaps frustrated with R.J.'s distance and lack of participation.

I went back up to my room and began to draft an e-mail to R.J.

> Dear R.J.,
> I'm sorry our first interview didn't go as well as we both hoped. I think e-mail will be a better platform for us. I've listed a few questions. Please answer at your discretion.
>
> All the best,
> Kate Corbin
> Chicago Crier
>
> 1. Can you give me any details about your personal life? Are you single? Do you live alone? What are your hobbies? Is your family involved in your business ventures?

2. Why did you decide to buy a winery?

3. Why did you sell J-Com Technologies?

When I hit SEND, an error message popped up reminding me that I still wasn't connected to the Wi-Fi. I fiddled for twenty minutes with it before finally resorting to typing the e-mail on my phone and sending it. Within half an hour, he responded in complete narrative form.

Kate,

I'm really sorry about yesterday. I didn't conduct myself professionally and I apologize. I'm trying desperately to keep my personal life private. I'll give you some background and then try to answer your questions as efficiently as possible. I was in the public eye from the age of thirteen when I graduated from high school. By sixteen, I had a degree from MIT and a brand new company, J-Com Technologies. After patenting new server technology, I was coined "The Boy Genius" in the media. It was a tough role to live up to. I was under a great deal of pressure, even with the unwavering support of my father, who essentially ran the company.

Although my love for discovery and science never died, my interests and focus began to change back then. There was a night when I realized that all of the glory of my early success translated into money, but the money only made me feel empty. I had to teach myself to look at it differently, to look at the money as representing something more basic: clean water, food, vaccines, shelter, and for the very lucky, education. It was the realization that a third of the world's population is poor, hungry, and dying of preventable diseases that pushed me to sell J-Com. I did not want to waste my time on what I felt were frivolous things, and that's why I got out when I did.

I took the money, started a foundation, and went to Africa, where I spent almost ten years traveling around, building schools and infrastructure. My foundation still provides vaccines for thousands, and we work tirelessly to provide small villages the proper resources to get plumbing and clean water. That is my passion. I spend several months a year there.

The winery is my escape. I've also used it to test clean energy theories, but mostly it's a home to me. I am single and live alone. My hobbies are typical. I am very close to my father, who lives in Portland. He's a retired Boeing engineer. My mother was killed in a traffic accident four years ago. She was hit head-on by a girl texting on her phone. Because of that, I spend very little time around the technological gadgets I helped to invent. My mother's death tore me up so badly that I needed to find something to focus my energy on, and that is why I bought the winery. I have one sibling, a younger sister in Boston. We're not close. I think that about wraps it up.

Again, I'm sorry for yesterday. I hope that experience didn't taint your view of the winery.

Kind Regards,
R.J.

And there it was. I had my story. I didn't need to write an article; R.J. had basically done it for me: philanthropist, genius, douche bag with a heart. That was going to be my angle. The tragedy of his mother's death drove him to buy the winery and escape into the hills of Napa Valley, leaving the tech world behind. I wanted to spotlight the winery in the article as well as the good he was doing in Africa with his organization, but I struggled with how R.J. had treated me during our meeting. I wondered if he really needed his ego stroked any more.

I glanced at the clock. It was three fifty. I showered in three minutes, threw on a coat of lip gloss and mascara, and got dressed in a T-shirt, jeans, and flats. When I got to the stairway, Jamie was there at the bottom. I reached for the banister but saw him slowly shaking his head back and forth.

"What?"

He pointed toward my door. "Back in there, lady. You need sneakers and a sweatshirt." I huffed and rolled my eyes like a teenager before turning and heading back to my room. When I came down the stairs, he was leaning his back against the banister with his hands in his pockets, looking relaxed and delicious. He was wearing jeans, a thicker black jacket, and his plain black baseball cap. He looked dangerous, and then he flashed me a dimple and it all went *poof. No more danger.* He grabbed my hand and pulled me toward the door.

"Where is everyone?" I asked.

"Everyone who?" he asked without turning to look at me. We passed the front desk and Jamie shot his hand up in a wave. "See ya, George." The same man who was working behind the desk the night before waved to us.

"Who all is going sailing?"

He stopped in the parking lot as we approached his truck and turned toward me.

"It's just you and me." He hesitated, searching my face. "Is that okay?"

"Yes, I just don't understand why you made such a big deal about dinner if you already had plans to sweep me away tonight?" I said, fluttering my eyelashes coquettishly.

"Dinner is intimate. This is sport. It'll be fun." He opened the passenger door. I hopped in. Chelsea sat on the sidewalk, glaring at us. He turned and spotted her. "You have to stay here, girl." And then he pointed toward the inn. "Go lay down on your bed." Her head dropped as she walked away slowly. She knew exactly what was going on.

As we turned onto the main road, I rolled down the window and stuck my head out, letting the wind dry my hair. Jamie turned up the radio.

"Who is this?" I shouted.

"The Amazing. It's a song called 'Dragon.'"

"It sounds old."

"It's not. What are you doing, crazy girl?"

"What does it look like, genius? I'm drying my hair."

He laughed, shaking his head. I closed my eyes and felt the wind whip my long hair all over. I listened to the music and let the lowering sun beat down on my face. When my hair was adequately dry, I rolled the window up and Jamie turned down the music.

"All right, Katy, we need to talk about a few things."

"Yes, because I have questions, too."

"Well, first of all, I need to talk to you about the diabetes." There were two rectangular canisters sitting between us on the truck seat, one orange and one black, both about the size of a sunglasses case. "The black case has my meter and insulin, and you won't need to worry about that because I can do that myself. When my blood sugar is high and I need insulin, I'm usually alert. When it's low, I can take these glucose tablets or drink some juice." He held up a bottle of glucose tablets. "If it gets really low, I get groggy. If it gets too low, there's a chance I could pass out." My eyes got huge. He glanced over at me. "I've never passed out, but I've gotten really low. If I pass out, you'll need to give me that shot in the orange case. It's a glucagon kit." He looked over quickly and then returned his gaze to the road. "Kate, are you okay?"

"Yes. Where do I inject you?" He pointed to his ass and grinned. "Of course it would have to be there."

"I don't think you'll need to worry about it, but since we'll be on a boat, I thought it was important to tell you."

"Are we going on R.J.'s boat?"

"It's my boat." He snickered.

"Yesterday, when you gave me the ride up the driveway, you called R.J. a douche." He didn't respond. I let a few moments go by. "Jamie?"

"He can be, but he wasn't himself in that interview. I think it was a case of paranoia, to be honest with you."

"He had a funny way of showing it . . . by hitting on me?"

Shaking his head back and forth, he said, "I know, he was an idiot. R.J. usually tries to do the right thing, but sometimes it just backfires."

I quietly watched Jamie for a few minutes and studied his tattoos as he turned the steering wheel.

"Where did you get your tattoos? They all look different."

"I've gotten them all over the world. I traveled a lot after college."

"They're really interesting. Not typical at all. Do they mean anything?"

"Yes. Some do." He looked over, wearing a small, sad smile, so I decided to drop the subject.

"Where are we going, exactly?"

"We're sailing out of Sausalito. That's where I keep my boat. We're almost there."

The sun was moving lower in the sky and the air was much cooler when we stepped onto the docks in Sausalito. "There she is." He pointed to what looked like a thirty-foot standard keel sailboat. When I got closer, I noticed that it was an older boat with beautiful, polished wood decking, sleek lines, and a very tall mast.

Once we reached the boat, Jamie immediately started unhooking cords and coiling up lines on the dock. He unhooked the safety cable and stepped on board easily, then turned and held out his hand for me. "Step up on the block there, Katy, and then onto the boat. You can have a seat. I need to get a few things ready." He gestured toward a bench in the cockpit behind the large steering wheel. I watched as he removed covers from the rolled-up sails, hooked lines, and then removed the door leading into the bedroom below. He went down the ladder and then returned a few moments later with a blanket and red wine in a stemless glass.

"Here you are. It's going to be really chilly out on the water."

"I feel so spoiled. Is this what you do for all the ladies who visit R. J. Lawson Winery?"

"Hardly," he said as he continued setting things up and tugging at lines. "I usually sail with Guillermo, sometimes Susan or her son. I don't really like going out alone, but I'll go on short runs with just Chelsea once in a while."

"Cute. She hates me, by the way."

"Maybe she's jealous of you."

"Are we really having this conversation about a dog?"

"She's like a person. You said it yourself."

"True. So tell me about the boat. How long have you had it? How long have you been sailing?"

"I learned how to sail as a kid with my dad up north, but it wasn't until last year that I had a boat of my own. I restored this beauty. I bought her for fifteen hundred dollars last year and spent three months bringing her back to life."

"Why am I not surprised? What's her name?"

"*Heartbeats*."

"Why?"

"You'll see."

The sun was setting behind the Golden Gate Bridge. To say it was picturesque would be a gross understatement. I was in awe. Jamie backed the boat out of the slip and then moved forward out of the channel to the open water.

"Katy, what do you know about sailing?" His back was to me.

"Nothing. I've never even been on a sailboat."

"You're kidding. Please tell me you know how to swim."

"Of course I do."

"Well, I don't think you'll want to swim in this water, but it's good that you know how. The life vests are under your seat just in case, and there's a little emergency beacon and radio that you can turn on if something happens to me."

"That sounds very scary."

"Everything will be fine."

"What shall I call you? Captain Jamie?"

"Or Captain Fantastic. Either one will do." He turned to me and smiled.

Once we were in the open water, Jamie stepped aside and said, "Okay, your turn to steer."

"Me?" I said with a shriek.

"Yes, I need to raise the sails. We're going to turn into the wind. See the arrow up at the top of the mast?" He pointed up.

"Yes."

"It's always pointing in the direction that the wind is coming from. If the arrow is pointing directly to the bow of the boat, then you're in irons; you're driving directly into the wind. That's what you want to do if you need to stop the boat—just turn the boat into the wind. Okay, now take the wheel." He put his arm around my shoulder, bending close to my face, and pointed. "See that buoy in the distance?" I nodded. "Just steer the boat in that direction. That's your heading. I'll get the sails up and then we'll kill the engine, my favorite part." He jumped up on the tiny decking space and held the safety cords as he walked along toward the sails. He removed some ties and quickly raised the mainsail and then returned to the cockpit. Standing right behind me, I felt him bend close to my ear and then I heard him inhale deeply. He put his hands over mine and turned the wheel about forty degrees to the right until we were heading right for the Golden Gate Bridge.

"Okay, baby, that big bridge is your heading now. You can't miss it, just steer straight for it."

"Ha-ha!" I said sarcastically. *Try me.*

He adjusted some lines, pulling them from the winches and cleating them off. He turned a key and pulled a lever, killing the engine before quickly returning to his spot behind me. There was silence for a few moments, followed by the light sound of the wind and the water lapping at the side of the boat.

"What do you hear?" he asked.

"Nothing."

"Listen closely," he said softly near my ear.

It seemed like every sound was shut out, every worry, every care . . . gone. Once Jamie turned off the engine, there was only peace from the quiet and gentle movement. The sound of the city was a distant hum across the huge bay. The world looked like a painting, and the only movement I could see was the water around us. It was as if we were sailing across a canvas, painted with Impressionist waves, with the San Francisco skyline in the background. Sunlight dazzled us through the giant cables of the bright red bridge, silhouetting the monster in an almost frightening way. It was overwhelming to be so close to the bridge. There were no cell phones, no horns honking. Nothing. And then I heard it. I took a deep breath and said quietly, "Heartbeats. That's what I hear. Yours and mine . . ." I turned to see him smiling.

The wind picked up rather dramatically. I shivered and he wrapped one arm around my shoulder from behind while he used his other hand to grab the wheel. "Ready for some fun?"

"I'm scared."

"I got you." As soon as he turned the boat into a better heading, we immediately began listing dramatically. The wind beat much louder against the sails, and the forward motion of the boat sped up. I lost my footing a little, but he held me tight to his chest. We moved closer and closer to the massive bridge. It became bigger and more intimidating with each passing moment, but the truth was that I wasn't scared at all. Jamie made me feel safe. Even against the rushing wind, the choppy waves, and the towering bridge, I felt bigger, like I could stand up to it all. The right side of the boat was way above us. We had all of our weight on our left feet when we started skipping, rising, and diving quickly on the waves.

I was laughing and screeching with joy. I saw Jamie smiling, his grin so wide and so proud that it made my eyes water.

"Are you enjoying yourself, Katy?"

"This is . . . amazing." At the last second my voice cracked, tears ran down my cheeks, and I shivered. I felt cherished, and even though I wasn't sure where it would go with Jamie, I was enjoying every minute of the ride.

He moved from behind me. "Here, sit, I'll wrap you up. It's getting cold."

I sat on the bench to his left on the low side of the boat. He handed me my wineglass from the cupholder and then quickly wrapped the blanket around me before getting back to the wheel. "We're going to jibe. Normally the captain would say 'prepare to jibe.'"

"That sounds fun," I shouted giddily over the sound of the waves.

"It just means we're turning with the wind, but the mast is going to swing around quickly. Keep your head down."

"Aye, aye, Captain."

We headed back to the docks in Sausalito. The entire way back, neither one of us spoke; we just took it all in. Every once in a while I would steal glances at Jamie, only to find him watching me and smiling. Once we parked in the slip, it took him about twenty minutes to put the covers on everything and tie up the sails. He slung an arm around my shoulders as we headed back to the truck, and then he opened my door for me. "Hop up, cutie." He ran his hand across my hair as I got in. I immediately looked in the visor mirror and discovered a red-cheeked, windblown, wreck of a woman. He was teasing me by making me self-aware about my hair. Quickly wrapping my frizzy locks in a bun, I turned toward him as he got in the driver's side.

"You were making fun of me, jerk."

"I was just playing with you." His eyes dropped to my mouth. I shook from a chill.

"You're still cold." He took off his jacket and draped it over my legs. I watched him, completely mesmerized, as he opened the black case from the compartment between us, pulled out the pen, and stabbed the skin on his stomach with a needle full of insulin. No blood that time. We were back on the road in seconds.

"Chef Mark is making us dinner but the restaurant will be closed. It closes early on Wednesdays for karaoke night."

"You're kidding?"

"Not at all. We take our karaoke very seriously at R. J. Lawson."

"I am the karaoke queen."

He laughed. "Well, I am known far and wide in these parts as the white Otis Redding."

"Oh, we are so doing a duet. Which song should we do?"

We were silent for a few moments, and then in unison both of us shouted, "Tramp!"

We practically skipped through the parking lot and into the restaurant, which was already full of people directing their attention to a small stage set up in the corner. Judging by the turnout, karaoke was a very popular activity with the locals. I started feeling nervous about my performance until a very drunk group of women, who looked to be in their fifties, sang a horrible rendition of "Vacation" by the Go-Go's.

We sat at the kitchen bar where a waitress immediately brought out the plates Chef Mark had prepared for us. I had seafood stew in a light tomato sauce with French bread on the side. It smelled divine. Jamie had some kind of white fish. When he saw it, he smiled. "Oh good, we can share," he said, boyishly. He grabbed a bottle of chardonnay from the kitchen. It was from a different winery, and I quirked an eyebrow at him. "We like to know what our competition is up to."

"Really?" I had to shout over the painful sounds coming from the speakers.

"No, we serve a few other wines here." He laughed. "Some of our neighborhood friends."

"I see," I said, smiling. The winery really was becoming a magical and friendly place in my mind.

He walked over and said something to the guy manning the karaoke equipment.

When he came back, he leaned down toward my ear. "It's so on." I laughed and dove into my dinner. I drank three full glasses of wine while Jamie sipped his tiny portion.

"Are you trying to get me drunk so you can show me up?"

"Yes, that's my strategy."

"But we're doing a duet. I could make you look really bad and tarnish your precious reputation."

He smirked. "I'm thinking of it more as a duel than a duet."

I leaned in toward him and deadpanned, "Bring it."

A moment later, the karaoke guy announced, "Captain Fantastic and Super Girl, you're up!"

Jamie grabbed my hand and pulled me toward the stage. "That's us," he shouted. I laughed and then my stomach dropped through the floor when I realized I was about to sing to a room full of strangers. Karaoke guy handed Jamie and me our mics, and then we stepped up onto the small rectangular stage. Jamie never looked over at me. He put his head down like he was about to deliver Hamlet's monologue to a room full of thespians. He clearly took his karaoke seriously. I had to play along, so I quickly choreographed a few steps in my mind.

When the music came on, I got the pleasure of singing the

first line. "Tramp!" I coated it with a thick Southern accent and then jetted my arm out, pointing at Jamie as I spoke the word.

Still with his head down, his right shoulder began bouncing to the beat as we exchanged the famous back-and-forth between Otis Redding and Carla Thomas. When it was time to sing, Jamie lifted his head, spun around, and slid across the floor, dropping to his knees in front of me as he delivered the line "I know, I'm a loverererer." He held his empty fist out and pounded his chest as he sang before winking at me and then hopping to his feet. He sang up to the ceiling dramatically during the second verse, which garnered him a lot of cheering from the audience, mostly from the women, but it was when he went out into the crowd to sing the last verse that he truly lived up to his reputation. He hovered around the ladies who had sung "Vacation," and I watched as they fanned themselves and laughed like schoolgirls.

When we were through, he grabbed my hand and held it all the way to the door while yelling back "Thank you!" to the crowd. We both bowed and then he said, "We'll be back next Wednesday for the encore." Everyone cheered loudly.

Once outside, he turned to me, "You were awesome." His eyes were gleaming.

"You're already promising I'll be back next week? Pretty confident of you, isn't it? I doubt I'll still be here next Wednesday. I'm on a serious budget with the paper." The idea of going back to reality in Chicago made my stomach hurt.

He drove his hands into his pockets, looked down at his feet, and shrugged. "Wishful thinking, I guess."

I was doing the same thing, hoping that there would be some reason to stay longer, to get to know Jamie better. "Well you, my friend, were truly fantastic in there, especially with those ladies."

His face went expressionless. "I had to work at that, Kate. It didn't come easily."

We both burst into laughter. I looked up at the sky and saw a hundred million stars shimmering brightly. We quieted, but I stayed where I was, staring at the sky, transfixed. I wondered if I had been at the winery for years. That's what it felt like. I couldn't believe I had only known Jamie since the day before. I knew so little about him but I didn't care because, when I was with him, I didn't feel alone.

"Kiss me," I said strongly. He took a staggering step back and then scanned my face but didn't respond. "You heard me."

"Is that how you ask nicely?" One side of his mouth lifted.

"Please kiss me."

"You have a boyfriend."

I didn't hesitate for a second. "Not anymore."

And then his lips crushed mine.

We kissed eagerly, clutching at each other. My hands went to his neck, tangling my fingers in his soft hair. His hands ran upward from the small of my back. His lips were softer than they looked and he took his time, moving from my mouth to my neck and then up my jawline to my ear, trailing tiny kisses before coming back to my lips. I could have kissed him like that for days. When he finally slowed, his fingers ran up my spine to my neck, and I shivered. When he let go, I stumbled to the side, not completely in control of my body. He braced me by the elbows. His eyes were wide and bright, and I could tell he was waiting for me to say something.

"That was nice," I said, still stunned.

"Nice?" he said in mock offense.

"Wondrous?"

"Mind-blowing," he came back quickly.

"Spine-tingling."

"Exploding stars."

"Intoxicating."

"Christmas morning."

"Chocolate lava cake."

"Potassium chlorate and gummy bears."

I squinted sharply. "What?"

"It's chemistry. Google it." He took my hand in his and pulled me along into the darkness.

"Where are we going?"

"Let's watch the stars."

We lay down on some blankets in the back of his truck, which was still parked in the main parking lot. We watched the stars, talked, and laughed as we heard the drunken ladies pouring out of the restaurant, talking about Captain Fantastic.

As the parking lot fell quiet, I decided to get personal. "Tell me your story, Jamie."

He didn't move for a few moments. "What do you want to know?"

"Tell me about your life and what brought you to this place."

"Well, I was adopted by two of the greatest people to walk this earth. I was their only child. I grew up on the West Coast, not too far from here, and aside from the diabetes, I had a truly idyllic childhood. When I was eighteen, I found my birth parents. They were married and had another child, whom I've never met because a month after I reconnected with my birth parents, they tried to steal money from me." I squeezed his hand, but he continued without pause. "I cut off all ties to them, not that there were many to begin with. I went to college on the East Coast and then came back to California for a couple of years. Before I found the winery, I traveled a lot and tried my hand at a few different things. I met Susan when I was going through a rough time, and she brought me to this place." He paused for just a second. "Your turn."

It seemed like Jamie was uncomfortable talking about himself or his life. I didn't get the feeling that he didn't want to share certain things with me; I just got the impression he was a live-in-the-moment kind of guy and didn't dwell on the past. Still, something about the way he described his life reminded me of my own, and the solitude I felt in it. I thought dreamily for a moment about how it seemed like Jamie and I were two lost and lonely souls finding each other in the vast wasteland of adulthood.

"No rebuttal questions?"

"I want to know about you, Katy."

"Well, I was raised in Chicago by my mother. I never knew my father. I don't even know his name, so I'll never find him. When I was eight, my mother died of cancer. After that, I went to live with her best friend, Rose. I have no family that I know of, my grandparents are dead, no siblings, no aunts or uncles. I was shy growing up so I didn't have a lot of friends. I came out of my shell when I went to college, but didn't have many lasting relationships from that, either. I've worked at the *Chicago Crier* for five years. I live alone." In that moment I wondered if I was scaring Jamie away, but he just continued listening and nodding every few seconds, so I went on. "I'm good friends with Beth, a writer at the paper. I'm pretty sure she's a closeted lesbian. I also have a pretty good relationship with Jerry, the editor you talked to yesterday. Let's see, what else? Oh, my ex, Stephen, just basically told me he never loved me and that he had been unhappy for a long time. So, that's my story. Pretty pathetic, huh?"

"He's an idiot," he said up to the sky. We were both lying flat on our backs, holding hands.

"Who, Stephen?"

Jamie just nodded.

"I can think of a few stronger words for him. We broke up last night and he was already at breakfast with another woman this morning."

"You deserve better," he said and then brought my hand to his mouth and kissed it. "Where is Rose now?"

"She's dead. She died nine months ago," I said, flatly. He turned his whole body toward me.

"Kate, I'm so sorry."

"I don't want to talk about her. It's too hard."

"I understand. Let's change the subject. What shall we talk about?"

"Um, what kind of music do you like?"

"A little bit of everything. Mostly indie rock, folk, that kind of thing." We lay on our sides, facing each other.

"Same here."

"So why'd you ask me to kiss you?"

I swallowed and made a loud gulping sound. "I . . . er . . . uh, did you not want to kiss me?"

"Are you kidding? Let me think . . ." He scratched his chin. "I've wanted to kiss you pretty much every second I've spent with you since we met, but that wasn't my question."

My heart was racing. I felt momentarily paralyzed with fear that I might accidentally blurt out that Jamie was the single hottest guy I'd ever been alone with. "I wanted you to kiss me," I said, shyly.

He touched his index finger to my bottom lip and tugged down on it. "I know, but why?"

"You know why."

"Was it my amazing karaoke skills?"

"No."

His face went expressionless. "Was it to get back at your ex?"

"No."

"Then what was it?"

I smiled giddily and tried unsuccessfully to stop. Finally giving in, I laughed and said, "I like you, okay?" I felt like the biggest dork in the world.

He smiled, kissed me on the nose, and then said, "I like you, too."

. . .

Later that night, Jamie walked me all the way to the door of my room. I opened it and asked in a confidential whisper, "Do you want to come in?"

"Yes . . . but I'm not going to." He took a step toward me, reached his tattooed arm out, and wrapped his hand around my neck, pulling me toward him, my mouth meeting his. He kissed me softly and slowly and breathlessly. "First, I want to take you on a real date tomorrow. I'll show you the city. There's somewhere special I want to take you."

"Okay," I said.

"Then we're set. What are your plans during the day tomorrow?"

"I was going to work on the article, and then unless I get an itinerary . . . I'll just be hanging around."

"Okay, I'll come and get you around four." He lowered his voice. "If I don't see you before then."

After he walked out, I looked down at my sneakers and my stupid college sweatshirt and laughed. I hadn't thought about fitting in or how I looked when I was with Jamie. He made me feel beautiful and alive. I decided to call Beth. I knew Beth liked to write into the wee hours of the night. She usually got to the office later than me but would proceed to brag to everyone about how many words she wrote the night before.

She picked up on the second ring. "Kate?" She sounded groggy.

"Oh my god, did I wake you?"

"No." She perked up. "I just busted out three thousand words."

"Nice."

"What's up? Are you bummed about Stephen, the jackass?"

"Actually, I was calling because I wanted to tell you that I met someone here."

"Man or woman?"

"Seriously, Beth? A man. I'm straight."

"I was just asking. I mean, I wouldn't blame you, with your history with men and all."

"My history? You've known one guy that I've dated."

"I was just sayin', I wouldn't blame you. That's all, geez, settle down. Tell me about the dude."

"Don't tell Jerry."

"I don't tell Jerry shit."

"Okay, it's this guy who works at the winery. He's gorgeous, but totally not what I'm used to. He's tall and thin but really muscly. His hair is kind of grown out and sometimes he slicks it back. He has a scruffy light beard and tattoos. Oh my god, his tattoos!"

"Whoa, Kate. Bad boy, bad boy, whatcha gonna do?"

"That's the thing. He's not. He's really sweet and sensitive, but confident and sexy as hell—and smart, too. I don't know what the hell he's doing here picking grapes."

"Get his history," she said urgently.

"I did. He told me all about his childhood and everything. He had a totally normal upbringing, besides the fact that he was adopted."

"I meant get his sexual history before you drop your panties for him."

I laughed. "What is it with you and Jerry? You guys think I'm some kind of slut."

"Do you know what a dental dam is?"

"I'm changing the subject."

"Get his history, that's all I'm trying to tell you. If you're going to have your little winery fantasy, then get the details."

"Now you really sound like a journalist. I'll let you go."

She got quiet for a few moments. "Kate, I'm happy for you. Seriously. Enjoy yourself for once. I'll talk to you soon."

Lying on the bed, I wondered where my little fantasy could take me. I had a life in Chicago, plants in my apartment that needed watering, and a career. There was Just Bob on the train waiting to give me some life-changing advice, and then there were Beth and Jerry. I thought about all of it, but when I added it up together, sadly it didn't amount to much. I loved Beth and Jerry, but they were colleagues. I could write anywhere; I could live anywhere. I wondered if Jamie liked me enough to see where things would take us or if he was looking at me as a fling, something temporary.

I thought about what it would be like to upend my life and move to California, but the idea of losing my rent-controlled apartment scared me. Then I thought about the holiday train. Every year the transit people decorate one train. They completely deck it out—even Santa Claus rides on it. My entire life, all I had ever wanted to do was ride the holiday train, but I'd never been able to catch it. When people would talk to me about how rad it was to ride the holiday train, I wanted to kick them in the face.

I was trying to convince myself, while lying on that bed, that I had enough reason to stay in Chicago because, hey, I hadn't ridden the holiday train, but I fell asleep thinking about Jamie and what his rough hands would feel like on my bare skin.

Exposition

Three knocks startled me out of bed. I glanced at the clock—9:01 a.m. I had never slept in that late. I bolted to my feet and headed for the entryway, wearing only a tight black crewneck T-shirt and black lace panties. I hid my lower half behind the cracked door and peeked out to find a smiling female member of the waitstaff holding a metal carafe.

"Hello, Ms. Corbin. I have coffee for you. And this." She handed me a folded-up piece of paper that had the word *Itinerary* written across it in messy handwriting. I opened the door wide and let her pass into the room. She set the coffee on the corner table and I scrambled into the bathroom, threw on a white terry robe, and came out, not bothering to tie it.

"Hi, um . . . ?"

"Lydia."

"Hi, Lydia. I'm having some issues with the Wi-Fi. I think I need a new code?"

"Okay, I'll check on that for you."

"Thank you."

"There's frittata and fresh fruit and muffins and scones in

the dining room when you're ready to come down. I'll be right back with that code." She passed me and headed out the door.

I stood near the entry and started to unfold the itinerary when the three knocks came again. *Wow, she's fast.* I opened the door wide to find Jamie on the other side, looking charming. I glanced down at myself and realized my robe was still hanging open.

"Good morning," he murmured distractedly. I didn't move. His eyes skimmed down my body and back up again. He put his hand over his heart and then turned around to walk away but quickly turned back and stood his ground in the doorway. He was trying to collect himself. He looked up at the ceiling and then back at me. When his eyes met mine, he smiled.

"See something you like?" I asked, using his line on him.

He cleared his throat. "You have no idea."

"I haven't read my itinerary yet so I don't know why you're here." I batted my eyelashes and smiled innocently.

"It's not about that. Although, right now, I'm wishing I'd made breakfast plans with you."

"I have work to do, young man."

He looked down at his feet and chuckled. "I just wanted to let you know that the rental company replaced your car." He pulled the black square key from his pocket. "It's in the parking lot if you want to go exploring today. Just be careful."

"Thank you. At first I thought you were Lydia at the door. I asked her to find out about the Wi-Fi for me. Maybe you can help?" He shook his head. "You don't know how the Wi-Fi works here?"

"No, I don't use it, but I can find out for you and send someone up if you want?" He rocked back onto the heels of his work boots a couple of times. It seemed like an impatient gesture.

"That's okay. I think Lydia will take care of it."

"Great," he said. "So I'll see you later?" I nodded. He turned around and then came right back again, pushing the door open. With a sweet look splashed across his ruggedly handsome face, he stage-whispered, "I can't wait," and then he was gone.

Lydia never came back with the code. I went downstairs and raided the basket of muffins and scones before scurrying back to my room to start work on the article. No Wi-Fi was going to pose a problem, but I didn't want to hassle anyone at the inn. Instead, I decided to hassle Jerry. I dialed his number with lightning speed.

"Jerry Evans."

"Jer, I can't get Wi-Fi here."

"You're kidding? Are you going to write that in the article?"

"I'm going to do this the old-fashioned way."

"What's that, carve it into a stone tablet?"

"Listen, I'm just going to jot down some notes on paper here and let this whole story marinate a little bit. I'll have one of the PAs at the office do some research for me and then, when I'm back in Chicago, I'll knock it out. Whaddaya think?"

"Do I hear a little spark in your voice?"

"If I had a dollar for every time you answered a question with a question . . ."

"You sound better already, Kate. Take your time. I'm not putting a deadline on you, but that doesn't mean you can take for fucking ever, either. All right?"

I laughed. "I know. You're the best, Jer."

By noon I had several sheets of notes scribbled out and strewn across the bed. I remembered that the itinerary was still lying half open on the long entry table. I skipped over and unfolded it to find a couple of simple lines in Jamie's scratchy handwriting:

> 4:00 p.m. Going into the city. That's it. That's all.
> Just relax and enjoy your day.
>
> Kisses,
> Jamie

My heart skipped a beat when I imagined him saying the word "kisses." I went back to my notes but couldn't focus. All I could think about was dinner with Jamie. I decided I'd put some effort into it and try to find a dress for our date. After throwing on a pair of jeans and my ballet flats, I headed over to Susan's office, hoping to get her input, even though part of me feared she wouldn't approve of our date.

When I reached the door I looked down the patio and saw Chelsea sitting on her dog pillow, looking queenly as ever. "That's it!" I said aloud. I marched up to her, dropped to my knees, and began scratching behind her ears. She melted into a puddle of Jell-O, all splayed out on her back with her legs in the air. "Oh, you're so much easier than you pretend to be, aren't you? Deep down inside you're just a sweet girl, lookin' for some love." Chelsea wagged her tail and stretched her arms as I scratched her neck and belly.

The moment I stood up she went right back to her regal pose, looking straight ahead and ignoring me. If she could talk, I think she would have said, *Don't think this makes us friends.* I brushed my hands on my jeans and headed into Susan's office, where I found her typing at the computer. She looked up at me over her square glasses. "Hello, Kate. What can I do for you?"

"Well, I was wondering if you know where I can get something to wear?" She stared at me, expressionless, so I continued. "I was hoping that I could find a clothing store nearby so that I don't have to go all the way into the city."

"Is that so?" Her eyes scrutinized me. I nodded shyly, wondering if coming to her might have been a bad idea. She didn't seem possessive of Jamie as much as overprotective. Whatever it was, it seemed like more than a working relationship. "What's the occasion?"

I thought about my answer for a few seconds and then decided to go with the truth. After all, she already knew. "I'm going on a date with Jamie, but you already knew that. I want to look nice for him." I held my head up high and watched as her expression turned from indifference to warmth. She smiled. I could have sworn that Susan liked it when I fought back.

"Well. There's a little boutique store in the town of Napa. They have some really cute dresses that I think would look stunning on you." She wrote the address down and handed me the piece of paper.

"Thank you . . . and I don't think of this as a fling, just so you know. I'm not like that. I like Jamie, and I think he likes me." She nodded but didn't respond. I was looking for validation from her. I had no plans to hurt Jamie, but I couldn't tell if she believed me. Worse than that, she didn't exactly verify his feelings for me. "Thank you again for this," I said as I headed out the door. I glanced into R.J.'s office and saw only an empty chair. *Hands-on? Yeah, right.*

On my way to the car, I spotted a familiar pair of work boots. Jamie was crouching by a long wrought iron fence that surrounded the pool. From where I stood, I could see little glimmers of light popping into the air. I walked toward him hesitantly. There was a square machine on the ground, and I spotted the welding rod in his hand. He was wearing a hood and gloves, but other than that, no protective gear, just a white T-shirt and jeans. I approached unnoticed and stood over him to watch as he welded a bar back into the fence. There were sparks flying all over, and some landed on his forearms, but he seemed unaffected by it. When he finally noticed me standing beside him, he stopped immediately and turned off the welder. He stood up with ease and pushed his hood back, revealing his damp face.

"You shouldn't look at the light. You'll get flash burns," he said.

"Where did you learn to weld?"

"My dad taught me." He wiped his sweaty face with the back of his arm. I noticed he had a six-inch hunting knife sheathed in a light brown leather holster attached to his belt.

"What's that?" I asked stupidly.

"A knife."

"What for?"

He smirked. "Cutting things."

I just couldn't imagine being with a man who welded fences and cut things. That might sound stupid, but it took Stephen three days to put together a piece-of-shit IKEA desk. He had to ask the super of our building what an Allen wrench was—just another reason the super couldn't stand him. Stephen didn't even own a pair of jeans. He got manicures and pedicures at the same nail salon as I did. But he was educated and business savvy—he had that going for him. Yet so did Jamie, it seemed. There was nothing businesslike about Jamie, but there was something mysterious and uniquely brilliant about him. He was the best of both worlds. In my tiny, thirty-second fantasy, as I stood there staring at his knife, I imagined him fighting off wild beasts with it. Shirtless.

"Katy?"

"Yeah."

"Does the knife bother you?"

"Well, it's not like you kill things with it," I said, even though I was fantasizing about him doing that very thing. He arched his eyebrows very slightly, but other than that, his expression didn't change. "Right?"

"Well, we have rattlers here and we raise animals . . ." His voice trailed off.

"You slaughter animals with that knife?"

"I'm not usually the person who does that. We have a professional. I promise you, it's very humane, but I've had to assist a few times in the past."

"I'm a vegetarian."

"I know, I'm sorry, but you asked." He paused, gauging my expression. "Killing is not always violent. Sometimes it's merciful." He seemed repentant.

"I was just surprised, that's all. One less rattlesnake in my vicinity is all the better." I smiled.

"Where are you headed to?"

"I'm going into Napa just to browse around for a bit."

"Don't run your car into anything," he said with no trace of humor.

I reached out to sock him in the arm, but he caught my fist midair, brought it to his mouth, and kissed it. My knees wobbled. I turned and began walking away, but when I looked back he was still watching me, just as I expected. He was smiling with curiosity in his eyes. "See you at four, sailor," I shouted back.

My driving skills had not improved since my accident. GPS lady got me to the boutique, but I drove half the speed limit. Cars whizzed by, honking at me the entire way. When I finally got inside the store, I spotted my dress immediately. It was a simple three-quarter-sleeve black dress with a plunging neckline. It came to just above my knee but was a little longer in the back. *Perfect*, I thought. Sexy, not slutty. I twirled around inside the dressing room for exactly ten seconds before changing back and heading for the register.

"Great choice," the young female clerk said. "Are you, by any chance, Kate from R. J. Lawson?"

"Yes. I'm a guest there. How did you know?"

"Susan asked that we bill your purchases to the winery. She said anything you want."

"Oh, I couldn't possibly. Is this something they do often?"

"No, I've never done this for them, but I know Susan. She comes in a lot. Did you want to add some shoes or jewelry?"

"Thank you, but I think the dress is enough." I hadn't even looked at the price tag before she clipped it off. She wrapped the dress in pink tissue paper, slipped it into a white bag, and handed it over to me. "Enjoy. Have a lovely day."

I walked out to my car, a little stunned. I didn't know if Susan was buttering me up or if everyone really was this genuinely nice at the winery. Except for stupid R.J., whom I had started to resent. Of course I had to write the article about him, because that's what my editor wanted. R.J. was the whole reason I was here. But I found myself dreading it. I wondered how I could twist the story so that I could tell the truth about him without negatively impacting the winery itself. I could say he was philanthropic and well meaning, but I knew deep down that being truthful about his personality would take away from that. Had I known how to spin the article, I would have written it already.

I didn't get back to the winery until a little after three. I was supposed to meet Jamie in less than an hour. I literally ran from my car, through the parking lot, and through the main room of the inn. George laughed at me from the front desk. "Hey, George!" I yelled, and then I took two stairs at a time until I was at my door. I showered in record time, but I took great care pinning up my hair and drawing little strands out around my face. I had the black heels that I brought with me, which went perfectly with the dress. I thickened my lashes with mascara and made a few passes with the blush brush. When I got to my lips, I slowly swept the translucent gloss across my bottom lip and thought about Jamie kissing it away.

Three knocks sounded right at four p.m. I skipped over to the door and opened it wide. The first thing I noticed was his eyes, which glimmered and squinted slightly with a look of wonder. He was wearing a black button-down dress shirt and black jeans cuffed over a pair of Converse. He looked sexy and hip, but a little dangerous, too.

"You look . . ." and then he paused.

"Handsome," I said with a brazen smirk.

"Stunning."

"Gorgeous."

His eyes glanced down to my lips. "There have been no women before you and there will be no women after you," he said, seriously.

I swallowed. "And he's poetic, too."

He moved into the room, put his arm around me, kissed my cheek, and whispered, "You inspire me." Once he stepped back, he opened a long black jewelry case revealing a delicate filigree chain with a floating peach-colored briolette bordered with marcasite along the top.

"Oh my god, this is beautiful. It looks like an antique."

"It is."

"This is too much, Jamie." I shook my head. "It's gorgeous, really, but I can't accept this."

"Of course you can, and you will. I have a friend who owns a little antique store in town. It's not a big deal, I promise."

"I can't even imagine how much this cost."

"Please, don't think about that." He took it out of the box and twirled his other finger at me. "Turn around, beautiful." He gently brushed the loose strands of my hair aside. I could feel his warm breath on the back of my head. When he clasped the necklace, he leaned down and pressed a lingering kiss on the side of my neck. "God, you smell good," he said softly.

I giggled from his ticklish breath. When I turned around he was smiling serenely, but he had an obvious look of desire in his eyes. "We better go now or we'll never get out of here," I said.

"You are so right about that. Come on."

We drove across the big, red bridge and into the city of San Francisco, with its steep hills, Victorian row houses, and the famous trolley cars coasting along the main streets downtown. The energy in the city was like none other I'd experienced. Rolling down my window, I took in the sights and smells. Every time a trolley bell rang, it transported me back to another time, a time when the black-and-white photos from the winery were taken, when life was simpler. The smell of saltwater, baking bread, and wet pavement overtook my senses. We drove deeper into the city through Nob Hill and past Union Square. Jamie didn't say much, he just let me take in the sights. We found a parking garage and parked, then he reached behind his seat and pulled out a woman's short trench coat.

"Susan thought you would need this, and I think she was right." It was chillier in the city than in Napa, and I was grateful for Susan's thoughtfulness. "It's a shame to cover you up, but I think you'll feel more comfortable where we're going." He held the jacket open for me. I slipped it on and tied the belt.

"Where *are* we going?"

"We're going to serve dinner to some of my friends. I'm taking you to GLIDE. It's a homeless shelter that I volunteer at." I stopped dead in my tracks. He turned to me, and for the first time since I had met him he looked unsure of himself. "I hope that's okay?"

I cupped his face and kissed him softly. "Of course it is. I volunteer in Chicago. I can't tell you how many times I tried dragging Stephen with me, but he wouldn't have it."

Jamie laughed once and looked down at his feet. At first I thought he was being bashful, and then he looked up and said, "This is our first date, Katy." He shook his finger at me. "No talking about exes." I took ahold of his finger and pretended to bite it. "Ooh, feisty, I like it," he said before pulling me out of the garage.

On the way into the shelter, we saw homeless people crowding the streets. Many of them shouted "Hi" to Jamie as we passed by. I even heard one woman say, "Ooh, Jamie's got a girlfriend." He squeezed my hand tightly after that comment.

Once inside the shelter kitchen, he handed me a white hat and apron to put on.

"I look silly."

"Not possible. You are the sexiest volunteer I've ever seen."

The kitchen was bustling with helpers. A very tall and extremely thin man with an intimidating stare came walking toward us. I looked at Jamie for reassurance and could tell everything was okay by the way the corner of his mouth quirked up. He was amused.

"You're late, my man," the tall guy said in a serious tone, which didn't hold long.

"But I brought an extra pair of hands. Charles, meet the lovely Kate Corbin. Kate, this is Charles, the man who runs this wonderful place."

He gave me an ear-splitting grin and then reached for my hand and kissed the back of it. "Lovely, indeed. Okay, let's put you to work, and let those hands give life to these hungry folks."

We jumped right into serving food to a long line of hungry men, women, and children. Every single person that I had the joy of serving food to said thank you with so much sincerity and gratitude, I felt a chemical change in my heart. I had volunteered in shelters many times before, but somehow there was a stronger connection. I realized it was because of Jamie's presence there beside me. He laughed and told stories to everyone in line. He teased all the little kids about eating their vegetables, and he heckled some of the men about the Giants and how there was no way they were going to win the World Series again. Evidently, Jamie was a Red Sox fan, and he assured me that if the Sox ever played the Cubs at Fenway, he would be there and I would personally be responsible for showing him around Chicago. Even during the light banter, I couldn't help but wonder if that's what it would take to see Jamie again once I left Napa.

When the line started dwindling, I spent a little more time observing each person. There was a young woman about my age who was alone, wearing tattered clothing. I wondered what her story was. When she reached me in line, I scooped a lump of mashed potatoes onto her plate. She gave me a satisfied smile and then said, "My favorite, thank you."

I was willing to spend the last moments of my life doing what I was doing with Jamie because it made me feel like I had a purpose. I felt more aware of the humanity in others, something I had lost sight of since Rose's death. Serving food to the homeless truly made me feel like I was connecting more deeply with others. It was one of the most authentic and satisfying feelings I'd had in a long time. I thought about Jamie comparing love to food, and now I was comparing charity to life through food. I looked at the blessings in my life, my ability to give my time, to have a stable job and support myself. I started to wonder if R.J. was so terrible after all. The fact that he spent so much of his own money to provide life-improving and lifesaving resources to the needy deserved some measure of my respect. He didn't need his accomplishments to be advertised—most people had no idea what he was doing. Maybe the goodness in R.J. had rubbed off on Jamie and Susan. I was seeing everything the other way around now. Writing the article weighed heavily on me, but being out with Jamie alleviated that.

"Katy, our replacements are here. Are you ready to go?" Jamie asked, snapping me back into reality.

"Yes, this was wonderful. Thank you for bringing me here." We walked hand in hand back to his truck, and I watched as Jamie metered and then gave himself a shot of insulin. We left the truck parked where it was and headed to Belden Place, a row of romantic restaurants tucked in an alley between two buildings. The area was crowded, but strangely it was one of the most romantic and intimate settings I had ever been in. Strings of twinkle lights hung across the entire width of the alley. We decided on a French restaurant, where the very young hostess greeted Jamie by name. She looked to be in her early twenties. Her short blond hair was pulled back in a slick, tiny ponytail. The collar of her black dress shirt was just low enough to reveal the cluster of pink cherries tattooed on her neck. She blinked several times in quick succession.

"Hi . . ." Jamie said. We both waited uncomfortably for her to answer. I was definitely picking up on a weird vibe.

"Izzy," the hostess said flatly.

"Right, Izzy. This is Kate." He rested his hand on the small of my back.

She smiled superficially at me and then shifted her attention right back to Jamie. "I'll get you two a nice romantic table in hell. How's that?"

He grabbed my hand and said, "Time to go."

We walked to an Italian restaurant in the same alley and were seated far enough away that we were sure to be out of Izzy's line of fire.

"What was that?"

"I dated . . . er . . . uh, I mean, I went on a date with her."

"So you had a one-night stand with her?"

"No, I didn't have sex with her."

"It's none of my business, and we aren't even supposed to talk about exes." I crossed my arms over my chest, failing to play it cool.

"It's nothing like that. This guy, Benny, from GLIDE set me up with her. She's too young for me. I tried to let her down easy. We had dinner once. I took her home right after, but she kept hassling Benny about me." He took a breath and paused and then shook his head slowly. "What a horrible way for us to start dinner. I'm so sorry. That was totally weird. Can we pretend that didn't happen?" His eyes were soft and pleading.

I believed him. His answers were genuine, and I couldn't see him being the type to have random one-night stands with women. Frankly, after Izzy's death threat, she seemed like she could be a bit of a loose cannon anyway.

Before I could answer, Jamie immediately ordered a bottle of wine and raw oysters on the half shell for our appetizer. Our table was so small that, if I wanted to, I could literally rest my head on his chest without being inhibited. Underneath the table, our legs carelessly tangled with each other's, even though I was still a little hesitant after our encounter with Izzy's wrath.

I smiled sincerely. "Yes, let's start over, but I'm ditching your earlier rule. It's time to come clean. Now I want to know everything."

His brow furrowed but he laughed. "Uh-oh. What have I gotten myself into? I'm on a date with the most curious woman in the world."

I looked down at my hands and fidgeted nervously. I felt a blush creeping across my face. "I promise, you'll only face this line of questioning once."

Just then, our oysters and wine came to the table. He had a self-congratulatory smile on his face while he poured me a very large glass.

"First, this." He put the oyster shell to my mouth. I opened for him as he tilted it up. The salty, slippery oyster went sliding down my throat. I watched him do the same for himself. We both took sips of wine and then he leaned in and kissed me like the whole world was crumbling away around us. His hand gripped the back of my neck and kissed me hard. We were all tongues and lips and light moans that only we could hear. Everyone in the alley disappeared except for us. He slowed and nuzzled my cheek and then left one last lingering kiss on my mouth. Stephen would rarely hold my hand in public, and although I wasn't a huge proponent of PDA, I didn't mind with Jamie. When he kissed me, no one existed but us.

"Did you have something you wanted to ask me?" he said with a sly smile.

"You did that on purpose, just to distract me."

"No."

"No?"

His lips flattened. "Katy, I want to kiss you like that every second of the day, even in my sleep." Had the waiter not shown up at the moment, there was a high possibility I would have stripped down naked and begged Jamie to take me right there on top of our tiny table.

We ordered mussels and pasta, and after we ate our dinner I excused myself to check my phone. It had been buzzing in my purse since we sat down. I headed to the bathroom and saw that it was Jerry. I dialed his number.

"This is Jerry."

"It's late there, Jer, what's up?"

"Beth told me you met a man."

I laughed. "I told her not to tell you."

"Why? I'm happy for you."

"Are you?" Sometimes I had to remind myself that Jerry was one of the most happily married men. He doted on his wife. He would often leave the office early and say, "I'm going home. I miss my buddy." His wife was truly *his* person, his partner, but Jerry never gave me advice on love. I knew he didn't like Stephen, so he minded his own business about it.

"Beth told me a little about the guy."

"It's nothing yet, I just met him."

"Well, all I wanted to say is give it a chance . . . I've watched you crawl inside yourself over the last few months." He paused again. I took in a deep breath and held it. "I heard a spark in your voice yesterday, and I think you're coming back to us. Maybe it has something to do with that guy."

"Uh-huh," I said, my throat closing up.

"Listen to me. Don't be scared. All of the skeletons and the blood and the guts and the emotions—that's the stuff that makes you human and alive. When I said you've lost your spark, I meant that you were shutting everyone out. That spark is the beauty in you, Kate. But sometimes when it gets too hot, when people get too close, and that spark gets too bright, you stifle it because you're scared."

In the cloudy bathroom mirror, my own reflection startled me. One beaming light showed down on my face, casting dark shadows under my eyes, hiding the tears pooling in them until, drip, drip like a faucet, the heartrending process began. I was crying. It wasn't an ugly cry; it was a bleak, emotionless cry where you feel your body surrender. Jerry was right, and I knew it. I was so scared of letting anyone in. I didn't make a sound, so he continued. "I've been so happy in my marriage and lucky to have found my person in life, but it's only because I realized a long time ago that if you keep all that stuff inside, the stuff that makes you most uniquely you, then you will never find *your* person. You'll just wither from within and forget who you are, and if you can't see you, then *he* can't see you. Don't be scared. I've seen you, Kate, who you really are, and you're worth it. You're worth all of it."

"My gosh, Jerry, thank you, but where is all of this coming from? Why are you telling me this now?" I sobbed.

"Because you're my friend, dammit. But now I'm pissed at myself for making you cry."

"I'm not crying," I lied.

"Are you with him now?"

"Yes, but I'm in the bathroom."

"Trust me on this." His voice got low. "Go back out there and just be yourself."

"I don't know what I'll do if I fall in love with him."

"If you fall, let him catch you." And then he hung up.

When I got back to the table, Jamie stood and pulled my chair out for me. "Are you okay?" he asked.

"Yes, I'm fine." I propped my elbows on the table and rested my chin on my hands. "It's time for questions." I laughed and a little lagging tear fell from my eye.

"Were you crying?" He looked pained.

"No, I'm laughing, silly and you're not getting out of this."

He smiled sullenly. "Okay, ask away."

"Do you date many women?"

"No."

"That's it? You're not going to elaborate?"

"I've dated a few. I had one long-term relationship for three years after college."

"What was her name?"

"Julia."

"What happened?"

"She left me."

"Why?"

"She wanted other things in life."

"Like what?"

"Material things."

"Were you in love with her?"

"Not when I realized what she wanted from me."

"Were you hurt?"

"Yes." He remained serious.

"So you don't sleep around?"

He chuckled. "I'm a man. I've dated, but I'm not interested in sleeping around. I want to be with someone who intrigues me, who I can have fun with, who I can laugh with, but who will challenge me. I've been looking for the same thing most of us are looking for."

"What's that?"

"Someone to come home to."

My eyes filled with tears. He leaned in slowly and cautiously and then he kissed me softly before whispering, "Can we have fun now?"

"Yes!" I said passionately. "What do you have in mind, sailor?"

"Well, first I'm going to feed you tiramisu. Then we're going to walk across the street and I'm going to kick your ass at shuffleboard and darts. And then, if you're lucky, I'll take you back to the winery and show you my barn." My eyes went wide. He laughed. "No expectations."

"That is by far the strangest offer I've ever had, but I'd love to see your barn. There is one thing you must know, though."

"Uh-oh. What?"

"I'm known as the shuffleboard champion east of the Mississippi."

"You're all talk. You said that about karaoke." He slipped a bite of tiramisu into my mouth.

"What are the stakes?"

He kissed cream away from the side of my mouth before answering. "If I win, I get to kiss you for as long as I want."

I nodded enthusiastically. "And if I win . . . then you get to kiss me for as long as you want."

"Deal."

We went to a little dive bar where I won two games of shuffleboard but lost three games of darts, so Jamie still claimed that he was the champion. He talked me into doing three Fireball whiskey shots, and every time I did one he kissed me for an entire minute afterward.

"I like the taste in your mouth," he said.

"You just like getting me drunk."

"It's not about that, I just want you to enjoy yourself."

"I am, but you're going to doom me all night." He laughed so loudly when I said it that I quickly realized what the words sounded like.

"Katy, I would love to, but don't you think that's a lot of pressure to put on me?"

I offered to settle the bar challenge score with a game of pool.

"I think I should get you back. Plus I'm ready to claim my prize. I won fair and square." Just as he said that, a short, stocky fellow took a seat at the bar next to me on my right.

The man next to me said, "Hi," in a kind, friendly voice.

I turned toward him slightly and said, "Hi," very blandly.

The man had one of those chests that stuck out in some futile attempt to make him look taller, and he wore a black muscle shirt that hugged his large, gunlike biceps. Not my style at all. "Do you live here or are you just visiting San Francisco?" he asked. I looked at Jamie first before turning back to answer. He swept his hair back out of his face and I could see his jaw flex, but his expression never changed. He looked unaffected.

I swiveled back toward the man. "I'm just visiting."

He put his hand on my leg and rubbed it up and down. "Can I get you another shot?"

I gasped and pulled my leg away. I blinked twice and Jamie

was suddenly standing on the other side of the man, gripping the back of his neck and pushing the guy's face to the bar. Jamie lowered his own face to the man's ear and spoke in a steely voice that was so quiet but so powerful that it gave me chills.

"You see that she's with me, don't you?" Jamie was looking right into his eyes. I could see the man struggling. He was breathing through his mouth. Jamie's grip on his neck was so strong, the veins in his forearms and in the man's neck were bulging and pulsing. "Answer me."

The man nodded.

"Then keep your fucking hands off her."

The guy stood from the bar and held his hands up in a defensive gesture. "Okay, man, back off."

I stood as well. "I have to use the restroom," I said quickly then marched off. I turned back just as I entered the bathroom door and saw Jamie standing at the bar, looking shattered as he watched me walk away. My heart was beating out of my chest. *What do I say? That was so weird and possessive.*

Gathering myself, I took two deep breaths and splashed cold water on my face. When I opened the door, Jamie was standing against the wall just outside the bathroom, waiting for me. His hands were in his pockets and he was looking down.

"I'm sorry," he said to the floor. When he looked up, I noticed his eyes were misty. "I didn't mean to scare you. I'm not a violent person at all. I would never lay a hand on you. I just want you to know that."

"Why did you do that?"

"I just thought he was being really disrespectful, and I wouldn't want anyone to treat you that way."

"We barely know each other, Jamie. You don't have to do that for me."

"Did I ruin the night?"

I walked up to him and pressed myself against his body. Looking up into his eyes, I brushed his hair back and said, "I have mixed emotions right now. It scared me a little, but no one has ever done anything like that for me." I kissed his cheek. "Thank you. It made me feel important."

"You are."

We walked several blocks back to the truck. Every time there was a shadow cast on the wall of a building, Jamie would push me into it and kiss me like Armageddon was around the corner. Once we were back at the parking garage, I felt like the world was spinning. I stumbled just before I got to the truck. Jamie braced me by the elbow. "I'm pretty drunk," I said to him as he opened the truck door for me.

He cupped my face and gave me the lightest kiss. "I'll take care of you." He helped me in and then went around to his side and gave himself a shot of insulin.

I scrunched up my nose. "Smells like Band-Aids."

"Yeah, the insulin has a really potent smell. Does it bother you?" He looked over at me apprehensively.

"Not at all. I was just making an observation, and I'm drunk. Just ignore me."

"Never." He winked at me then pulled the truck out onto the street and into the bustling city traffic.

"Didn't you do that before we ate?"

"What?"

"Use the insulin pen."

He looked up. His eyes were wide, and there was a faint look of fear in them. "Did I?"

"Yeah, you did."

"I felt hot, so I thought . . ."

I giggled. "Maybe it was all the kissing." His expression never changed. He looked bewildered. "Are you okay, Jamie?" I asked.

"Yeah," he said quietly as he looked up into the rearview mirror and over his shoulder to change lanes. "I'm fine."

We were approaching the Golden Gate Bridge. Jamie was very quiet. I started to fade, and the last thing I remembered was laying my head in his lap and him stroking my hair.

Cutline

The first thing I noticed when I woke up was that my head was pounding from the alcohol. The second thing I realized was that we weren't moving. I was still in Jamie's lap. His forehead was resting on the steering wheel and his right arm was on the dashboard out in front of him. My initial assumption was that he was sleeping. I shimmied out from underneath him and saw that he was clutching the bottle of glucose tablets in his left hand. We were across the bridge in the parking lot of Golden Gate Overlook, facing the city. I looked closely at Jamie and saw that his eyes were very slightly open.

"Jamie."

"Mmhmm."

"Jamie, are you okay?" I grabbed the bottle from his left hand and discovered that it was empty. I became frantic. I put my hand to his forehead, and he tried to give me a weak smile.

"What is it?"

"Low," he mumbled, barely loud enough for me to hear.

It occurred to me, very brutally, that Jamie had given himself too much insulin. I started searching the car but couldn't find the glucagon kit. "Jamie!" I screamed, but at that point his eyes were closed and he was unresponsive. He started to lean left. I gently laid him against the driver's side door and then glanced out at the bridge. The traffic had stopped; the pedestrians were frozen in space and time. I felt frustrated and powerless, like in a dream. I screamed again, "Where is it?" And then I prayed and reached for my phone, but just before I dialed 911, I visualized the orange case under the seat. *Visualize to realize.* When I looked, it was there. Yanking it from below and popping it open, my motions were fluid and precise, as if I were on autopilot. Somehow I knew exactly how to pump the liquid into the vial of powder. I filled the syringe and pushed a drop up through the needle, removing any air. I unbuckled his belt and yanked at his jeans to where I could see just enough skin below his hip to give him the shot, and then I jabbed the needle into his flesh and pushed the liquid through. I was crying, panic-stricken. *Please be okay. Please be okay.*

I dialed 911 on my phone, just in case, but right before I hit SEND, I heard Jamie speak.

"Katy?" he murmured.

"Yes?" I slid toward him. He sat up against the seat, his head falling back, and took two deep breaths. I straddled him and cupped his face, searching his eyes. They were dilated and he was clammy, but he was conscious and watching me.

"Oh my god, Jamie! Oh my god!"

"I'm okay," he mumbled. Between each loud sob, I kissed him all over his face and neck. His hands rested on my thighs. He let me smother him with kisses while my tears spilled all over his face. I wanted to cradle and rock him like a baby. I wanted to soothe him. But at that point I was the one who needed the soothing.

"Baby, stop crying, please. I know that was scary for you, but

I'm okay. I messed up. That's never happened before." He became more alert. He brought his hands up to my face and wiped away the tears. "I'm sorry I couldn't take care of you."

"We can take care of each other," I said instantly, and then as if a new portal in my brain had been unlocked, I remembered my dream. *The whispers.*

It was a moment, like so many I'd had before, where I'd go the entire day not remembering my dream from the previous night and then suddenly, it would be triggered by a smell or a song or a comment made by a colleague and the dream would rush back to me, like a tidal wave of memories. That's what happened in the truck that night. I remembered my dream—*the* dream. I was there again, hovering over Rose's body, the sound of heartbeats streaming loudly, except I realized there were two sets beating. I leaned down over her to listen, but the sound wasn't coming from her. It was a human sound, a living sound. My memory of the dream was clear, finally. When she spoke, her voice was soft and melodic, but pleading.

Take care of each other, she said, and then she glanced at the figure standing next to me. It was Jamie, and the heartbeats were ours. His and mine.

In the truck, still straddling him, I held my hand to my heart.

"What is it?" he asked.

"Nothing." I shivered.

"Calm down. Everything is okay."

"I know." I laid my head on his chest and he held me tightly. An hour must have passed. Every few minutes I would look up at his face to check on him and he would smile at me every time, but we remained quiet and still, just holding each other.

Finally, I crawled off of his lap. "Shouldn't I take you to the hospital?"

He shook his head. "I'm okay. I just need to eat something."

"Oh yeah." I pulled a Balance bar from my purse, unwrapped it quickly, and held it to his mouth.

He laughed. I knew he was going to be okay. "I can feed myself. Thank you, Katy." Before he reached for the bar, he swallowed and then stared sharply into my eyes. "I mean it. Thank you."

I shook my head. "I know, I know. You don't need to thank me. Here, eat this, please." He bit off half of the bar and then set it on the dashboard. I looked at my phone. It was two a.m. He pulled his jeans down to where I had given him the shot and looked at the injection site. He rubbed the area and winced a little.

"You're going to have a bruise. I jabbed you really hard."

"You did," he said with a hint of amusement in his voice. "You got me good, lady." He buckled his belt and pulled out his meter to check his blood sugar. "Do you always carry food in your purse?"

I blushed. "I read on the glucagon kit the other day that sometimes you have to give diabetics food right away."

He looked up beatifically. "God, you are the sweetest thing."

I smiled, but a tear fell from my eye at the same time. "How's your level?"

"I'm good."

"I think I should drive, Jamie."

"Sweetheart, even if I were half conscious, our odds of getting home safely are much higher with me behind the wheel." He smiled playfully. "No offense."

"You're probably right."

"Did you pull over here because you felt groggy?"

"Yeah. I should have metered earlier. Sometimes it gets confusing, especially if I'm distracted, and then I ran out of glucose tablets. It was stupid, I'm really sorry."

"Stop apologizing, you did the right thing by pulling over. Next time wake me up."

"I promise."

It was a promise for a next time. That was all I could think about in that moment. Not a next time Jamie got that low—just a next time, period.

Jamie drove us back to the winery with his window all the way down and the heater cranked up so he could keep himself alert without freezing me out. I kept my eyes on the road along with him. He pulled up the long driveway and then continued onto a dirt road until we were parked in front of the barn.

He looked over apprehensively. "Do you want to stay with me tonight?"

"It's already tomorrow."

"Do you want to stay with me tomorrow?"

"Mm-hmm."

He held my hand until we were inside the barn, and then he flipped on the lights and watched me take it all in. It was no barn on the inside. Whoever the brilliant designer was, he left the natural beams exposed but finished the walls with white slate wood. The floors were aged teak and there were large rustic chandeliers hanging from the highest points of the ceiling. It was at least forty feet high in the center. Above one set of beams in the gable space were shelves filled with books and a little ladder leading up to it. I walked around, fascinated. The décor was warm, rich, and masculine. It was an immaculate snapshot of a Restoration Hardware catalogue. The kitchen followed in the same vivid design, with a farmhouse sink and Shaker cabinets. Jamie leaned against the wall with his hands in his pockets, watching me.

"It's amazing. Who did this?"

"I did."

I laughed to myself. Of course he did. "R.J. let you have this space?"

He nodded.

The entire floor plan was open. There were only partial walls dividing the spaces, much like a loft, except for the bathroom, which had a modestly designed door compared to the rest of the barn. In one corner there was a drafting desk with all kinds of drawings of machines on it. There were some framed drawings on the walls above the desk that I recognized almost immediately as copies of da Vinci. I saw the sketches for the water-lifting machines and the Vitruvian man in the circle representing the ideal proportions of a body. Jamie was a thinker, there was no doubt. I realized at that moment that, even though he could be social when he needed to be, he was a little bit of a loner, too . . . like me.

I walked toward the opposite end of the barn, and in the process, tripped over my own damn feet. I stumbled but quickly regained my balance. I looked back and caught Jamie smiling. "Oh, wipe that smile off your face. I'm clumsy, okay?"

"You're adorable," he said.

In the center of the opposite wall was the bed. I walked toward it and felt Jamie following me. The lights behind me went off one by one until there was just one tiny desk lamp on, filling the space with a faint warmth like a glowing ember in the darkest night. We shuffled around for a few minutes and then stood on opposite sides of the bed. He untucked his shirt, I took off my coat, and we both kicked off our shoes.

"It's beautiful in here."

He came toward me without hesitation and lifted my dress

from the bottom. I raised my arms to accommodate him. He never took his eyes off me as he threw the dress onto the chair next to him. "It is now," he said.

I stood in my panties and bra and didn't feel a modicum of shyness. I unbuttoned his shirt and pushed it off of his shoulders, letting my hands linger there. His hair had fallen down against the sides of his face. I pushed it back, slowly and sensually. He kissed me while he unbuttoned his jeans, only breaking the kiss to step out of them.

"Do you feel okay?" I asked.

"Yes. Let's rest for a bit, though." He pulled the duvet back and slid in wearing only his boxers. "Get in here, Katy," he said with a lazy smile. *Who would say no to this man?* I glanced at the old-fashioned clock on the nightstand before slipping in beside him. It was three thirty a.m. We were lying on our sides, facing each other, but our bodies were flush. I fit perfectly into the space of his chest. We dovetailed our legs, and then I felt him kiss the top of my head.

"We can stay like this all day. We have nowhere to be but here. Sleep, angel." And just like that, I was out.

It was morning twilight when I woke. There was a glow coming through the window shades. Our bodies started moving at the same time—he was waking up, too. We were hyperaware of each other's presence, of skin against skin, of heat radiating from our bodies. We started moving more intentionally. He rolled me over until we were spooning. He kissed my neck and behind my ear and pressed himself forward, and I felt him hard against me. I moaned so faintly, I thought only I could hear, but he responded to it by pushing against me again, harder and more urgent. He unhooked my bra and it disappeared.

He rolled on top of me and trailed light, slow kisses over my breasts and down to my stomach and down further. I fixated on the muscles in his arms as he held himself above me effortlessly. I felt him kick off his boxers; he was very good at that. He was also very good at making me crazy. He was kissing me through my panties, right there in that perfect spot. I felt myself moving toward him, bucking slightly and encouraging him to continue teasing. He rolled my panties down and those disappeared into the galaxy as well. There were hands and lips and teeth and tongues everywhere, but it was slow. He stopped and hovered over me, gazing into my eyes, but he didn't say anything.

"Do you like me, Jamie?"

"Yes. A lot."

"What blood type are you?"

"O positive." He shook his head and laughed.

"Do you have a savings account?"

"Yes."

"And health insurance?"

"Uh-huh," he murmured as he kissed his way down my body and back up again.

"And you've had a checkup recently?" When he looked up, I opened my eyes wide so he knew what I was talking about.

"Yes, of course."

"What's your last name?"

"No more talking." And then his lips smashed into mine and I felt him enter me, filling me until my back arched. He moved fluidly, like perfection mixed with just a tinge of pain from the newness. He kissed my lips like they were cherished, priceless jewels, and then he kissed his way to my ear. We breathed heavily, and I moved with him, letting him in deeper and closer. It felt so right. There was something so natural about the way our bodies moved together. There was no awkward clashing of teeth as we kissed, or confused, fumbled movements. It was like we had relinquished control to some power stronger than us. He grabbed both of my hands, interlacing his fingers with mine, and stretched them above my head.

"Open your eyes. I want you to see me when you come."

I did, and my toes pulsed, shooting waves of radiation up my spine until I felt that buzzing tempo between my ears and in the back of my throat. Gazing into his eyes made it so intense. There was the familiar pounding heartbeat between my legs. He jerked and drove deeper but watched me intently, then he gripped my hip. That's when we both came undone. It was slow, sweet, sleepy sex, but it was more powerful than anything I'd had before. I thought maybe that's what making love was supposed to feel like.

My hands grabbed his hair as the last tremors left my body. He finally closed his eyes and collapsed, burrowing his face in my neck. We fell asleep again just like that, with him still inside of me, but I didn't mind because I didn't feel alone.

There were a few hours filled with hazy memories of the sun blasting us through the blinds and Jamie getting up to shut them. He brought me water and juice. I heard him talking to Susan on the phone before coming back to bed, and then the next time I woke up I heard him tinkering in the kitchen. I smelled pastries and became convinced that I had died and gone to heaven. I slithered out of bed and searched the space for my undergarments. *Do people just walk around naked in heaven?* I used his toothbrush covertly and then quickly realized how stupid it was to be sneaky about it after what we had just done.

When I walked back toward the bed, I noticed a sliver of sight line from which I could watch Jamie in the kitchen, about twenty feet away. He was wearing flannel pajama pants. *Not fair.* When he saw me, I froze. He stalked toward me with an intimidating look on his face. I couldn't move. I felt myself flush all the way down to my toes. My heart skipped and stuttered. What happened next was a bit of a blur. I could have been dreaming, but I'm pretty sure I watched Jamie stop halfway and slip easily out of his flannel pants. We were standing in the bright light, completely naked and staring at each other. I could hear our shallow breaths and the faint thumping of our hearts. His hair was tousled loosely and the scruff he wore so well was thicker and darker than it had been the day before. An unintentional moan escaped my lips. He stared at me for just a second longer and then took three long, quick strides before lifting me from the back of the legs to straddle him. He pushed me against the wall forcefully.

"You are so beautiful. God, you are so fucking beautiful," he said with a sigh.

We ravaged each other for hours, moving from space to space. On the bed again, he pulled me up to straddle him and then he pushed my chest back so that my entire body was on display above him. I leaned over and guided him inside of me, filling me to the hilt. He pushed me back again so that I was sitting more upright on top of him.

"Close your eyes, Jamie."

"No, I want to see you."

I felt self-conscious but let some of that go when I saw how adoringly he gazed at my body. His eyelids were heavy; he looked spellbound as I began to move. I ground down slowly and felt a small whimper escape my lips. There was already a numbness and pulsing throughout my body, but the position and Jamie's roaming hands had set the pace much quicker. He finally reached down and touched me where we were connected. I writhed and increased the pace, threw my head back, and lost it. He sat up almost immediately and buried his face in my neck. We stayed that way until the minutes and seconds meant nothing. Time was measured only by the sound of our beating hearts.

When we finally broke our embrace, we fell lazily to each side of the bed. Jamie turned and propped one hand on his elbow and fed me pieces of chocolate croissant before insisting that we take another nap. *Still pretty sure this is heaven.*

"Where's Chelsea?" I asked in a sleepy daze.

"With Susan."

"That's probably a good thing." Out of the corner of my eye, I could see him smiling.

We were lying on our backs, staring up at the high, beamed ceiling. He reached for my hand and kissed the back of it. "Hey . . . let's do this forever."

My eyes widened. "Do what forever?"

"Lay around like this and sleep and eat and fuck."

"Oh."

He turned his body toward me and searched my eyes. "I'm sorry, that wasn't very romantic."

"That's okay."

"I can be romantic . . . but first let's sleep." He kissed my forehead and tucked me into his chest.

When I finally woke up from the dreamy sex-and-sleep fest we'd had, I realized Jamie was gone. There was an old hardback book on the nightstand and a folded note sitting on top of it. I reached for it and read:

My kingdom for one more minute with you. Please stay put. leaving you lying here like an angel in my bed is the hardest thing to do. I'm sorry. I have to help Guillermo with something. Here's one of my favorite books to pass the time, so you don't get bored and leave me. Maybe you can tell me if you agree that the poets are right.

The last line was a riddle of some kind. I found my dress and put it on and then shuffled through Jamie's closet until I found one of his flannel shirts. I slipped it over my head and scribbled a note for him.

I'll be in my room. I'm definitely not bored. Come and see me when you're done. ~Kate Kisses, Katy

I set it on his nightstand next to a picture of him in a cap and gown standing with an older woman, who I assumed was his mother. She looked beautiful, vibrant, and proud. Jamie's arm was around her shoulders, embracing her. From the picture, you could tell they were close. Someone once told me that you can gather all you need to know about a man by the way he treats his mother and his dog. There was something oddly familiar about the photo but I couldn't put my finger on what it was. I grabbed the book and looked at the title. *A Room with a View. How very romantic of Jamie,* I thought. I had read it, so I searched my mind for the answer to his riddle but came up with nothing.

In the fading sunlight, I meandered back toward the inn, barefoot, twirling my slingback heels around my index finger. There were the distant sounds of birdcalls and a light breeze caressing the vines. The sky was an ocean, crystal blue with giant, heavenly clouds floating about. I watched as a flock of birds danced in perfect unison, swooping down, up, and around against the stark white clouds like a child's drawing set in motion.

When I passed the last row of vines, I spotted Jamie about forty yards away with his back toward me. I approached him slowly and quietly and watched him stare into the sky, mesmerized by the birds the same way I had been. At the exact moment that I stopped, he turned and looked over his shoulder. He walked toward me with pure determination. There was no hesitation. He just took me in his arms, dipped me slightly, and kissed me hard. When I caught my breath, I smiled.

"Do you get it yet?" he asked.

"Not yet."

"You will, except there's no one here to stop us but ourselves."

"Hmm. Jamie, your riddling prowess is quite impressive." He smelled musky, and I could feel the dampness of his sweat through his shirt.

"Where are you headed?"

"To my room."

We were both smiling giddily. "Can I come to your room when I'm through here?"

I held my hand to my mouth and gasped in mock horror. "But, Jamie—what will the town folk say?"

"That's true. I can just hide your clothes again, lock you in my barn, and fuck you silly." His dimple was deeper than I had ever seen it.

I socked him in the arm. "I knew you hid my clothes."

"I had no choice. I needed you naked." His boyish charm was in full force.

"I'll let you stay with me in my room, but I'm making no promises beyond cuddling. We can always cuddle," I said with a hint of amusement.

"That's enough to keep me going for a hundred years."

Blank Pages

There were at least twenty random pieces of paper spread throughout my room. Several contained quick notes from my observations at the winery, some were Jamie's itineraries that I couldn't part with, and some were just blank pages or pages filled with doodling from my brainstorming sessions gone awry. I cleaned up quickly, tossing the papers on the desk and chair, and then I stripped down and jumped in the shower. Before I was able to thoroughly dry my hair or throw on a coat of lip gloss, the knocks came.

He was still wearing his work clothes, and I was only wearing a tiny white towel.

He stepped into the room without a word and then flicked the top of the towel, causing it to fall open and onto the floor. He took a deep breath as his eyes traveled up and down my body. "You need a shower," he said.

"I just took a shower."

He bent down and effortlessly threw me over his shoulder and then stalked into the bathroom. I protested while he turned the shower on and waited for the right temperature. He managed to kick his shoes off with me hanging over his shoulder and then he put his mouth on my hip and bit me. "Ouch!"

"Oh, sorry, baby." He sucked on the same spot until I was writhing around like a maniac suspended in the air. I beat my fists against his back and butt, but he just laughed. Once the water was perfect, he dropped me in and then removed his clothes in five seconds flat. Before I could blink, he had me against the wall of the shower.

"Whoa, Jamie!"

"This is like cuddling, right?" he said with a devilish smirk.

"You are dangerously close to breaking my rule."

"Okay, let me just wash you."

"I'm clean."

"I think you need a once-over."

After thirty minutes of washing each other's hair and bodies, we made it out of the shower, but Jamie insisted on drying me in the most painfully slow and gentle manner. We were torturing each other.

"I'm saving you for later," he said as he helped me into one of the terry-cloth robes.

"What shall we do for dinner?"

"It's on its way. I'm going to feed you naked."

He was still wearing nothing. "You're going to feed me while you're naked?"

"No, I'm going to feed you while *you're* naked."

"I heard it the other way around," I said accusatorily.

"Okay, how about I feed you while we're both naked?"

"That's a good compromise." I rolled forward on my tippy-toes and kissed his cheek.

When our food came, I insisted that we eat dinner at the table with our robes on like civilized human beings, but I promised him we could eat dessert his way. He immediately called the restaurant and ordered one of each kind of dessert, a scoop of each flavor of ice cream, and a bowl of whipped cream.

"Aren't you embarrassed? You work here," I said after he hung up.

"Embarrassed about what?"

"You'll have to see Chef Mark, and he'll wonder what you're doing with a giant bowl of whipped cream."

"I'm going to eat it." He smiled innocently. "What'd you think I was going to do with it, Kate? God, you have such a dirty mind."

"Ha-ha."

"Truthfully, who cares? Chef Mark has seven kids. I'm sure he knows his way around this kind of thing." He smiled and then slipped his hand inside my robe and up my thigh. "Especially when you add food to the mix." He scrunched up his nose and shook his head. "Ugh, I don't want to think about Chef Mark anymore. I just want to think about you and me and dessert."

As promised, Jamie ate the entire bowl of Chef Mark's special sugar-free homemade whipped cream off of my body while I squirmed around underneath him. He made it more silly than sexy, so when we were both thoroughly sticky and full from dinner, he ran a bath and poured us each a glass of wine. We sunk into the bubbles in silence. I rested my head back, closed my eyes, and thought about what would become of Jamie and me. Thoughts of Chicago invaded my mind. I sat up abruptly and opened my eyes.

Jamie watched me with concern. "What is it, Katy?"

"Nothing." I shook my head in exasperation.

"Tell me." His eyes were pleading as he pulled me onto his lap.

"What are we doing, Jamie?"

"We're taking a bath." He dropped his head and circled my nipple with his tongue. I didn't stop him as he slowly kissed his way up my neck.

"I want to talk to you."

"Talk."

"How long should I stay here?"

"As long as you want."

Wrong answer.

"Jamie," I said in the most serious tone I could muster.

He pulled away and then cupped my face. "When do you have to be back?" I just shrugged. "Well, when do you have to turn in the article?"

"I should go back sometime next week, maybe Tuesday, to turn in the article, and then I don't know what."

"Well, today is Friday, so we have some time." By that point Jamie was kissing me all over. Between nuzzling my neck and biting my ear, he said, "Doesn't it feel good to just be . . . together?"

"Yes," I said. And then I scooted forward and guided him inside of me.

After sloshing water all over the bathroom floor, Jamie picked me up sopping wet and carried me to the bed, pausing only to say, "This is one of the nicer rooms here. You have a view." It was a gorgeous view, especially at that time of day when the sun had gone down but the sky still glowed with the memory of light. It was magic hour as we looked out at the expansive vineyard, with its endless rows of vines. It was like watching a Terrence Malick film: quiet, poetic, reflective, and the imagery overflowing with beauty.

Our bodies dried quickly. We fell back into lazy mode, like

we had that morning. He kissed my back and shoulders and I flipped through a brochure of the winery while he explained the fermentation process to me. I learned everything I ever wanted to know about the difference between naturally occurring yeast and cultured yeast.

"God, Jamie, you could teach a class on this stuff. What was your major in college?"

"Seducing young journalists," he said just before he disappeared under the covers.

. . .

I only remember hearing my room phone ring once. I was in a deep, comfortable sleep, nestled between Jamie's arm and his chest. When he picked it up, he was abrupt. "Yes? Okay. Okay." He hung up and I dozed off. I don't know how much later it was, but I stirred in the middle of the night and felt the empty space beside me. I sat up. Jamie was still naked but sitting at the end of the bed with his feet on the floor. His elbows were propped on his knees, his hands holding his sunken head.

"Jamie?" I said as I shuffled out of the comforter and moved to the end of the bed next to him. He wiped his face. "Are you okay?"

"Yes."

I kissed his back once. He turned immediately, stood, and lifted me from under my arms, tossing me up higher on the bed. I couldn't see the expression on his face as he crawled up between my legs, but I could feel his intensity.

"Jamie . . ."

"Shh." He kissed me hard and fast on the mouth, then moved down my body, rubbing his face against my bare skin between kisses. It was like he was consuming me and he couldn't get enough. I tangled my hands in his hair as he moved down my body, kissing and sucking. He sat up quickly and then leaned back on his heels. A small amount of light from the moon was peeking through the side of the curtain and lighting Jamie's face just enough so that I could see his expression. His eyebrows were downcast and his mouth was very slightly open. The movement of his chest pumping in and out looked dramatic as he took long, deep breaths. He stared down at me.

"What is it?" I whispered.

Without hesitation or words he took me forcefully over the edge. Reaching behind my bottom, he yanked my open legs toward his body and sat up on his knees, entering me at the same time. He stayed above me, looking into my eyes as he thrusted into me. Our breaths became louder and louder. I felt a yearning to have his whole body against mine. I tried to pull him down but he resisted. Instead, he brought my foot up to his mouth and kissed it gently, before extending my leg to rest on his shoulder. I was completely open to him and exposed as he took me over and over. Somehow, I felt totally unself-conscious. He held my leg against his chest and anchored his other hand on my hip, reaching his thumb down between us and drawing deep and deliberate circles until I was writhing against him uncontrollably. Arching my back, bringing our bodies a millimeter closer, I gripped the sheets and came hard, without shame.

I felt him tense as my body pulsed around his. He let out an exhausted breath and then collapsed onto me, burying his face in my neck. We were still for several moments while I held his big body, damp with sweat, against mine. He sank down lower, then rolled off of me and onto his side so he could take my nipple into his mouth. He kissed and sucked sleepily until I dozed off. With his head on my chest and my hands tangled in his soft hair, I fell into a heavy, dreamless sleep.

. . .

I felt alone before I knew I was. I rolled out of bed and opened the drapes. It was dawn and the light was almost as beautiful as it had been at dusk the evening before. I knew Jamie was gone, but before I turned around for visual confirmation, I stood at the door looking out onto the vineyard. My mind wandered back to the night before. Jamie seemed vulnerable and withdrawn sitting at the edge of the bed, and then suddenly undeterred, hungry for comfort, and a release. I looked around the room at the evidence of our night and wondered how, in such a short time, I could feel so connected to him. Clothes littered the floor, plates from our dessert covered the table, and notes that I had taken and informational pamphlets about the winery were strewn about. I figured Jamie must have gotten up early and gone to work in the vineyard. I took a long, hot bath and waited to hear from him.

At noon, I was starving and bored, so I decided to take my car into town. Driving was still a terrifying experience but it helped to roll down the window and focus on breathing in the clean, warm air. It was a perfect day to walk around the little town. I found my way into a used bookstore, where I discovered a copy of some of da Vinci's published journals. I bought it for Jamie and then browsed the other stores on the street. It seemed like everywhere I looked, I was reminded of him. Seeing a couple holding hands, or eating in a sidewalk café, I thought of Jamie. On my way back, I visited three other comparable wineries and found that they all lacked the magic I found at R. J. Lawson. Perhaps Jamie was responsible for that as well.

When I got back to the winery, I noticed that his truck wasn't parked in its usual place.

I headed to my room and found that housekeeping had already cleaned it. There was no record of Jamie and me in bed. It was made with the perfect hotel folds.

A feeling started building in my chest. I looked out the window and searched for Jamie among the many rows of vines. It started to occur to me that he hadn't called or left a message. His truck was gone and it was getting late. I picked up the phone and called the front desk.

A man's voice came through the receiver. "Hello, Ms. Corbin. How can I help you?"

"I was wondering if you could connect me to Jamie, uh . . . Jamie, the guy who works here."

Oh my god, I don't know his last name. I'm so stupid!

"One moment." I exhaled, relieved that the phone was ringing.

"This is Susan, how can I help you?"

"Susan, hi, it's Kate."

"Hello, Kate." She sounded weirdly apprehensive.

"I'm looking for Jamie."

"Oh . . . well, Jamie had to leave."

"Why?"

"I'm not sure I can . . ." her quiet voice trailed off.

"Can you give me his phone number?"

"Kate, let me get back to you."

"Get back to me?" I wanted to say, *Give me his goddamned number, I just spent the last two nights naked in bed with him.* "Never mind." I hung up and slumped onto the bed and waited for him to call.

What began as a tired sadness eventually morphed into anger.

All of my feelings of insecurity came rushing toward me at once. The memories of our last conversation in the tub, Jamie acting dodgy, the girl in the restaurant—all of those thoughts hit me at full speed. I began breathing loudly, anxiety coursing through my veins, my heart beating out of my chest. He wasn't coming back, I convinced myself. *Who would want me?* I was a shell of a person, plain and simple, not worth coming home to. Within a matter of a few days, both Stephen and Jamie had proven that to me.

I wouldn't need to learn how to be alone. I knew how to do that, but I was mad at myself for believing that Jamie and I had something. He was too good to be true, all good things . . . blah, blah, blah. When I saw him on the edge of the bed the night before, I should have known he was contemplating something that weighed heavily on him. It's not easy to crush someone's heart, no matter how spineless you might be. I wondered if he had snuck out just moments after I had given myself to him in such a raw and emotional way. He had rested his head on my chest as I fell asleep. I had thought he was mine. Then he had left, and now I was alone again.

In roughly four days, I had gone from believing that I should live a solitary life to having faith in love. With every inch closer to Jamie, I had approached a greater sense of peace. I couldn't explain how he had taken the pain of being alone away, but he had. Yet he had made no promises to me. I had believed that we had something bigger than words, that there was no need for conversation. I had believed, like a fool, that it wasn't possible to walk away from what we had. I guess the pull I had felt was stronger than what we'd actually had, which was quickly turning out to be nothing. Isn't that how it always is? The two parts inevitably make up one hundred percent, but that doesn't mean that the parts are equal. Someone is always giving more to make up for the deficit from the other. That's what blinded me—my own silly, romantic fantasy about a guy whose last name I didn't even know. I had given myself entirely to Jamie, and he had left without even asking for my phone number. I stood in the middle of the room, stunned.

I threw on jeans and a sweatshirt and scurried down the stairs to the inn lobby, where George was now manning the desk. "Hi, George. Have you seen Jamie?"

"No, dear."

"So you didn't see him sneak out of my room in the middle of the night?"

With a look of pity on his face, he slowly sucked air in through his teeth. "I just got in a half hour ago, so no, I didn't."

"Okay."

I marched over to Susan's office. As usual, she was tucked behind her computer and already peering at me over her glasses.

"Where's Jamie?" Without knocking, I opened the door to R.J.'s empty office and peeked in while I waited for her response.

"I'm not sure I'm the person to answer that."

"Why is that?"

"Because it's not my place to discuss his personal matters with you."

Heat, anger, and embarrassment flooded all of my senses. I could barely hear her because the sound of my own rapid heart-beat was pounding in my ears. "Do you have any idea what a co-lossal waste of time this entire thing has been for me? I came here to get a story on R.J., who is never fucking here." I started to raise my voice, but she didn't cower. "I got five rude minutes from him and one abrupt e-mail. Did you guys plan this? Did you use Jamie to distract me? Lighten the blow of not getting what was prom-ised to me? Your 'resident jack-of-all-trades'—well, that's no lie, is it? He's here to fuck lonely women and then fuck them over? Poor diabetic Jamie who lives in a barn and picks fucking grapes all day can fuck you against a wall like no one else." She didn't even raise her pencil-lined eyebrows at me, so I continued my rant. "What is this place? Is this some kind of joke? How could Jamie do this to me? I thought he was one of the good ones." Tears I had forced back finally sprung into my eyes.

In a low voice, she simply said, "It's not what you think. I'm sorry, Kate." In my mind, that was enough of an admission for both of them.

"Me, too. This thing with Jamie just made it all worse."

"That wasn't the intention. I didn't 'sic' Jamie on you." She made air quotes around the word "sic."

"Well, maybe not, Susan, but I still need to write an article about this godforsaken place. I'm leaving for Chicago tonight." *I'm not going to lie down and take it. I've done enough of that.*

She didn't try to stop me as I left the building. I spotted Chelsea lying on her bed outside.

"Bitch," I said under my breath and then kept walking, determined to continue my streak of vengeance.

I left a note for Chef Mark that said:

> Thanks for the whipped cream. I'm sure it wasn't the first time you fulfilled a special request like that from Jamie.

Poor Guillermo was my next victim.

"I don't know anything, *mija*. I just work here."

"Does Jamie have a lot of women in and out of his barn?"

"No." He shook his head convincingly. "Maybe your curiosity is getting the best of you," he said.

"I'm not the one with the problem."

I turned to walk away and stumbled past the row of vines where Jamie had kissed me so passionately. I paused and pressed my fingertips to my lips. Through tears, I wondered how I could have been so stupid. I promised myself that after I wrote the article, I would never think about that place again. I wouldn't think about how he took the pain away for a little while, like a needle in the dark.

It all came back as the sun blasted me that morning in the vineyard. The dream was wrong. I wanted to believe that Rose prayed for me to find someone to share my life with. I wanted to believe that there was a cosmic force drawing Jamie and me together, but that's not how things work. I shivered, even with the morning sun blaring down on me, because I realized there was no room for pain in love. Love is not the same thing as a marriage or a relationship or having children. Love is not work. Love is a feeling, pure and simple. It's a feeling you can have one moment, in which you believe you could throw yourself in front of a speeding train for someone; and it can vanish the next, when they tear your heart out and steal every last beat for themselves. If I had any love for Jamie inside of me, I ripped it out of my heart that morning as I stood there among the sea of vines. Every last bit of hope I had for a relationship evaporated into the atmosphere like a memory forgotten.

I walked toward the inn thinking, *I'm all I've got.* I never should've let go of that mantra.

No one would ever know what Jamie and I had shared. The moments of closeness, the things he whispered to me, the way he said I was beautiful with so much conviction. Who could prove or deny it? Back in my room, I stared at the bed, thinking it had only been hours since we had lain there wrapped and tangled in each other, the way lovers do. I felt like we had grown together like a couple of trees planted too closely together, our branches mingling so that we didn't know whose limbs belonged to whom. But it didn't matter now because Jamie had uprooted himself. I had thought there was a chance we could stay that way forever. *How naive of me. How sad. How pathetic.*

The maid had tossed all of my belongings into a neat pile on the dresser and desk. It made packing up simple. I dialed Jerry.

"Jerry Evans."

"Can you get me a flight tonight?"

"What? You and the winery guy want to elope to Cancun or something?"

"No." *Don't cry, don't do it, Kate!*

I started crying.

"Oh shit," he said, quietly. "Go to the airport. I'll text you the details in a few minutes."

"Thank you," I said through sobs, and then I hung up.

I stuffed all of my belongings into my tiny suitcase, including the numerous pages of notes and doodling. I drove all the way to San Francisco International Airport with a newfound confidence. I honked at shitty drivers; I even gave the finger a few times. It was only after I began screaming at an elderly woman in a green Chevy Nova that I decided I had a legitimate case of road rage and should probably cool it before I got myself shot.

At the airport desk, I upgraded to a first-class ticket, thinking it would be easier to drown my sorrows with the free, unlimited booze. I tucked myself into my giant seat. The flight attendant brought me a blanket and pillow. I asked for an extra blanket and then I proceeded to wrap myself into a fleece cocoon. I managed to pin my arms against my body inside of the blankets, which was wonderful. If only it didn't slightly resemble a straitjacket. When we got off the ground, I undid the seat-back table with my teeth and ordered a double scotch on the rocks. *I don't even drink scotch.* When my drink came, I leaned over and sucked the entire thing through the straw in three large gulps. It was then that I noticed there was a passenger seated next to me.

She was staring at me with round, giant blue eyes. "How old are you?" I asked.

"Twelve," she said.

"What's your name?" I cocked my head to the side as if I were interrogating her, unconcerned that I must have looked ridiculous.

"Aurora. Are you a crazy person or something?"

"Takes one to know one, kid." Her eyes widened even more. "I'm just kidding. No, I'm not crazy . . . yet. Anyway, crazy people don't know they're crazy, so that's a silly question." She nodded in agreement, a thoughtful expression on her face. I could tell right away she was one of those kids who are wiser than their years. "The truth is that I just got my heart trampled over. I had a rough day. You know how that is?" I arched my eyebrows for emphasis.

"Yeah," she said and let out a deep breath. "I know exactly what you mean. This boy in my class, Genesis, told me he liked me and then told everyone else that I wouldn't leave him alone."

"Genesis? That's his name? Um, red flag right there. What kind of name is Genesis?" She just shrugged. "Well, I'll tell you. That is an English New Age rock group from the seventies and eighties. His parents are either really old or they've been dropping acid for way too long. My guess is the latter, hence Genesis's bizarre behavior. Don't sweat it. Someone else will come along. Unless, of course, you realize now that being alone is better than having your heart broken over and over again. Realize that now, kid, and save yourself the trouble."

"So being alone is better?" She was looking me right in the eye. Could I really lie to her?

"Are your parents married?"

"Yes, they've been married for twenty-two years," she said with a smile.

"Well, I guess it's a case-by-case basis. Don't listen to me. It happens for some people. Maybe you'll be that person."

"Maybe you will, too. You just can't let all that bullshit make you hard." That, from a twelve-year-old.

"You're probably right. Hey, do you want to help me? I have to write this article . . ."

Never Start a Sentence with "So"

After traveling most of the day and scribbling the article down on the back of a couple of flyers I grabbed from the rental car company, I finally made it back to my cold, dark Lincoln Park apartment. I immediately opened my laptop, shot an e-mail off to Jerry, then went to sleep and stayed that way for the next two days.

To: Jerry Evans
From: Kate Corbin
Subject: Fuck it!

This is it, Jerry. I don't even know what to call it. This is all I have. I'm sure I'm fired or severely demoted. Maybe I can be the coffee cart girl? I know R.J. won't approve of this, so I feel like I've totally let you down. I have some vacation time accrued and I'd like to take next week off if I still have a job. I need to get my head straight. I fucked up, Jerry. I shouldn't

have gotten involved with that guy. I fucked up and I'm
sorry. —Kate

UNTITLED ARTICLE ON R. J. LAWSON AND WINERY

*So you have two birds. One is long, lean, and powerful,
with sheer physical strength on its side. The other is
colorful, small, and fast, and prized for its beauty. Who
will win? First, you must know that the challenge is the
game of business, otherwise known as deception, and
the winner of this game will always be the more cunning
player, regardless of his physicality. Forget what you've
seen—looks can be deceiving. You have to search inside
the competitor's heart. You have to detect the rhythm
that drives him, what fuels the challenger's willingness to
sacrifice dignity and integrity for money. That's what it all
comes down to in the end. The winner of this game gets
a gold, diamond-encrusted cage. But success comes with
a price—in this case, the freedom to fly. He may have
the promise of admirers, but his majestic wings will never
dance across the sky again.*

 *The world wants to know why everything R. J. Lawson
touches turns to gold. Well, I'll tell you: he's the more
cunning bird. He was a genius who peaked at eighteen,
made his money, and now proudly waves his wallet at
anything that interests him—in this case, wine. I spent
one week at R. J. Lawson's famed Napa Valley winery
during the harvest season to learn more about him and his
seemingly worthwhile cause. While there, I observed that
he spent little time at the winery, but he does take credit
for all the work. He described his approach as hands-on,*

yet I didn't see him complete a single task during my visit, with the exception of sipping a glass of Pinot.

His image is held together by a few loyal pawns who are willing to do his dirty work. I saw right through it. I saw that R.J. had mastered the game of buying people and buying success. Maybe inside the man there is a boy whose curiosity earned him a great deal of adoration and money, but there is no trace of that exceptional wonder and gift in the man I met.

If R.J. had shown me a modicum of brilliance or even humanity, aside from rapping off the many charities he's donated to, maybe I could write a nicer article about him, but the truth is this: he acted as though I wasn't worth his time. He was misogynistic and degrading toward his staff. He was pompous and put out while answering a few questions. From afar, one might envy what R.J. has acquired. It's no lie that the wine is fantastic and the winery itself is something of a shining gem among the hills of Napa Valley, but that doesn't mean R.J. is not paying a price for all of that perfection. His shrewd cunning has condemned him to the confines of a cage. He may sit perched above all that beauty, but he's in that cage alone.

The staff at the winery made a pathetic attempt at hospitality in the wake of my awful experience with R.J. Sadly, I found their strategies to be somewhat elaborate. So, my conclusion is that R. J. Lawson's big ego was probably responsible for orchestrating all of the backpedaling and ridiculous behavior from the others at the helm. Although the facility seems unmatched in the region, you might be gambling with your happiness by taking a trip to R. J. Lawson. Before you do anything, you

*have to ask yourself about that bird, the one who is willing
to sacrifice the freedom to fly for the material facade.
However mesmerized you are by the glittering gold of that
cage, the only question you need to ask is: Where does
that bird shit?*

*My advice about R. J. Lawson would be this: drink the
wine, but don't drink the Kool-Aid.*

Kate Corbin
Chicago Crier

. . .

On Monday morning, when I finally woke from a depressing slumber, I opened my computer to find a new e-mail from Jerry. He always gave it away in the subject line; maybe that's why he made a better editor than writer. I appreciated it in that moment and was able to let out a huge sigh of relief when I realized that, at the very least, I still had my job.

To: Kate Corbin
From: Jerry Evens
Subject: You still have a job!

It's brilliant, Kate. I don't know what we'll do with it, but it's the most inspired work I've seen out of you and that's all that matters. R.J. may have done his best to make getting the details nearly impossible, but you proved that as long as you can capture the essence of a situation, a story will be born from it.

I agree that it's best you take a week off. Apparently

you left your luggage at the airport. There was no name on the tag, just the address to the paper, so the airline delivered it here. I opened the suitcase when it arrived today and realized quickly that it was yours from all of your notes and belongings. I'll lock it in the storage room until you get back, unless you need it right away. Just let me know.

I'm worried about you, Kate, but I know how strong you are, and I know we'll get you back on track soon. Beth has some ideas.

Your Loyal Editor,
Jerry

There was nothing particularly heartfelt or touching about Jerry's e-mail, but for some reason it made me cry. The truth was that I didn't want anyone worrying about me or pitying me. I wanted to stop feeling like I was searching for something else or some answer to the meaning of it all. The expectation that life should be more than waking up alone, riding the train to work, and then going home to fall asleep alone had been weighing on me for so long, but I always found myself back at my apartment . . . alone. Everything in between was just heartache.

I shuffled down my short hallway to the kitchen, where I scanned the barren refrigerator. Staring at the same jar of jelly for ten minutes, I contemplated eating it with a spoon. There was little I was willing to do to keep myself alive at that point. I hadn't showered in two days, and aside from a couple of stale crackers and an old skunky beer that had been in my fridge for a year, I had consumed nothing. The jelly seemed appropriate, until I finally allowed my most basic survival instinct to kick in. I threw on a pair of sweats and a jacket and headed to the market and produce stand on the corner. There was an older man at the counter making fresh homemade salsa, so after picking up a banana, some Fig Newton–like cookies, and a bag of pretzels, I figured: *What would go better with all of that than salsa? Am I losing my mind?*

"Excuse me?" I asked. He looked up through his dark lashes. His eyes were almost identical to mine. A hazel that looked spectacularly green in the light, but sort of a dull brown in the shadow.

"Yes, ma'am, what can I help you with?"

"Are you my father?"

He chuckled but stopped immediately when he saw how serious I was. "Oh, hmm, no, dear. I've been married for almost forty years and we have three children. I'm sorry."

"Oh, well, shot in the dark, you know?" He nodded, but his eyes still held the same pitying expression he had on before. "Do you sell beer here?"

"No, but there's a wineshop about half a block down."

I shook my head frantically. "I'm detoxing, I can't have wine."

"Okay, well, there's a liquor store about three blocks from here that sells beer."

"Yeah, I know that one. Thank you, sir."

"You're welcome."

The liquor store was more like five blocks, but I skipped along, eating my banana and fig cookies. I felt extremely pissed at the universe when I saw Stephen and some chick about half a block down, walking in my direction. Hoping they didn't see me, I slipped quickly into an alley. As I waited for them to pass, I scanned my attire. I was wearing the oldest pair of gray sweats that exist on this planet, a yellow T-shirt with the sunshine Care

Bear on it, and my powder blue skiing jacket, although that wasn't the worst of it. I had on two different socks, one black and one light purple, and an old pair of black Chucks with black laces. I was the twenty-six-year-old Punky Brewster. I quickly felt the top of my head. *Phew.* No pigtails, but it was topped off with a messy bun. *Please do not let them see me.*

"Kate?"

Fuck!

I shoved the last cookie into my mouth and mumbled, "Hey, Stephen."

"This is Monique. I work with her."

"Hi, Monique." He never hung out with female colleagues outside of work. She was a tall, blond beauty wearing an extremely narrow pencil skirt and stilettos. There was a brief moment where I thought how perfect she and Stephen looked together, the epitome of working professionals in Chicago. My disheveled ass had taken sulking and letting myself go to a new level, and I could tell that Stephen had picked up on it.

He squinted. "Are you okay, Kate?"

"Yeah, I'm fucking dandy, Stephen. You?"

"Fine. Where are you off to?" he asked. I glanced over at Monique, who was scanning my clothes. I saw sadness and pity wash over her face.

"I'm going to get a forty."

He pinched his eyebrows together. "What's a forty?"

"A forty of beer." He still looked dumbfounded. "It's forty ounces of beer in a bottle. Not everyone can afford to indulge in expensive spirits."

"I've never seen you drink beer."

"Well, I guess there's a lot you don't know about me. Why would you care anyway? You never loved me, remember?"

Monique's eyes shot open. Stephen's jaw twitched. "I said I wasn't sure. Plus, we were fighting when I said that. This is not the time or place to pick at old wounds."

"Old wounds? That was six fucking days ago." He shook his head in a warning gesture. "Well, you two enjoy each other," I said as I walked away.

Still within earshot, I heard Monique ask, "Who was that?"

"Nobody," Stephen said. *Ouch.*

At the liquor store, I purchased a giant can of Budweiser, some tortilla chips, and a total of eighty lottery scratchers. My thought was that each scratcher would take me roughly thirty seconds to complete. That meant that it would occupy at least forty minutes of my time. Forty minutes I wouldn't have to think about Jamie. It was two thousand four hundred heartbeats I wouldn't be listening to.

I walked back to my apartment, sipping my can of Bud from the crumpled paper bag it was housed in. When I entered my apartment, I could hear my cell phone ringing incessantly from the bedroom, but I didn't answer it. I finished my beer at 11:43 a.m. and then went back to sleep. The doorbell startled me awake. I glanced at the clock on my nightstand. It was six thirty p.m. As I slowly inched my way to the door, I breathed into my hand. My breath was horrid. Had I brushed my teeth in three days? *Probably not.* The doorbell rang again.

"Coming." I opened it one inch and peeked through the sliver of space into Beth's peering eyes.

"What up, sister? Are you gonna let me in?"

I slammed the door shut and removed the chain and then opened the door wide for Beth to enter.

"Christ, Kate, you look like death warmed over."

"Thanks, Beth."

"Dear god, what is that smell?"

I lifted my shoulders to my ears. "I don't know."

"It smells like burnt hair."

Then it hit me. "Oh yeah, Dylan from 5B came over earlier and we smoked some pot. You know Dylan, that kid who plays the bucket on the corner? He lives in my building."

"Isn't he a teenager?"

"He's twenty."

"Since when do you smoke pot?"

"Since earlier, when Dylan from 5B came over."

Beth shook her head in disapproval. "Did you do anything else with Dylan from 5B?"

"Jesus no, Beth—who do ya think I am? He just showed me some rare comic book he bought with the money he made on the corner, and then he pulled a tiny bong from his pocket. I said what the hell, why not, and took a hit, but I didn't really know what I was doing with the lighter." I pointed to the half of my eyebrow that was completely singed.

"Oh shit, girl, you need to pencil that in."

"It could have been worse. He asked me if I wanted to do X and then go roller-skating." I shrugged. "He's a nice kid, though."

Beth walked through my apartment, scanning the disarray. She opened the refrigerator. "You have no food in here. Let's go get a hot dog."

"There's salsa, plus I'm a vegetarian. Actually, I'm a pescetarian, but that's just semantics." Then I smiled really wide. "You know what? Fuck it! Let's go get a hot dog."

We went to an old hot dog joint called the Dogfather. It looked like something out of an episode of *The Sopranos*. The room was dark with red leather booths. They served every kind of hot dog imaginable. You ordered at the counter, where they had about a hundred different toppings and thirty different kinds of beer. I chose the foot-long spiced dog called Sal's Hit. Beth got the kielbasa named the Kill Mob Bossa. We slipped into a booth and ate in silence for a few minutes. After the initial disgust I felt over chomping into meat encased in pig intestines, I decided it was the best goddamned food I'd ever had.

I washed Sal's Hit down with three twenty-four-ounce Belgian beers, none of which I could name. I was thoroughly drunk. Beth talked me into hitting up a gay bar with her that Friday night, and staying true to my motto of the day, I told her, "What the hell, why not? So you're outta the closet, I take it?"

"I was never in the closet. I just don't do relationships. I've kept my life simple."

"I totally get that," I deadpanned.

"I'm worried about you, Kate." I had never seen Beth that serious.

"What are you talking about?"

"I just think you spend a lot of time alone."

"That's not by choice, Beth. And anyway, you do, too. You just said you don't do relationships."

"But I go out and have fun and cut loose. You used to, re-member? We used to do karaoke? You laughed more then."

"Everyone keeps telling me I'm lost and my spark is gone and I'm crazy, but every time I take a chance, every time I go out on a limb, I fall. I slept with a guy I didn't even know. I mean I really slept with him, Beth." I opened my eyes wide for emphasis.

"You mean, fell for him?"

"Yes, that's what I mean. I'm always the one to fall."

She looked very thoughtful for several moments. "At least you get to enjoy the view, even if it's brief. I don't think taking chances is such a bad thing. Maybe you're stronger now. I just don't want you to give up."

"This, coming from the girl who doesn't do relationships."

She bit her bottom lip and nodded. "I might change that and check out the view sometime."

Beth walked me to the door of my apartment. I took one step in and then my body reminded me that I hadn't eaten red meat in ten years. My stomach rumbled and turned violently. I honestly didn't know which end it was going to come out of, and then to my absolute horror I realized it was both. Sitting on the toilet, I managed to puke into the sink. And even though there was about three inches between my mouth and the edge of the porcelain, I was able to projectile vomit perfectly into the basin.

Beth stayed with me for part of the night, bringing me clean washcloths and water. My body thoroughly rid itself of Sal's Hit. I swore off meat for another ten years and then told Beth she was free to go. She left but came back ten minutes later with Popsicles, Seven Up, and saltines.

"You're a good friend," I told her.

"I just want you in tip-top shape so I can take you to Lady Fingers on Friday."

"Are you kidding me? That's the name of the place?"

"You won't be disappointed." She smirked. I hiccupped and burped and wondered what I was getting myself into.

After she left, I slumped onto my bed and stared at the ceiling, thinking about Jamie. I thought about him whispering, "I'll take care of you," and then I cried myself to sleep.

Tuesday and Wednesday flew by. Dylan from 5B came over on Thursday. I didn't smoke any pot, but I let him hotbox my apartment so I was even more completely stoned than I was the time before, except this time my eyebrows remained intact. We watched three episodes of *Whose Line Is It Anyway?* and laughed our asses off. Dylan was actually pretty cute. He was tall and skinny and pale with buzzed hair, but he had these really blue eyes. That night he helped me carry my laundry to the basement.

"Hey Kate, you wanna go to the skate park with me tomorrow night?"

"I can't, I have a date with a lesbian."

His eyes shot open. "Oh, cool."

"It's not what you think."

He smiled and shrugged. "It's your business. Aren't you still dating that douche wad in 9A?"

"Stephen? No, he dumped me last week. He's dating someone else already."

"His loss." He said it so quickly and nonchalantly that I almost believed him.

We got to the basement door. Dylan pushed it open and walked in but paused in front of me. I leaned around his body and saw Stephen making out with a different girl than he had been with earlier that week. At first I didn't recognize her, and then I saw her token pink scrunchie bobbing above her head. It was the bimbo from the sixth floor. Every time I saw her she was with a different guy.

Stephen turned and spotted me. "Kate, I thought you did your laundry on Mondays?" I contemplated sharing my thoughts on women in their thirties who still wear colorful hair pretties, but I chose to take the high road. Anyway, one or both of them would undoubtedly have a venereal disease by the end of the week, and that was my silver lining.

"Don't talk to me, Stephen." I coughed and mumbled, "Pencil dick" at the same time. Dylan stayed near the door. Everyone in the room watched me as I emptied my laundry bag into a washer. I added soap, stuck some quarters in, closed the lid, and turned to walk out. Just as I reached the opening, Dylan pushed me against the doorjamb and kissed me like he had just come back from war. I let him put on a full show until he moved his hand up and cupped my breast. I very discreetly said, "Uh-uh" through our mouths, and he pulled his hand away and slowed the kiss. When we pulled apart, I turned toward Stephen and the bimbo and shot them an ear-splitting smile.

"Hey, Steve"—I'd never called him Steve—"Will you text me when the washer is done? I'll be busy in my apartment for a while."

He nodded, still looking stunned.

I grabbed Dylan's hand and pulled him into the elevator. Once the doors were closed, we both burst into laughter.

"You didn't have to do that," I said.

"I wanted to. That asshole had it coming."

"Well, thank you. You live with your mom, right?"

"Yeah."

"Please don't tell her about this. I can't imagine what she would think of me."

"I'm not that much younger than you, Kate." He jabbed me in the arm playfully and smirked. "You need to lighten up. Anyway, my mom would be cool with it."

"Well, I hope I didn't give you the wrong idea."

"Nah. We're buddies, I get it. I'm kind of in love with that Ashley chick from the fourth floor. I just have to wait until next month when she turns eighteen, you know?" He wiggled his eyebrows.

I laughed. "You two would make a cute couple." *If only it were that simple.*

Rowback

Throughout that week, I occasionally pulled out a few lottery scratchers to pass the time. By Friday, I had scratched all eighty and there was a healthy amount of the sparkly silver shavings littering my apartment. I didn't care. I'd won thirteen new tickets and forty-four dollars. It was like I'd hit the jackpot, even though technically I'd lost twenty-three dollars.

As promised, I met Beth at Lady Fingers, although I can't say I put much effort into my look. I wore black skinny jeans, the same grungy Chucks I'd worn all week, and a gray hoodie over an old Ani DiFranco T-shirt. Beth was waiting for me at the bar.

"You . . . look hot!" she said, scanning my getup. "I really have turned you, haven't I?"

"What are you talking about? I've been wearing these jeans for three days."

"Well, casual works for you. These ladies will be all over it."

Beth was wrong. I must have been putting off the bitch vibe because I sat at the bar, unapproached, while I nursed a pint of Guinness. I watched Beth dance and mingle. She got the entire dance floor going when she busted out an extremely en-

177

thusiastic rendition of the African Anteater Ritual. I smiled and laughed but couldn't help wondering what I was doing there.

"I'm gonna head back."

"Already? The night has just begun."

"I'm sorry, Beth. I'm just really tired."

"Oh, hey—I read the piece you wrote on Lawson." A smile touched the side of her mouth.

"Well?"

"It's good, Kate. Short, but good. Jerry's printing it. It goes to press Monday."

"What? Are you kidding me?"

"Why are you so surprised? Jerry loved it."

"I'm shocked because R.J. himself had to approve it, and I tore him to shreds."

"I guess Jerry found some loophole." *Of course he did.*

There were a few dozen emotions flowing through me in that moment. I felt a twinge of guilt for so publicly bashing R.J., but I let it slip away when I started to feel the pain seep in. I was angry at what the winery represented in my mind. When I thought about all of the moments with Jamie, his sweet vulnerability after his insulin level had fallen, all the laughs and physical closeness I had felt with him, it was like a flurry of knives stabbing my heart. I couldn't think of those times without thinking about how he slipped out without leaving me so much as a phone number or his last name.

"Well, it is what it is, I guess. I'll see you Monday, Beth."

"See ya, Kate."

Back at my apartment, I finally switched on my computer and checked my e-mail. Jerry had sent the article back to me with a few minor editorial notes. I approved his changes immediately and sent it back to him.

The rest of the weekend got lost in my foggy memory. I cleaned and tried to create some order in my apartment. I saw Dylan talking to Ashley on the street, which put a huge smile on my face. I went grocery shopping and then took flowers to my mom's grave. That Sunday was her birthday. Why we acknowledge birthdays after death makes no sense, but I guess it's a way to stay committed to remembering somebody. Maybe it's because, after we die, we are so easily forgotten. I wondered who would remember me.

I leaned up against the blank side of my mother's tombstone. When I did that, it gave me the feeling that we were sitting back-to-back. When I would visit her grave as a teenager, I would pretend to have conversations with her. I made her up in my mind to be the perfect mother. She would always have the best advice, the perfect answer to some dilemma I was facing.

"Hi, Mama." She died when I was so young that I never started calling her Mom, the way older kids do. She would always be Mama. As I sat there, a sad realization washed over me. "I didn't really know you. I remember you, but I didn't know you. I wish I did." The mother I had made up in my mind was probably nothing like the woman she was. "I'm twenty-six now, but I still feel like I need my mama." *Maybe I always will.* Tears rushed down my face. "I don't want to spend my life alone." That was the last thing I said aloud. I stopped talking but sat there for an hour with my head resting on my propped-up knees.

After collecting myself, I walked to Rose's grave. She was in the mausoleum at the same cemetery. Her name placard still hadn't been placed on the marble, a reminder of how recent her death was. I couldn't even go near the wall. I felt like she was still haunting me through the dream, the nightmare. I wondered if I would hear her pleas if I got too close. A cemetery worker passed me as I stood there, rocking back and forth on my heels.

There was at least a fifteen-foot barrier between the wall and me, so I wasn't surprised when the worker looked at me curiously.

"Can I help you, ma'am?"

"Do you know when they'll put the placard up? It's been almost nine months since her death." I pointed toward the marble wall.

"That usually means the bill hasn't been paid. You'll need to talk to someone in the office."

I marched up to the office and spoke to a mild-mannered woman who informed me that there was a balance on the account of forty-seven cents, which was why Rose's placard hadn't been placed on her tomb. I felt like the worst human being on the planet. How could I have let that happen? I handed the woman twenty dollars and said, "Keep the change and apply it to any other accounts that have small balances like this. Some people don't have anyone to look after them after their gone, but they still deserve their goddamned placard."

The woman looked shocked at first, but then nodded fervently. I could tell she agreed.

"When will they put it up?"

"They have another one to do on that wall, so it should be done by the end of the day." She reached into a file drawer and pulled the placard out. They'd probably had it sitting in there for eight months, all because of forty-seven cents. She showed it to me and I was suddenly taken back to the days after Rose's death, when I'd had to make the decisions about her funeral. I had chosen to include her name and birth and death dates, like on most gravestones and placards, but I'd also had them add the simple word "Beloved" at the top, because she was.

"Is this the one?"

"Yes."

"I'll have them put it up."

"Thank you," I said quietly and then shuffled out the door. It was getting dark as I headed back to the L station. I felt cleansed, as I always did after visiting my mother and Rose. On the train that night, I decided I would walk into the *Chicago Crier* the next day with my head held high. I had a job, an apartment, and a few devoted friends. I feared the general reaction to my article from R.J. and the public would be that it bordered on libel or defamation, but I had written nothing more than my observations, which would be impossible to refute, and I knew that the crowd at the *Crier* would appreciate the risk I had taken. I told myself there would be no more article pitches for fruit-flavored gum. I was going to be a serious journalist.

The next day I hit the Brown Line and searched for Just Bob. I needed a heavy dose of the inspirational self-help mumbo jumbo, but I couldn't find him. I searched the entire length of the train twice, but he wasn't there. I even missed my stop looking for him. I had to walk three extra blocks to the *Crier*, so I didn't roll into the lobby until well after ten. I knew by that point in the day that everyone would have seen the article, so my nerves were on extra high alert. The security guy held up the paper as I walked past.

"Pretty bold one, Kate."

"Thanks, I think."

As I entered the *Crier* bull pen, as we called it, the music went off the overhead speaker. Jerry's voice came on.

"She's back, people." Slowly, each head rose above the cubicle partitions to face my direction, and then the clapping began. I heard someone shout, "Glad to have you back, Kate!" and someone else yelled, "Great article this morning!" Beth grinned at me as I entered my cubicle.

I stood on my chair to thank everyone for the warm welcome back. It tipped and I almost fell, but I quickly regained my composure. Everyone laughed. "Yes, I'm still clumsy!" I shouted. I was known as the office klutz. People would see me coming and move things out of my way. I laughed at myself for a few seconds longer. "Okay, I just want to say thank you, I'm glad to get back to work."

I stepped down as Jerry came toward my desk, rolling my suitcase behind him. "I guess there was nothing in here you needed too desperately," he said.

I glanced at the suitcase. "I'm actually terrified to open that thing."

He leaned against the cubicle wall and peered over me as I sat at my desk. "What happened out there?" Out of the corner of my eye, I could see Beth's chair roll a little ways into the aisle. She was eavesdropping.

"Just get in here, Beth. I know you're listening." She came in and leaned her backside against my desk. I huffed, "Nosy journalist."

"Well, I need the details so I can have your back."

"I fell hard for this guy, Jamie, who worked at the winery. I guess it was just a fling. He acted dodgy when I asked him personal questions, and then he slipped out in the middle of the night."

"Why do you think?" Beth asked.

"I thought maybe R.J. or Susan, the general manager, put him up to it as a buffer between R.J. and me, but the more I think about it, the more I realize it wouldn't have helped. I don't know. We really clicked. I don't get it. It was only a few days. Maybe it was too much, too soon."

Jerry had a slightly penitent look on his face. "I'm sorry, I feel responsible."

"Why?"

"Because I told you to go for it. I guess you have to kiss a few frogs first, but I think you deserve to find your prince."

"Do I?"

Beth reached down and gave me a sideways hug around the shoulders. "You absolutely do," she said.

"I think I need to get you working right away. Start coming up with some pitches, Kate. Let's meet in my office tomorrow morning."

"You got it, Jer." They both left my cubicle just as Annabel, the young research assistant, came in.

"I guess you won't be needing any of this. Congrats on the article," she said as she plopped a stack of research on my desk.

"Thanks. Sorry you did all of that for nothing."

"Yeah, this guy's info was seriously buried. It took me forever just to find a picture of him. Someone must be a little paranoid."

"He probably invented some super amazing computer gadget to protect his identity. I really am very sorry."

"No worries, Kate. I like the angle you took on the piece, and if we ever want to run another article on him, we have a couple weeks' worth of research here."

"Thanks."

After she left, I glanced down at the stack. My intention was to slide it entirely into the trash, but something caught my eye. It was an obituary from the Saturday before. The headline read: R. J. LAWSON SR., FATHER OF FAMED TECHNOLOGY IN-VENTOR, PASSES AWAY AT 68.

I skimmed past the section on Sr.'s contributions to the

world of aviation engineering to his relationship with R.J. It said he was survived by his only son, Ryan James Lawson Jr., an extremely private technology inventor and philanthropist. Just over a week after his father's death, I was libeling him in a worldwide publication. I moved the article aside. The next piece of information was a spreadsheet of the organizations R.J. had donated to. It was in order from the largest donations to the smallest. At the top of the list, under his own foundation, was the American Diabetes Association, and underneath that was the GLIDE homeless shelter.

My stomach began turning, but it completely dropped through the floor when I moved the spreadsheet to reveal a picture glued to a piece of paper. At the top, Annabel had written, *R.J.'s graduation from MIT. Pictured here with his mother, Deborah.*

Underneath the picture there were more notes.

It's public record that R.J. was adopted as an infant. His adoptive mother, pictured here, was killed in a car accident four years ago. After reuniting with his biological parents, they tried to extort money from him. Both were given jail time. He has a biological sister in Boston, and even though he went to college and spends some free time there, he does not have a relationship with her. She testified in her parents' favor at the short, unpublicized extortion trial.

I looked at the picture in disbelief. It was the same picture I had seen on Jamie's nightstand in the barn. Suddenly, I remembered the picture I had seen before going to the winery, the one of R.J. as a young boy at the science fair. That boy at the science fair and the young man at his college graduation were clearly the same person. *Jamie.* Even now, I had a hard time seeing them in the man I had spent several intimate days with. Jamie couldn't be a computer genius—he didn't fit the stereotype. And I had seen R.J. with my own eyes in an interview . . .

I stood up on shaky legs and pushed my chair away. *It can't be.* The room started spinning.

Beth spotted me over the partition. "You okay?" I nodded and then sunk to my knees on the floor. I tore open my suitcase and began rummaging through all of the notes and papers I had shoved in there from my room at the winery. I looked at the sheet where I had taken notes from R.J.'s e-mail to me. When I thought back to what Jamie had told me about his life, it matched or somehow fit into the outline R.J. had given me.

Giant puzzle pieces floating above my head started moving into place.

Jamie: Ryan James.

MIT: College on the East Coast.

Building schools in Africa: Tribal tattoos. *I've traveled a lot.*

Hands-on approach: *I clean this pool, I can swim in it anytime I want.*

Me: *Is this R.J.'s boat?* Jamie: *It's my boat.*

Me: *What's your last name?* Jamie: *No more talking.*

Tears began falling onto the papers in my hand. I looked down at the smudge I'd created in Jamie's handwriting. It was a note—one I hadn't seen. The morning I had left, the maids had cleaned before I packed. They had gathered all of my paperwork into a pile, and this note, the note that could have changed everything, got lost in the mix somehow.

Katy, my angel,

I had to go to Portland. My father had a heart attack, and they don't know if he's going to make it through the night. Please don't leave. If I can't get back by tomorrow, I'll send a car and get you a flight up here. Please, please don't leave. I have something really important to tell you, besides the fact that I am completely in love with you.

—J

I sobbed loudly. Beth was hovering over me within seconds. "What's wrong?"

"J . . . Jamie is . . ."

"What, Kate?"

"Jamie *is* R.J." I finally got it out.

"You mean the guy, the one you fell for?"

"Yes," I groaned.

"Well, then, who was the R.J. you met?"

"I don't know."

"Are you sure?" I nodded. "So if Jamie is R.J., then the article . . ."

"Oh my god, I thought he destroyed *me*, but I've destroyed *him*. He's not that man." I pointed to the article pinned to the cubicle partition. "He's a good man with a big heart." I sniffled. "He's brilliant and he works so hard. How could I have not put it together?" I held the note up. "And on top of everything else, he's in love with me!"

"Shit, Kate. Why did he lie to you?" I swallowed back the lump taking over my throat. I stood and looked up at Jerry's office, which sat perched above the bull pen. Jerry was standing at the large glass window, talking on the phone and staring down at me. He pointed to the receiver at his ear and mouthed, *Lawson. He's here.* I flew toward the bathroom. Beth followed. She held my hair while I puked the entire contents of my stomach into the toilet.

"You should go home. I'll talk to Jerry."

"Thank you," was all I could get out. I went back to my cubicle and grabbed my coat but left my suitcase and paperwork, except for the note. When I glanced up at Jerry's office, I could see that Beth was already there, talking with a sober look on her face.

I darted out of the bull pen and chose to use the service elevator, hoping to avoid Jamie, or R.J., or whoever he was. I beelined through the lobby, pushed both glass doors open forcefully, and headed out onto the street. I stopped within a few feet of the entrance when I spotted him. He was leaning against a concrete wall, looking down at his feet. He was wearing a black suit with a white dress shirt. The top buttons were undone and his hair was slicked back.

His eyes were sad and shadowed with dark circles. I stuffed the note into my pocket and began to rush past him with my head down, hoping he wouldn't see me.

He stood up to block me. "Wait," was all he said.

I squared my shoulders and put my hand on my hip. "Why are you dressed like that?"

"I flew straight here after my father's funeral." His voice cracked at the last second.

"I'm sorry, Jamie . . . R.J. . . . . whoever you are." I had sympathy for him, for his loss and for the stupid article, but I was so hurt by his lies and the problems they'd caused. I turned to walk away. He grabbed my shoulders and turned me back toward him.

"Everyone I know calls me Jamie. And I'm sorry, too, Kate." He tried to pull me closer.

I pounded my fists against his chest. "You're a liar." I started to cry. "You lied to me while I was naked in your arms. And the article . . . you made me a fraud, and you ruined my career." I tried to pull away but he held me. "Why did you approve it?"

"I didn't. If I didn't respond within forty-eight hours, he had a right to print it. It was in the contract." He stepped away and looked down at his feet. "I was busy mourning the only family I had left."

Wiping the tears from my face, I stood up straight and re-gained my composure. "I am truly sorry for your loss. I'm sorry for this whole big mess. I wish I had never gone out there. I wish I had never met you."

"How can you say that?" He gripped the outside of my arms and stared down at me with a desperate pleading in his eyes. "Do you really mean that?"

"If you hadn't lied to me, I wouldn't have written a fucked-up fake article about you." I yanked my arms out of his grip. "Who the hell was that guy I interviewed?"

"His name is Bradley Reis. He's a friend of Susan's—or was, I should say. She thought he would fit the part."

"Fit the part?" I shook my head.

"I know, it seems so stupid now. I didn't want to give up my privacy. I wanted to be able to walk around the winery and just be myself, just be Jamie. I was afraid if I met with a reporter, everyone would know who I was and hound me."

"That's not what would have happened."

"I panicked. Susan said all we had to do was write down information about the winery and Bradley would just try to avoid all the personal questions. I never liked him and shouldn't have trusted him." Jamie was staring at his shoes. "I don't think he expected you to be so persistent. I think he thought he could charm you." He looked up and smiled timidly.

"Your little plan backfired, didn't it? Now you've ruined your reputation and my career."

"Jerry said Beth could write a rowback."

"That's great for you. Your name will be cleared, but I'll still be out of a job."

"I'll do whatever I need to do to make this right." His eyes watered a bit and then he swallowed. In a low voice, he said, "Why did you leave?"

"I didn't see the note until today, but everything happens for a reason, doesn't it?"

I turned to walk away but he followed. "Katy, I know you don't believe that."

"Don't call me that," I said without turning back. He grabbed my arm and swung me around. I gasped. "What do you think you're doing?"

"Stop this now! This is crazy," he growled. He searched my eyes, still holding my arm tightly. "Just stop and give me a fucking chance."

"You're hurting me." He let go instantly. "I barely know you. It was four days. Four days I wish I could get back," I said in a calm, even tone.

He straightened up and squared his shoulders. "You're a liar."

"You're the fucking liar."

"I don't care about the article. They don't need to correct it. You can call me a liar, an asshole, whatever you want, but I know that four days meant something to you. I don't care about my reputation or the money. Nothing!"

"What do you care about, Jamie? Making wine, singing karaoke, lying about who you are?" I continued walking quickly ahead of him.

"I care about you." His tone wasn't soft; it was matter-of-fact, the way a person sounds when they're telling an absolute truth.

I turned on my heel and grabbed the lapels of his jacket. "Listen to me, Jamie. Do nothing. We are not meant to be. I live here and you live there. You are some insanely rich genius, and I don't even own a car. I probably don't have a job, either." It was the first time I had seen him clean-shaven. I leaned up on my toes and kissed him softly then whispered, "You fucked with me. You fucked with us. And now we can never be."

He stared down at me, looking somber. "Just tell me one thing."

"What?" I seethed.

"Am I the only one you think about?" Tears filled my eyes again. I put my head down quickly and turned to walk toward the L station. He didn't move but instead shouted, "I won't give up. The poets are right!"

I got on the wrong train, so it took me an extra half hour to get home. When I entered my building, Jamie was sitting at the base of the stairs. He had ditched his suit jacket and rolled up his shirtsleeves. He looked the part of the CEO millionaire for once, except for maybe the tattoos and his tanned skin.

"Go home, Jamie."

He got up and followed me toward the elevator. "Kate, please. Let's go get a coffee and talk about this."

"No." I continued walking past him.

"I thought I scared you off with the note. I thought maybe it was too soon for you, and then when I read the article I realized how upset you were."

"I told you, it doesn't matter now. All of it is too fucked up. I thought you were someone else. I don't even know you."

"You do know me. I'm the same person. I'm Jamie. Nobody cares who R. J. Lawson is. It's just a name. You know the real me."

"I thought I knew you." I stopped at the elevator.

"I am so sorry. I know I should have told you before we . . ."

I turned around, crossed my arms, and yelled, "What? Fucked?"

Staring into my eyes, he moved toward me and touched his fingertips to my cheek. "Calm down, please." He tilted his head and let his gaze drop to my mouth. "You know that's not what we did."

"Yes it is. You said it yourself." I pulled his hand away. "Please go home. We had a fling. It's over now. *Go. Home.*" I stepped into the elevator and held strong until the doors closed and then I collapsed against the wall in sobs.

I hit the button for the top-floor roof deck, but the elevator came to a stop on the fifth floor. Dylan and Ashley stepped in. I didn't make eye contact with them.

"You going to the roof, Kate?" He bent slightly to look at my face.

I sniffled. "Just goin' for a ride. The roof deck is all yours."

"You know Ashley, right?"

"It's nice to meet you," I said.

She seemed timid. "Same to you."

When the elevator doors opened, Ashley stepped out but Dylan remained inside. "I'll be right back, Ash. I'm gonna walk Kate to her apartment."

Shaking my head frantically, I pushed against his back. "No, you guys go, I'm fine."

I held the open-door button and urged him to exit the elevator. "Kate, you are not fine. I can see how upset you are. Was it Stephen? I'll kick his ass." He pushed my hand away from the button and then kissed the air in Ashley's direction. "I'll be back in two minutes, babe." She smiled longingly at him as the doors closed completely.

When we reached the door of my apartment, he wrapped his skinny arms around me and tucked me into his chest. "Whatever it is you're going through, I'm sorry." I cried quietly. He reached into his pocket and pulled out three pills: two yellow and one blue. "Here, you can have these."

"What is it?"

"They're benzos."

"What's that?"

"Those two are Ativan and that's Xanax." He pointed to the blue pill. "They'll relax you and help you sleep. Just take one at a time."

He dropped them into my hand. "Where do you get this stuff?"

"From my grandma's stash."

"That's terrible, you being so young and . . . all of the drugs."

"It's cute that you're worried about me. I actually haven't done any drugs in the last couple of days. Ashley makes me want to be sober." He smiled coyly. "*She's* like a drug to me."

"You're sweet." I pushed him toward the elevator. "Now go to the roof and make out with Ashley."

"Okay, see ya. Call me if you need anything, or if you just want to hang out," he said as he walked away.

I chased the blue pill with a large gulp of beer and the rest of the night was a blur.

Enterprise Copy

A month went by before I started feeling normal again. I easily fell into the same old routine, except I was condemned to the Arts and Leisure section of the paper. I didn't mind—at least Jerry hadn't fired me. He understood that I had been duped by everyone at the winery. I got to see Will Ryan and his wife play in Chicago, and Jerry printed (without question) my very gleaming review of the concert. Beth ended up writing the rowback for the R.J. article. That's when a newspaper tries to correct a story without indicating an error to begin with. She managed to imply that we were deceived, even though she didn't say it outright. To our complete amazement, there was little response to my article or the rowback, so that was a relief. We realized that the whole thing was very dramatically blown out of proportion, thanks to my personal involvement with the subject. Still, Jerry and I agreed that it would be best for me to lay low until it all was completely forgotten. R. J. Lawson, whoever he was, fell easily off the radar once again, but the wine and winery didn't stop getting praise. After my article ran, several Napa magazines featured full spreads of the Lawson winery and the gorgeous vineyard surrounding it. It continued to be recognized like it had been before, but R.J. the man was never mentioned in those articles. Jamie maintained his privacy after the rowback. I looked at each picture of the winery with a strange feeling, like I had never been there. My memories of that beautiful place had been tarnished.

I never went to another gay bar with Beth, but we made a pact to have dinner once a week. True to her words at the Dogfather, she finally started dating someone seriously, and for the first time I was actually producing more words than her on the weekends. I'd march into work every Monday and lean over her cubicle and say, "I busted out eight thousand words."

She would always chuckle. "Yeah, but I got laid."

"That's overrated," I would say. Lying, of course.

It was hard not to be happy for Beth and Jerry and Dylan, who had all managed to find their people, so I devoted myself to positively supporting all of their relationships. I added another houseplant to my apartment, along with a betta fish that I named Anchovy. Just getting a fish equaled more commitment than Rose had made in her whole life. I figured I was easily on my way to twenty cats. I wondered about Rose's dream all the time. I still had it, but it would always end before she'd open her eyes. The terrifying and touching moments in the dream were gone, but the sadness remained.

Stephen stopped screwing women in the basement after Dylan and I sent around a petition requesting that the door to the basement laundry room be removed. The super, who was not a fan of Stephen, gladly took the door off. Jamie continued leaving me messages, begging me to call him. That lasted two weeks, and then he resigned himself to simply calling and saying, "Good night" or "Good morning" or "I'm thinking about you," on my voice mail. The messages made my heart ache, but it was a good ache. Somehow it felt like a healing ache. It's like the pain you feel when the skin around a wound tightens up. I got to work on time every day because I stopped searching for Just Bob. I didn't stop searching for the holiday train, though. My pathetic goal in life became sitting next to Santa on the god-damned L, and I wouldn't stop until it happened. I made myself believe that searching for a fake Santa on a train was enough to live for.

Time sidled by like I was watching my life as a rerun in slightly slower motion—until the morning when I saw a familiar face on the L. It was December and freezing in Chicago, but I was sweating. There's a constant adjustment of your body temperature when you live in a cold place. I like to pile on layers of clothes because I hate stepping out into the cold, but then I always end up half walking, half jogging to the train. By the time I board I'm usually sweating profusely. On top of it, the transit system pumps heat into the subway portals so there's no ice buildup on the tracks. There's sometimes a stuffiness in the stations, and then if a train is crowded and you've been running for four blocks and you're wearing a parka, there's a good chance you will either pass out or puke, and that's what almost happened the morning I met Christina.

I recognized her right away but couldn't place her. She looked to be in her thirties, with strawberry blond hair and a perfect complexion. She recognized me instantly but continued to scrutinize me. My heart was beating out of my chest from running. I wiped a bead of sweat from my brow and began frantically removing my coat. She was still watching me, and then she tilted her head to the side. I felt like she was studying me.

"Are you Kate?"

"Yes," I said through heavy breaths. She grinned knowingly, so I moved across the aisle to sit next to her. I turned and stuck my sweaty hand out. "I'm sorry, I recognize you but I can't figure out where I know you from."

"Does Robert Connor ring a bell?"

After removing my giant coat and catching my breath, I looked down at my hands while I searched my mind. "Uh no, sorry."

"Bob, from the train."

"Oh, Just Bob. Yes! Yes, I know him. I remember you now. You used to sit with us. I haven't seen Bob. I couldn't find him. I just figured he had started taking a different line."

Her face changed and her lips turned down. "I'm glad I found you, even though I'm so sorry to have to tell you this. Bob passed away a month and a half ago."

Fuck. I knew something had happened.

"Oh no." My eyes started watering. "What happened?"

"We think he died a peaceful death from natural causes. He was older than he looked. He was ninety-five but sharp as a tack."

"Yes, he was."

"Well, he didn't have any close friends or family so his body wasn't found for quite some time." She furrowed her eyebrows and puckered her lips, clearly still emotional at the idea.

"That's terrible."

"Yes, Bob lived a very solitary life. I only found out after they were clearing his apartment. At some point I had given him my business card. You see, I'm a lawyer, and Bob wanted me to write his will. We never got around to a meeting, but he must have known his days were numbered because he wrote his own will right on the back of a paper plate." She laughed and looked up to the ceiling of the train. "Bob didn't have much, but he sure wanted you to have a few of his things. His apartment was full of books." My eyes widened. She reached out and grasped my hand. "Most of the books were donated to schools and libraries, but Bob had set a few aside in a little shoebox with a note. On the plate he wrote 'Please make sure Kate from the train, the young girl with big eyes and dark hair gets the shoebox.' It was luck that they contacted me after finding my card and that I remembered you, but I didn't know if I would ever find you. I just made a silent promise that I would watch every person that got on and off the train."

"So what does the note say?"

"I haven't read it." She stood up. "This is my stop. Can we meet tomorrow?"

"Sure."

"Okay, meet me at the Rosehill Cemetery mausoleum at ten a.m. You know where that is?"

"Yes." I knew it well. "Thank you," I said as I took the card. I stared at it for several minutes before putting it in my pocket. I wondered why Bob had singled me out of the group of followers.

After work, I went home and slid into bed. I opened my phone to three new voice mails. One was Dylan. *Hey, chica. Ashley turns eighteen tomorrow, holy shit!*

His voice got super high. *I wanted to know if I could borrow your apartment. I'll pay for you to go to a movie or something.*

I texted him back:

> *Me:* So you want to use my apartment to have sex with your girlfriend?

He responded almost immediately.

Dylan: Um yeah. Is that bad?

I laughed to myself. Dylan was always so innocently honest. It was kind of charming. I think if I had met Jamie in the right circumstances, I would have felt the same way about him.

> *Me:* Fine. You better wash the sheets and you better be safe with her.

> *Dylan:* I'm no dummy.

> *Me:* You should make her dinner. My kitchen is stocked. Be a gentleman.

> *Dylan:* You read my mind.

> *Me:* I'll leave around six. You have a key, right?

> *Dylan:* Yeah, from that time I had to feed Anchovy

> *Me:* K. Have fun.

I listened to the second voice mail from Jerry. *We're cleaning out the stockroom. Your suitcase is still in here. Seriously, Kate, I'm trashing it if you don't come and get it. I'm working tomorrow for a couple of hours. Maybe you can pick it up and we can grab lunch?* The suitcase was packed with everything from my time in Napa and all of the R.J. research. The dress I'd worn on our date was in there, as well as the necklace and note from Jamie. A lump began to form in my throat. *Why am I not over this yet?*

As expected, the third voice mail was from Jamie. *Hi,* —He paused and took a deep breath.—*I went to GLIDE today. A few people asked me about you. I had to tell them that I was a fool . . . and that I let you slip away.* I heard a subtle change in his voice, like he was choked up. *Night, angel.*

That's why I wasn't over it yet. But I didn't cry that night. There were no tears left.

I met Christina in the entry of the mausoleum at Rosehill the next morning. She held the box out to me as I approached. There was a folded note taped to the top. "Good morning," I said to her as I took the box and peeled the note off. I unfolded it immediately and read:

Kate from the L,

I remember when I first met you months ago. You seemed so disconsolate and distant. I know we didn't know each other well, but I felt a desire to help. Now I fear I may have failed you. You see, you reminded me of someone I used to know. Her name was Lily and she was beautiful, young, and vibrant, and she was the love of my life. You look like her—same warm eyes and dark hair. I used to get lost in her eyes. I wasn't always such a lonely ogre. I was full of life once, but I lost my Lily too soon when she passed away just after our wedding. I saw you in the same kind of pain that I'd felt. I didn't want to see my Lily in pain. I thought if I made you believe that there was happiness in solitude, that you couldn't and shouldn't rely on another human being, maybe you would stop feeling that pain. I was wrong. What I really want you to know is that I would have traded a lifetime with my books, alone in my apartment, for one more minute with

Lily, even if it meant I had to feel that pain over and over again. Don't give up, Kate. Don't stop searching. Find him, take care of each other, hold on to each other, and never let go.

I hope this finds you well and still hopeful.

Your friend,
Bob

To say I was a blubbering mess would be putting it lightly. Even Christina was crying just from watching me read the note.

I looked up at her. "Wow, Bob was romantic."

"You're kidding?"

"No, read it for yourself." I handed her the note.

As she read, I opened the box and fumbled through the books Bob had left me. There were a few old paperbacks I didn't recognize and then I got to *Possession* and *The English Patient* and *A Room with a View*. Perhaps it was a whisper.

When Christina was through reading, she folded the paper and handed it back to me. "I didn't expect that."

"Right?"

She pulled me along into the building and said, "Come on, let's thank him and pay our respects."

We took a familiar path. "Where are we going?" I started to get a very strange feeling.

"It's just around this corner." Soon, we were facing the spot where Rose's placard finally had been placed.

I looked up to the wall. Gleaming two rows above was a placard with the name ROBERT CONNOR and the dates of his birth and recent death. Bob and Rose were on the same wall.

Another whisper. It was a coincidence, but it brought back so much emotion. The dream with Rose flashed through my mind, as well as Bob's words. Those two lonely souls were reaching out to me in death and urging me to open my heart. I put my hand over Rose's name and then reached up with my other arm and touched Bob's placard. "Take care of each other," I said very quietly.

"I've got to go, Kate." Christina had been silent while we stood there facing the wall.

I turned toward her. "Thank you so much for holding on to this. It means a lot that he wanted to share his feelings with me. I only wish I could show him my gratitude now."

"You can—by taking his advice." She pointed to the note.

"Yeah." I smiled sincerely, but taking his advice at this point would open up the wound all over again.

Walking to the L, I held my head up and let the cold wind chafe my face. I needed, more than anything, to make a concerted effort to put things behind me and look forward. If I let myself be open to another relationship, I had to get over Jamie completely. Step one in that process would be addressing the suitcase.

I entered the open door of Jerry's office at the *Chicago Crier*. "Hey, kid." He removed his bifocals and stood up from behind his desk. "What do you say we get sandwiches and hit up Millennium Park?"

"It's freezing out."

"All right. Shedd Aquarium, then?" Clearly, Jerry needed a distraction, which wasn't usually hard for him. Maybe he knew I needed one, too.

"That sounds good."

"Should we pick up sushi and freak out all the animals?"

"No, that's terrible." He was such a kid at heart, albeit a

weird one, but a kid through and through. "Let's get grilled cheese sandwiches and tomato soup from Ma's."

"Comfort food it is."

I slurped my soup from the bench facing the dolphin aquarium. "Did you know dolphins have sex for pleasure?" Jerry said through a mouth full of grilled cheese.

"Yeah, I've heard that."

"They're the only animals besides people that do it for pleasure. Do you think they're capable of love, too?"

I huffed. "Do we have to talk about this?"

"I was just wondering what you thought."

"Well, I guess you would have to define love for me to answer that question."

He popped the last of his sandwich into his mouth and looked around contemplatively while he chewed. "Love is a thing that you can't take out of you. Once it's there, it doesn't go away, no matter what. Love can morph into hate and resentment, but it will always be there, buried under the bad feelings."

"Hmm, very poetic, Jerry, but I think love is just a feeling."

"That's lust. That's why dolphins have sex."

I choked on my soup. "You're funny."

"I'm serious. Love isn't just a feeling, otherwise it would come and go much easier."

"I guess what I had with Jamie was lust."

"Maybe so." He continued looking forward but elbowed me in the arm. "I guess that's why it's been so easy for you both to let go, huh?"

I faced him with a scrutinizing look. "Do you think I'm being unreasonable?"

"Yeah, I do. Not just to Jamie, but to yourself, too."

"He lied to me."

"He tried to tell you."

"How do you know?"

"Well, he's called me about three hundred times since your little article faux pas."

"About what?"

"Lots of different things. He wanted me to know that he was sorry for hurting you. He also wanted to make sure that you were okay, since you haven't returned any of his calls." I shrugged. "You know, Kate, I find him fascinating. Who would have thought young Ryan Lawson would grow up to be this kind of person? He was such a geeky kid. He's still brilliant, don't get me wrong, but he's really a guy's guy, you know?"

"Maybe *you* should date him, Jerry."

"I'm surprised, that's all. I don't think any of us would have suspected Jamie. I should have given you more time to research before I sent you out there."

"Maybe. Probably. They definitely didn't expect that Jamie and I would . . ."

"Fall in love?"

I face-planted into both of my hands and leaned over my knees. "I was going to say hook up. Enough with the love stuff."

He stood and brushed the crumbs from his clothes, seemingly unaffected by my dramatics. "You'll figure it out, kid."

Jerry drove me back to the office, where I collected my suitcase. I wheeled it past the closest L station, which was closed due to construction. I let myself absorb the cold again. I glanced at my watch. It was four thirty. I had a little time to get back to my apartment before I would have to disappear again so Dylan and Ashley could have their date. I was thoroughly freezing when I reached the second closest L station. I waited at the platform with the toes of my shoes peeking over the yellow line. It was starting to get dark out. I heard the train coming, so I leaned out to look down the track. To my absolute joy and wonder, pink lights were reflecting onto the shiny tracks just before the train came into view. Even though I had never seen it before, I knew, as if it were the absolute truth of the world, that the holiday train was coming my way.

I started giggling uncontrollably. Some schmuck next to me in a beige trench coat said, "Dammit, the holiday train again. This is the second time this week for me. The damn thing is slower than molasses."

"Oh, bah humbug, you asshole!" I wheeled my suitcase over his polished dress shoes and began running down the length of the train to where I could see an open train car. On the outside of each car were painted twinkle lights and holiday scenes. The sounds of "(It Must've Been Ol') Santa Claus" by Harry Connick Jr. started pumping through the speakers. I was running past the lights, smiling exuberantly, like I was in a Hallmark Christmas movie, about to be reunited with my love. *Seasons Greetings* flashed in bright white lights on the last car before I reached Santa's sled.

Just as I got to the end, a transit worker jumped down from the train and the lights and music went off. "What's going on?"

"She's broken down. That's it for the holiday train tonight."

"What?" My voice was at its highest pitch, piercing the silence. The rest of the train riders were walking past me to the stairs to exit the platform.

"You have to be kidding me!" I shouted.

"I'm sorry, honey, we're having some trouble on the tracks. You'll have to catch her the next time around. Maybe tomorrow when she's up and running. We have engineers working on her right now, but we got to let Santa have a break."

I looked back at Santa's sled and he was already gone.

"I can't believe it," I kept saying. "I've waited years for this, years!" *Fucking bullshit.*

I walked all the way back to my apartment, cursing at the sky and rolling my suitcase behind me. I spotted a large Dumpster in a dark alley near my building. *To hell with it.* I took the box that Just Bob had given me out of my suitcase. I lifted my five-hundred-dollar luggage into the air and heaved it over the Dumpster wall with surprising ease and then headed toward my apartment without looking back. I freshened up and headed out with Just Bob's copy of *A Room with a View*.

There was an old café on the corner of my street called the Living Room. It was one of those coffee houses with big cozy armchairs and the smell of roasting beans wafting through the air. Before I reached the door, I could hear Miles Davis coming from the outdoor speaker. It was "Someday My Prince Will Come."

Ha! I laughed out loud as I entered the café. Several people looked up from their newspapers and laptops. Smiling really widely, I pointed up and shook my finger at the speaker. "Love this!" I saw a few smiles before everyone went back to their business. I plopped into a giant purple chair with an ottoman and kicked my feet up.

"Can I get you a coffee?" a waitress asked, hovering over me.

"A cappuccino, please."

"You got it."

Minutes later, she brought my coffee back. I wrapped my hands around the warm mug and took a sip. It was divine. Closing my eyes and inhaling, I took another sip and said, "Mmm," very quietly.

"You enjoying that?" A man's voice. I opened my eyes to see a young guy in an identical armchair across the table.

I coughed, clearing my throat. "Yes." He was good-looking in a preppy way. He reminded me of Kevin McDonald, my first boyfriend in high school who taught me how to drive. I smiled.

"Whatcha reading?" he asked, nodding toward the book on my lap.

"*A Room with a View.*"

"What type of book is that? I'm not familiar."

"Well, I guess it depends on your belief system. It's a love story, so one might consider it science fiction."

"So skeptical," he said, shaking his head in mock disappointment.

"For example." I flipped the book open and noticed Bob had highlighted quotes from it. "Let me read you a bit." My eyes fell on the words:

Mistrust all enterprises that require new clothes.

I laughed to myself. Bob was right on highlighting that quote. I flipped through the book some more to find a bigger section to share.

"Okay, here," I said. "'It isn't possible to love and part.'" I paused when I felt my heart start racing.

"Please continue," he said.

"'It isn't possible to love and part. You will wish that it was. You can transmute love, ignore it, muddle it, but you can never pull it out of you. I know by experience that the poets are right: love is eternal.'" A huge lump began forming in my throat. It was actually painful.

It was the answer to Jamie's riddle. Had I known at the time what the poets said, I might have agreed that they were right, but did I believe it as I sat there in that coffee shop? Is that why

I couldn't let the memory of a few short days with Jamie escape my heart? Because it was impossible to push real love away?

"Gotta go." I jumped up and headed for the door.

"Wait a minute. Can I get your number?"

"Sorry!" I said as I rushed out onto the street. I ran back to the alley. It was completely dark at that point, and I had to step over a couple of homeless men. "Excuse me, I'm sorry." One of them grumbled something before I strapped my purse across my body, placed my hands on the disgusting edge of the Dumpster, and jumped up and over, landing dramatically in the knee-high trash.

Quickly realizing my suitcase was gone, I hopped back out and wiped my hands down my jeans.

"Excuse me, guys? Did you happen to see someone take my suitcase from the Dumpster?"

"Nah, we didn't see nothin'," said a toothless man. His beard moved up and down when he talked, like he was a puppet. It was frightening in the dark, but I swallowed back my fear and pulled out ten dollars. They both immediately threw their arms in the air, pointing behind me, and said, "She went that way!"

"Yeah, it's Darlene. She's got it," said toothless man number two.

I dropped the ten dollars and turned in the direction they pointed. I didn't see anyone but continued toward the light of a record store farther down the block. About halfway, a woman darted out of another alley. She was wheeling my suitcase, and from where I stood I could tell that she had on my jacket. As I got closer, I could see that she was also wearing my black dress over a grungy pair of sweats.

"Darlene!" I shouted.

She turned quickly, walked right up to me, and cocked her head to the side. "How do you know my name?" she barked out. Her voice was deep and rough.

"That's my stuff." She had on the necklace Jamie had given me. She was obviously homeless. Her skin had that dark, weathered, dirty look to it, and her hair was stringy, greasy, and gray, hanging down past her shoulders. My necklace glimmered against her neck.

"No, this is *my* stuff!" she screeched out.

"Look, there is stuff in there with my name on it. I can prove it to you."

"I don't care if you're Barack Obama. I got this from the Dumpster. One man's trash is another man's treasure. People don't throw away things they want."

"Listen. You can have it all. I just need the paperwork and that necklace. Please, it's sentimental."

I pulled out my wallet and handed her three twenties. She took off the necklace, handed it back to me, and set the suitcase flat and unzipped it. I grabbed the papers and realized that one of Jamie's white T-shirts had made it into my suitcase. I reached for it.

"Uh-uh, I don't think so, little girl."

My eyes welled up. I let go of the shirt and took a step back. Tears dropped from my cheeks onto the woman's back as she started to zip the suitcase up. She turned and looked up at me. I was standing in the light of a streetlamp but my face must have been shadowed from her view.

"Are you cryin'?" she snapped.

I shook my head. She yanked the shirt out and handed it back to me without turning around.

"Thank you," I managed to say.

When she stood up, she huffed, "Cryin' over a goddamned T-shirt. Imagine that."

I held it to my face and inhaled. It still smelled like Jamie— like the earth, but warm and spicy, too.

I walked three blocks out of the way before heading back to my apartment building. Not wanting to surprise Dylan and Ashley, I took my book, T-shirt, necklace, and all of the papers up to the roof and waited for him to text me. I was freezing my ass off for the sake of teen love and premarital sex. I started feeling a little shame about that, so I was relieved to get a text from Dylan.

> *Dylan:* It's all clear. We didn't do it. We had a nice dinner and watched TV. She's not ready so we're gonna wait. I have a major case of blue balls.

I chuckled.

> *Me:* Don't tell her that.

> *Dylan:* I'm not an asshole.

> *Me:* I know. TTYL

> *Dylan:* Later, chica. Thanks again.

It's Fiction

Dylan left my apartment exactly how he found it. I took a shower, threw my covers back, and slipped into bed wearing nothing but Jamie's T-shirt. I clutched the note to my chest as I pressed the button to listen to my nightly message. *I went sailing today with Chelsea,* he said. *I thought about your hair whipping across your face, your pink cheeks, and the huge smile you had on your face as we sailed across the bay. I just wanted you to know that I was thinking about you. I can't get you out of my mind. I'm always thinking about you.*

Me too.

I pressed END and reached down beside the bed to where I had set the note. When I read it again, this time I cried.

> Katy, my angel,
> I had to go to Portland. My father had
> a heart attack and they don't know if he's
> going to make it through the night. Please
> don't leave. If I can't get back by tomorrow,
> I'll send a car and get you a flight up here.

Please, please don't leave. I have something really important to tell you besides the fact that I am completely in love with you.

—J

In the morning, the note was crumpled up on my chest. I got up and spread it out on the counter. I underlined the last line and then wrote *WHY?* underneath it. I stuffed it into an envelope and mailed to it the R. J. Lawson Winery. I laughed to myself as I wrote *Attn: The Owner.* I spent Sunday in my apartment, not moping. I did a yoga video, edited some of Beth's latest article, and then devoted the afternoon and evening to a marathon of *MythBusters*, during which I learned that Jack's death in *Titanic* was totally unnecessary. Had that selfish bitch, Rose, given up her life jacket to tie under that wooden door, it would have been buoyant enough to hold them both. Damn her. I slid into bed at seven and listened to Jamie's latest voice mail over and over.

I can still smell you on my pillow. I can still see you standing in my room, the light caressing your smooth legs, your dark hair cascading over your shoulders, and your gorgeous mouth smiling so effortlessly. I miss you. I ache for you, and I'm bordering on crazy without you. Come back to me.

I had to clear my mind, so I called Dylan. "Hello."

"Did you know Jack's death in *Titanic* could have been prevented?"

"That might have been true if Jack were a real person. Are you drunk?"

"No, just bored."

"Oh."

"Hey, you want to go up to the roof?"

"I'm about to walk into a movie with Ash."

"All right," I said, sullenly.

"Everything okay?"

"Yeah."

"You want to meet us?"

"Nah, I'll see you later, buddy."

Two nights later I found myself in the same position, bored and lonely and watching too much television. After a *Law & Order* marathon, I found *Titanic* playing on cable.

"Just put the life jacket under the door. Dammit, Rose, he's freezing!" I yelled at the TV before bursting into tears. I cried through the last twenty minutes of the movie. I even cried when old Rose tossed the Heart of the Ocean overboard. I called Beth but her phone went straight to voice mail. "Beth, it's me. You don't need to call me back." I sniffled. "I just don't understand why Rose threw the necklace overboard. I've never understood that." I hiccupped and then my phone beeped. Without looking at the caller ID, I immediately clicked over.

"Hello," I said, my voice shaky.

"Baby?" His smooth, rich tone floated through the receiver and sent a blast of warmth all the way down my spine to my toes.

"Jamie?"

"Hi, Katy." His voice sounded different. I could hear hope in it. He must have gotten my note. "I just called to say good night."

"Oh."

"What's wrong? You sound sad."

I started laughing through my tears. "I was watching *Titanic*."

He chuckled. There was an awkwardness to our conversation. "I think they could have made the piece of wood fit for two, don't you?"

"Absolutely."

I laughed some more. "Had Jack been a computer engineering prodigy, maybe they could have figured out a solution."

"Maybe," he said unenthusiastically, and then changed the subject. "'Why' is an easy question to answer. I could have written a thousand pages on my feelings, but I didn't. I hope it will be enough to convince you when you get it. I'm sorry again for everything I put you through."

"I'm sorry, too," I said quietly. "Jamie, why are you so desperate to run from your past?"

"I'm not. I've just changed a lot from the time I was sixteen. I'm not that kid anymore. I don't want to sit around and play video games. That's what it was to me, a game."

"I don't know how we could make it work. We barely spent four days together, and every minute of it was under false pretenses. I'm not even sure I want a relationship."

"What we had wasn't false. That was me. That was the most real version of me. I felt more like myself, more content, confident, and happy when I was with you than any other time in my life. I just wish I could have been up front."

"Why weren't you?"

"I was scared. I didn't expect to fall so hard for you. From the moment I met you, I couldn't stay away. You were the one person I tried to avoid, but once I saw you, you were all I could think about, and everything else just got mixed up in it. I always planned to tell you the truth but I wanted you to know the real me first. I didn't want you thinking about the article and my past while we were getting to know each other. Almost everything I told you was true."

"Except for who you really are. That's a big one."

"You know the real me. We'll get through this, and you'll learn to trust me. I know you feel the way I do or you wouldn't be sitting on the phone with me now."

"You're pretty confident about that, aren't you? Is that why you keep calling?"

"No, I just can't get rid of my thoughts of you. I don't fucking want to. I used to think people shouldn't need each other, but I need you, Kate. So we only spent four days together. What does that even mean?" He started to raise his voice. "I knew in five fucking minutes that I had to know you, that I needed you in my life. I've never felt that way about anyone, ever. Whatever happens will be up to you, but I'll be a different man if I can't have you. I will never breathe as deeply as I did when I was with you. I'll never see the range of color on a perfectly cloudless sky. I will never smell anything as sweet as you or hear a voice that fills my heart up as much as yours does. That night in my truck, when I had the low, I knew without a doubt, even though I had never been in love before . . . I knew that I was in love with you."

"Jamie, please." I could barely speak.

"I'll do anything."

"I have a life in Chicago."

"I'll move there," he said instantly.

"You can't."

"Yes, I can."

"I don't know what I want."

"You will, I promise." We both went silent for several seconds, and then he said, "Night, angel."

"Good night."

At two o'clock in the morning, I woke up sweating. I'd had the dream again. This time Rose didn't struggle to speak. Her voice was musical. *Take care of each other.* She said it the same way she had before. In this version of the dream, I looked down at my neck and could see the necklace Jamie had given me shining brightly. So bright that it looked like the light was coming from the necklace itself. I could hear two sets of heartbeats. When I put my hand over my heart, I felt arms wrapping around me from behind. I looked back and up to Jamie's face. He held me passionately, but his attention was on Rose. I focused on his lips as he mouthed the words *Forever, I promise.*

My first instinct after I woke from the dream was to make sure my necklace was still on. It was there, and it felt like a little piece of Jamie was with me. I got out of bed and went into the bathroom for a drink of water. I stood in front of the mirror for exactly two seconds before abruptly turning and stalking back into my bedroom for my phone. I dialed his number.

"Hi," he said groggily.

I took a long, cleansing breath. "You didn't name one specific thing you liked about me."

"I did. You just don't remember."

"Well?"

"I like your spontaneity and feistiness." He sounded half asleep, but sincere. "I like the fact that you called me in the middle of the night because you had to know the answer to this right now."

"So."

"Remember that list I started making when you were out here?"

"I guess I do remember that." I had tried so hard to push the good memories of the time we had together out of my mind, but clearly it hadn't worked.

"The list is long, but I'll give you a preview. I like that you're confident with your body. Jesus, I can't stop thinking about your body. Do you know what it's like to walk around here with images of your naked body floating around my head?"

I'd had the same thoughts. Jamie stood so tall and lean and muscular that his body left a visual imprint in my mind. I yearned to feel the strength of his rough hands around my arms. I sometimes closed my eyes and my mind would go directly to images of his cut stomach and the aptly named trail that ran downward. "Uh-huh," I said, urging him on.

"I love that you have a big heart and that you try to be tough. I love that you cry when you're touched or moved or saddened or thrilled. I love that you're so high-spirited that you almost bounce when you walk. I love how strong you were when I had the low."

"Jamie?" I interrupted him.

"Yes, angel?"

"Do you believe people are made for each other, like there's a force we can't see that brings us to the person we're meant for?"

"Is that what you believe?"

"That's what I want to believe," I whispered.

There was a long pause. "My parents were so happy and in love, it's hard for me to believe that they weren't made for each other. When my mother was killed, my father began to die, too. He couldn't live without her."

"That must have been hard for you."

"Yes, but in a weird way it gave me hope that there's a bigger plan for us. I think it gave me faith in love. I can't imagine that what I'm feeling for you isn't because of some kind of infinite power over our souls. You were the light coming toward me as I stood in the darkness. I only got through losing my father because I thought I was coming home to you. When I found out you were gone, I was crushed. I was fucking crushed, but not ruined, because I still had hope. Just the thought of you gave me enough light to see things clearly."

"What was the hope?"

"That you were feeling the same thing I was, and that the love couldn't be torn out of you the same way it couldn't be torn out of me."

"I'm overwhelmed."

"Please don't overanalyze this. Take your time. Call me when you're ready."

After a few moments, I finally resigned myself to Jamie's suggestion. This wasn't going to be fixed in a day. "Okay. Sweet dreams," I said.

"Only about you."

We hung up. Jamie was truly a conundrum. What a life he had already lived, and now he was this old soul who believed, from the depths of his heart, that I was the one for him.

Coming out of my apartment the next day, I spotted Darlene, the homeless woman, selling a random selection of items on the street corner. She had several articles of clothing, two pairs of shoes, and a few pieces of jewelry spread out on a thick wool blanket. I spotted my black camisole and black T-shirt right away. I also noticed that she was still using my suitcase to cart things around in.

"Hey! Girl!" she shouted at me. "Come over here. I have something you'd like." I was wearing Mary Jane heels and a black leather jacket over a black-and-white polka-dotted wrap dress.

As I approached her, she held up a pair of bright red cowboy boots. "You're a seven, right?" She knew that because she was in possession of at least three pairs of my shoes.

"Yes."

"These would be adorable on you."

"I don't know, Darlene. Cowboy boots aren't really my thing."

"They'll keep your legs warmer."

I laughed and thought, *Why not?* I was feeling bold. "How much do you want for 'em?"

"A hundred bucks."

"Ha. You're insane."

"Maybe so. Whaddaya got?"

"Five bucks, and I'll give you these Mary Janes."

"Deal."

I looked at the bottom of the boots; they were brand new. After I handed over my shoes and money, I slipped the boots on and clunked my way toward the L.

When I got to the *Crier*, Beth said, "What's with the shoes?"

"I'm a little bit country, I'm a little rock and roll? Lay off." I turned to find Jerry leaning against my partition, smiling.

"Aww, Kate. Remember when you first started working here and you tried to get everyone to wear certain colors on certain days of the week?"

"Yes, I do remember that. What's wrong with a little team spirit? The assholes in the design department said it would hinder their creativity. Come on."

"And remember when you petitioned the coffee cart girl to sell gluten-free pastries?" He smirked.

"Those scones were hard as rocks," Beth said.

"Yes, but the chocolate croissants were to die for."

"What about when you asked if we could have a mascot and then dressed in that stupid outfit all week?"

"What stupid outfit?" I squinted my eyes.

"It was a pink rabbit, right?" Beth asked.

"No, that was Easter." Jerry held his stomach and started laughing.

"That was fun, guys," I fake-whined. "Tell me your kids didn't love that, Jer."

"My kids didn't love that," he said seriously. "My son Davey was traumatized. He kept saying, 'Dad, why does the Easter Bunny have boobs?'"

"You should have told him the truth, that the Easter Bunny is a girl. It would have been the perfect opportunity to discuss the birds and bees."

"He was four years old, Kate."

"What's this all about, Jer?"

Beth winked at me while I waited for Jerry's response.

"I just saw you in those red cowboy boots and thought maybe you were gettin' your spark back, that's all. Have a good day, ladies."

"You, too," I said as he walked away.

"You want to get a hot dog at lunch?"

"Beth, seriously?" I skipped back into my cubicle and opened a fresh Word document on my computer.

I titled it "Whispers in the Dark." I wrote two, then three, then six, then nine thousand words before shutting down and going home. The next day, I repeated the same thing. There was a story forming, purely fictional, but one that echoed so many themes in my life at that moment. I was getting work done at the paper, but between completing short tasks I would go back to the story, and the words would flow right out of me. On the third day, I had written roughly five chapters. I e-mailed them to Beth without telling her anything.

She came over to my desk, clutching the printed pages. "What is this?" she asked.

"I don't know."

"It's fucking awesome. It's fiction?" she asked.

"Yeah, I guess."

"You have to keep going."

"I don't know what I'll do with it."

Beth crossed her arms over her chest. "You're writing a god-damned book, Kate. Keep going and figure that out later."

What I wrote was dark and unsettling at times, but that's how my life had been. The only brightness and warmth I could remember was being in Napa. My memories of the beautiful connection Jamie and I had shared started coming back to me, coursing through my veins like a rushing river. I would day-dream about his lips on my neck, so tender and warm, and his strong hands on my waist, making me feel safe. The story was about the pain we sometimes have to endure before the universe rewards us with real love. Through the writing, I was able to let go of the idea that I should be alone. I purged all of the feelings and preconceived notions I'd had going into my adulthood. The characters from the story and the memories of my time with Jamie brought me back into the light. They showed me that love was real and burning inside of me, and that no matter how hard I tried, I wouldn't be able to stifle it.

I avoided Jerry, but I had a feeling he knew what was going on, and I knew that I would be faced with some serious deci-sions. The *Crier* wasn't going to pay me to write love stories, and the idea of writing one more article on the dangers of trans fats made me want to stick pencils in my eyes. On the fifth night,

I woke from the fog of writing and realized Jamie hadn't left me a voice mail in two days. I scurried from my apartment and headed for the mail slots on the first floor.

When the elevator doors opened, Dylan and Ashley came into view. He was standing tall with a self-satisfied smirk on his face. Ashley was pink all the way from her cheeks to her neck and down toward the low cut of her shirt. Her long blond hair was pulled back into a messy ponytail. They had done it, was my guess—maybe on the roof, maybe in the doorless laundry room—but I was sure, with every ounce of my being, that they had done it.

"Hey, kids," I said with an ear-splitting grin.

"What's up, chica?"

"It's a beautiful night, isn't it?" I asked.

"Yes," Ashley said so softly I barely heard her.

Dylan gave an awkward, nasal laugh and then cleared his throat. "Where are you headed to?"

"Getting my mail."

When we reached Ashley's floor, Dylan turned toward me. "I'm gonna walk her to her door. Hold the elevator and I'll come with you."

I held the open-door button and watched as Dylan and Ashley walked hand in hand down the hall. He whispered something in her ear and she smiled with a peaceful and content look on her face. They kissed tenderly for just a few seconds and then he kissed her forehead before she turned and entered her apartment. *So sweet.*

He ran back toward the elevator, grinning the entire way.

"Well?" I said.

"I'm so fucking in love with her." He sighed.

"Do you really think it's love?"

He looked over at me pointedly. "Oh no, you're not gonna start your cynical shit with me now, are you?"

"No, Dylan, it's just that sometimes it can be hard to tell the difference between love and lust."

"I don't care what the difference is. All I know is that I can't stop thinking about her. I want to be with her every second of the day. Not just in that way, either. I want to talk to her and laugh with her and see the world with her. If that's not love, then I don't fucking know anything."

"Why are you so sure?"

"I have to be. I know she's amazing and she likes me. I don't think there's any room for fear or doubt when it comes to love. I'm willing to take my chances. You should be, too," he said just as we reached the mail slots.

When I stuck the key in and turned the little lock, the door practically jumped off the hinges. The slot was jammed full of mail. Most of it was junk mail that I managed to catch as it came spilling out. One envelope fell to the floor. Dylan and I looked down simultaneously. The return address was the R. J. Lawson Winery. It was Jamie's answer.

"Is that the guy?"

"Yes."

"Are you gonna open it?"

"I don't want to cry in front of you."

"You've cried in front of me about four hundred times since I've known you. You're the biggest crybaby I know."

"I'm tough," I declared.

"You wish. Just open the damn envelope."

I shoved my armful of mail into Dylan's hands and reached down for the letter. As I tore the flap from the back, I got a paper cut.

"Goddammit, it's a sign." I shoved my bleeding finger into my mouth and sucked. "Cay u beweve it?" I mumbled over my finger.

"For the love of God, Kate, open that letter right now."

I huffed and then finished opening the envelope. I took the familiar paper out and unfolded it. My eyes first went to where I had underlined Jamie's words, *I am completely in love with you*, and then in my big letters the word *WHY*? Underneath that was Jamie's response. It was two words. That's it. Two. Simple. Words. *MARRY ME.*

I'll admit, it wasn't exactly the proposal every girl fantasizes about, yet somehow it was better. It was totally unexpected but completely fitting for the way things had gone down. He knew I needed it all. I put my hand over my heart, took a step backward, and leaned against the mail slots.

"What? What does it say?" I turned the page toward Dylan and began crying. "Holy shit. I mean, wow!" He scanned my face and then one side of his mouth turned up into a lopsided grin. "You're crying. Are those happy tears?"

"Yes," I blubbered.

He pulled me into his chest with his free arm and held me tightly.

"What will you do?"

"I'm gonna go out there and . . ." I hiccupped and took a deep breath. Dylan rubbed my back, soothing me. "I'm going to quit the *Crier*, go to Napa, finish my book, and say absolutely, one hundred percent yes to Jamie."

"Attagirl."

I pulled back and wiped the tears away with the back of my sleeve. "Will you do something for me, Dylan?"

"Anything."

"Will you take care of Anchovy for me?" I asked, sniffling.

He laughed. "You're such a drama queen. Of course I'll take your fish."

"And will you promise me that you'll always stay this honest and sweet?"

"I'll do what I can."

He walked me to the door of my apartment and handed over the giant stack of mail before leaning down and kissing my cheek. "You deserve to be happy. Keep in touch, okay?"

"I will. No more drugs, right?"

"Nah, I'm done with that. I think I'm gonna go to college with Ashley next year and study music."

"Good boy," I said, breaking down into tears again. "These are happy tears."

He smiled. "I know."

I closed the door and immediately ran for the phone to call Jerry.

"Hello?" Jerry had six adorable kids, and they all happened to be talking at the same time when I called.

"Jerry!" I yelled over the noise.

"Hey, Kate. Let me go outside, hold on."

While I waited, I heard at least three different tiny voices yell, "Daddy!"

"What's up?" he asked.

"I don't want to bother you while you're with your kids, but I'm going to need to talk with you soon. I've made some decisions."

"Well, I'm going to put the kids down and then meet Beth at Harvey's to go over a breaking story. Do you want to meet us there at nine?"

"That would be perfect. I need to tell her as well."

"Okay, I'll see you there."

I hung up, threw on a pair of jeans, my red cowboy boots, and my winter coat, and headed out into the freezing Chicago air. I contemplated going back up to my apartment to grab a scarf, but I didn't have much time so I made my way toward the L. Walking into Harvey's, I instantly spotted Beth and Jerry seated at the long oak bar. When I approached Beth, she stood up and moved down one stool so I could sit in the middle.

"Well, what's this all about?" Jerry asked.

"I'm going to do it!" I said triumphantly. The bartender turned and looked in my direction. I waved him toward me. "I'll take the Lawson Pinot," I said, then faced Jerry and grinned. "It's a sexy wine." He nodded, looking somewhat bewildered.

"I have a feeling you're going to give us some bittersweet news," Beth said.

"I want to see about finishing my book."

"I knew it." Jerry smacked the bar top. "I knew you were up to something. I guess this means you're done with the *Crier*?"

"You both have given me so much support. You had faith in me when I was producing crap. When I could barely formulate a coherent sentence, you continued sending stories my way, Jerry. And Beth, you are an amazing writer and a serious inspiration to me. I *am* done with the *Crier*, but I'm not done with you guys."

"What about Jamie?" Beth asked.

"I'm gonna see about him, too." I looked down at my fidgeting hands. "He asked me to marry him." Beth almost spit her mouthful of beer out, but Jerry wore a knowing look.

"Well, kid, I couldn't be happier for you. Congratulations. We'll miss you at the paper, but I think you're doing the right thing."

"That's amazing, Kate," Beth said sincerely once she regained composure.

"I wanted to tell you both right away because I plan on flying out as soon as I can, possibly tomorrow. I want to say 'yes' to Jamie in person."

Jerry smiled. "My little Kate is going to marry R. J. Lawson . . . unbelievable."

"Yeah, you're going to be a bazillionaire." Beth snickered.

"I don't care about that. I love him." It was the first time I had said it out loud. "I love him and I can't wait to tell him."

We left each other with huge hugs in front of the bar and then went in three different directions. I headed toward the L feeling as light as air. I literally bounced up the stairs to the station. I felt myself smiling even though I wasn't trying to. It was quiet and empty on the train platform as I waited. I entered the third car, which I thought was empty, but realized very quickly that there was a man sitting in the very back. There was a brief rush of Chicago wind through the back of my hair just before the doors closed. The man's long black peacoat contrasted severely with his white, almost translucent skin and hair. Sitting all the way across the train car, I could see the ice-blue depths of his eyes. He looked haunted as he stared back at me. I broke the uncomfortable staring contest first by looking out the window. Buildings and tunnel walls zipped by like film in fast motion. I watched the lights string neon webs through the sky as the train picked up speed. I kept the man in my peripheral vision but tried to look fearless and confident.

Relief washed over me when a couple got on at Belmont. They stood near the door and kissed for about sixty seconds until they got off at Wellington, two stops before mine. The fear was back, and with good reason. I should have stepped off with them. Once the train was in motion again, the man stood up and stalked toward me. I backed up until I was almost against the door. *Hurry, open,* I kept chanting in my head, hoping the next stop would come soon. I stuck my hand into my coat pocket and pulled out the note from Jamie.

When the man was inches from me, he reached toward my neck. I took another step back. I clutched the note and covered my necklace with my right hand and held my purse out to him with my left.

"Here, take it," I squeaked.

"I want the necklace." His voice shot down my spine, raising warning alarms throughout my body.

"Please, I have money and credit cards in here. Please, take it."

"I said I want the necklace!"

I was shaking, and I couldn't move. In one fluid motion he reached into his pocket, pulled out a pistol, and held it up. I cowered and squeezed my eyes shut with all of my strength. I heard him shout, "Stupid bitch," and then I felt an overpowering force to my head, and that was the last thing I remember.

Irony

To what degree do we really shape our own destiny? Are the people who seem down on their luck unable to see the signs, unable to hear the whispers? Would I have been laying in a pool of blood on the Chicago subway in my red cowboy boots if I had listened more closely to my instincts?

I floated into the darkness, where I stayed for an immeasurable amount of time. Time didn't seem to matter and neither did my physical being. I was warm and in no pain, and although I was seemingly alone in that wormhole, I could sense that someone was with me. I wondered if it was my mother or Rose. There was no fear, just a sensation that I was loved. I felt I needed to wish, pray, want, and try hard to see a light in all of that darkness, but when I did, it came with the most excruciating pain. I recoiled again and again and went back into the blackness, where I spent what seemed like an eternity lost in my thoughts.

I wondered who would bury me. Who would make sure I got my placard? I wondered if Jamie would be at my funeral. Would he cry? Would he be able to go on with his life?

The thought of Jamie losing me was harder to accept than the thought of losing Jamie. Not because I didn't care for him, but because he would be in pain, and that gave me more strength to fight than anything else. I loved him and could not stand the thought of causing him pain.

There were two bright lights that came into my view first. Both were completely haloed and foggy. One was shining down on me from above what I quickly realized was a hospital bed, and the other was coming from the window to my left. My head was screaming with excruciating pain. I saw a figure sitting in a chair a few feet away. He was hunched over, resting his head on the foot of my bed. I thought it was Jamie. I sensed that it was him, but I didn't know for sure. I blinked several times, trying to refocus my eyes, but my vision was still so muddled, and the light was increasing the intense throbbing in my brain.

I closed my eyes and drifted off again. The next time I stirred, I kept my eyes closed but heard voices.

"She's my fiancée. Please, you have to tell me something."

"We cannot release information to anyone other than family."

"She doesn't have any family. I'm it. Please." The tone of his voice was so pleading that it made my heart ache.

"Okay," the woman answered. "I can get in a lot of trouble for this."

"I promise, I won't say a word. I just need to know. Is she gonna be okay?"

I tried to speak but couldn't form the words. I felt paralyzed by the pain.

"She was beaten severely with the base of a pistol. The trauma to her head has caused critical swelling and leaking of spinal fluid into her brain. She has what's called posttraumatic hydrocephalus." He gasped and made a guttural sound. I opened my eyes for just a second to see Jamie leaning against the wall across from me. His arms were crossed and his head was down. He looked broken. "Her prognosis depends completely on her own body. We'll be monitoring her very closely and doing scans every day. If the swelling doesn't start to go down with medication, then the doctors will have to perform brain surgery. They'll drill a hole and put shunts in to drain the fluid and alleviate the pressure." I couldn't tell for sure, but it sounded like he was crying very quietly. The tone in the nurse's voice changed. It became soothing. "Stay positive. Keep talking to her. The best-case scenario is that she could make a full recovery and be home in a week."

I made one heartbreaking attempt to open my eyes and speak, but I was crushed again. The pain was just too much. The pounding in my head became so loud it was deafening. I couldn't hear or feel anything else. Jamie's voice, the light and the feeling of the hospital sheets on my skin, were all gone. I went to the void, where everything was black and warm and painless.

I wasn't sure how many days, months, or years had gone by before I was able to sense my surroundings again, but when I did I could hear Dylan, Ashley, Jerry, and Beth talking to one another. They were talking about me as if I weren't there—nothing bad, just a general conversation about my apartment and things that needed to be taken care of. On my health insurance form I had named Jerry as my next of kin and said he was a relative.

"Did you see that? She moved her hand," Dylan said excitedly. "Kate, can you hear me?" I squeezed his hand and tried to open my eyes. The pain was searing. I blinked several times before finally focusing. Dylan was holding my hand in both of his, and Jerry was leaning over me with eyes as big as sand dollars. "Hey, kid."

I swallowed and tried to clear my throat. "Hurts," I said. My voice didn't sound like my own. It was raspy and strained.

"Get the nurse!" Beth shouted to Ashley, who turned immediately and went running out the door.

"Just close your eyes and rest and get better. Jamie will be back in a few minutes." Dylan smiled warmly at me. He looked relieved. And then I faded away again. I don't know for how long, but when I came to, Jamie was sitting in a chair on the other side of the room. Susan was also there, sitting in a chair opposite him. Everyone else was gone. He was leaning over and his elbows were propped on his knees. He was wearing a T-shirt and flannel shirt with dark jeans and tennis shoes, the way I had remembered him so well from the winery. It was just Jamie, not R.J.—just my sweet Jamie. The scruff on his face was at least five days old, and his hair was slicked back from his face. His head was down, braced by his two hands. He was looking at the floor but talking to Susan.

Two instant but conflicting feelings washed over me as I absorbed Jamie sitting in my hospital room. One was that our souls were connected so deeply that I could sense his presence before I knew for sure that he was there. Merely being in the same room with him made me feel more complete. One brief glimpse of him was enough to warm my blood and increase my heart rate. The other feeling was that we barely knew each other. The concept of "us" was so new. I still had that tingling feeling of excitement, like I hadn't yet explored all of him. My head throbbed with the beat of twenty thousand drums, but somehow Jamie's presence alone dulled the roar and made getting better my number one goal.

I watched for a few seconds in sympathy. He was shattered. It was hard to hear every word of their conversation, but I picked up enough.

"I'm cursed," he said softly. "And I've cursed everyone who loves me."

"That's not true," Susan said.

"I've done this to her." He looked up and ran his hand through his hair. "She wouldn't let go of the necklace I gave her. Did you know that? I'm telling you, it's because of me that she's lying there, broken."

"I'm not broken," I whispered. He stood instantly and was at my side in two strides.

"Baby, don't move. Don't strain yourself." He leaned over and kissed my forehead. "Get the nurse," he told Susan.

"I think I'm okay."

"God, I'm so relieved to see those brown eyes. You are so lucky to be alive."

"Come here." I opened my arms. He bent over and gently nuzzled his face in my neck. "How did I get here?"

His head jerked back. "You don't remember?"

"No."

The nurse walked in behind Susan. Both came over to the other side of my bed. "You okay, honey?" the nurse asked. She checked my vitals and then propped my bed up so I could sit.

"My head still hurts a bit."

"That's to be expected, but you're doing remarkably well. I'll let the doctor know you're up," she said and then walked out.

Susan smiled down at me. "I'm glad you're back with us, Kate. I wanted to say sorry about all the confusion at the winery. I wasn't completely informed and I didn't want to interfere."

"It was my fault, I didn't tell Susan what was going on," Jamie interrupted.

"Well, I didn't help matters. I knew something big was happening between you two, but I'm used to protecting Jamie's privacy."

"It's water under the bridge," I said sincerely.

"I hope so. I'll let you two have some alone time."

"Thank you." We squeezed each other's hands and then she left.

"Jamie, tell me what happened." He scooted a chair right next to my bed and sat down, holding my hand in his.

"You were attacked by a man on the subway. He hit you with his gun repeatedly, and the attack caused some swelling in your brain. But you're going to be okay, the swelling is going down on its own."

I remembered little bits and pieces about what happened, but it was hard to put it all together. "I must have a really hard head." I smiled.

One side of his mouth turned up. "Yes, I'm sure of it, and thank God for that hard head of yours. I think you're going to be fine."

"I should have worn a scarf that night." I reached up and ran my fingers down his rough jawline. He grinned into my hand.

"Why didn't you let him take the necklace?"

"I can't remember what I was thinking. But wait, how did you know it was over the necklace?"

"Because they found you clutching it, and the transit system has video footage of the assault." I felt my bare neck and started to panic. "They took it off when you came in. Beth has it, along with the rest of your stuff. It's safe, angel, but no material object is worth this. That necklace could have been replaced. You can't be."

I started getting choked up. "Jamie, I'm sorry." Tears began streaming from my eyes. My head was pounding again. I moved my hair away from my face and felt the bandage on the side of my head.

"Please don't cry. I wasn't mad, I was just scared. I thought I was gonna lose you."

"I know." I sniffled. He reached his hands down and wiped the tears away with the pads of his thumbs. I felt for the bandage at the back of my head.

"They had to shave a little of your hair to put the staples in."

"Staples? Oh my god, I must look like Frankenstein." I breathed into my hand. "Oh, and my breath is terrible. I feel like I have little sweaters on my teeth, they're so fuzzy. Can you get me some mouthwash?"

He laughed and went into the little bathroom and came back holding mouthwash and a cup out to me. "You can barely see the staples. Your hair covers that spot. And you don't look like Frankenstein at all. You're beautiful, and you will always be beautiful." I smiled with cheeks full of mouthwash. Are you feeling better?"

I spit the mouthwash into a little cup Jamie held out for me. "Yes. Where was I going on the L that night?"

"You were going home. You were only one stop away when it happened."

"Going home from where?"

"You'd met Jerry and Beth at a bar. They said you quit the *Crier* because of the note I sent you."

"Note?"

"I asked you to marry me. Do you remember that?" At that point he was sitting on the chair next to the bed, staring up at me. He looked boyish for once.

"I don't remember." I put my hand to my head, which had

begun to pound loudly in the front. I closed my eyes and winced. "I'm sorry, I can't remember much, just bits and pieces. My head hurts so bad." *Oh my god, he asked me to marry him.*

He stood up and lowered my bed. "Close your eyes, baby. You don't need to think about anything right now." I felt him gently climb up next to me and lay on his side. He draped his arm across my waist. I dozed off, feeling safe and protected.

There were a couple of days of tests and scans before I was scheduled to go home. I realized that I hadn't had a serious conversation with Jamie about the note or what our plan was. He had been at the hospital every day, only leaving briefly to shower at a nearby hotel. Beth, Jerry, and Dylan popped in and out a few times to check on me. Dylan was taking care of Anchovy and my apartment, and Beth had proudly proofread the first thirty thousand words of my novel. I was excited to get back to writing, but I knew there were things that needed to be decided first. I still didn't remember much from the night of the assault, but the police detective did show me the note I was clutching. The words *MARRY ME* were smeared in blood, which gave me a strong feeling of unease.

The day before I was scheduled to leave the hospital, they brought a plastic surgeon in to remove the staples from the back of my head and to add tiny sutures to the gash in my forehead. When the doctor left the room, I looked over at Jamie, who was flipping through *Techworld* magazine. "Hey, handsome. I thought you were done with all that?"

He jerked his head up, closed the magazine, and flung it onto a nearby table, then he looked down at his hands in mock horror, like he had been infected. We both laughed. I stood up next to my hospital bed on wobbly legs. I was still naked underneath the ridiculous hospital gown. Jamie came to my side instantly and held my arm as I walked toward the bathroom. "I just want to brush my hair out," I said.

"I can brush it for you."

"I have to do some things on my own, Jamie." I stopped halfway, feeling dizzy. Jamie had a scared look on his face as he braced my arm and shoulder. I tried to lighten the mood. Smiling up at him, I said, "It's kind of drafty in here," and then I reached behind me to feel my naked rear end. His adorable dimple that had been hiding for so many days behind a worried frown revealed itself.

He leaned back to catch a glimpse as I began to shuffle again toward the bathroom. "I've missed seeing that cute little ass." I giggled when he smoothed his hand over it.

"I hope you'll stay for a few days after I'm released?" I shot him a hopeful look. "You can get reacquainted with my ass."

"Katy, of course I'm staying. I'm not going anywhere. You're going to need help. I planned on staying with you at your apartment." He looked discouraged.

"I just didn't know if you'd want to." He was standing behind me as I looked in the mirror and brushed my hair.

"What are you talking about? I asked you to marry me. I was pretty sure you were gonna say yes."

"Everything seems so jumbled up now." I felt the familiar stinging of tears filling my eyes.

"You don't have to decide anything, but I told you, I'm not going anywhere."

"Don't you want to be in Napa?"

He stepped toward me confidently, turned me to face him, and reached for my hand. He placed it over his heart and then pressed his other hand to my heart. "There's nowhere but here. Nothing else matters, you have to see that. We'll figure everything out together. I want to get to know you all over again, but first let's focus on getting you home and well." He bent over to kiss me. When our lips touched, I immediately pressed my body to his. I took his hand and placed it on my bare butt. He smiled against my lips.

Dr. Coco, my regular trauma doctor, came whistling through the door. We both pulled apart quickly and Jamie folded the back flaps of my gown over each other so my backside wasn't exposed.

"He's my doctor, Jamie."

"This is my ass now." He smirked and then pinched my butt cheek.

"Ouch!" I yelped. "Excuse us. Hi, Dr. Coco."

When I first met my doctor, he had to tell me his name about ten times. I just kept laughing after he said it, and then I would say, "No. Tell me for real. I have a brain injury and I don't think I'm hearing you correctly."

He had a great sense of humor. Instead of being offended, he had mimicked a cuckoo clock and said, "My name is Dr. Cuckoo."

"Dr. Coco, I need to talk to you," Jamie said. "In private."

"You don't get to talk about me in private." They both stood there, staring at the ground. "I know what you want to ask him. Very sneaky of you," I said as he shoved his hands into his jean pockets and teetered back on his heels. I looked over at the interested doctor and blurted out, "He wants to know when we can have sex."

Dr. Coco chuckled. "Well, you, little missy, are free to do whatever you feel comfortable with, but you should probably take it easy for the first couple of days you're home."

"Oh, we'll go slow," Jamie chimed in. "I mean, we'll take it slow." He was beet red.

The doctor smiled and walked out, laughing to himself.

I clutched my stomach, laughing. "I don't think I've ever seen you this frazzled."

"Baby, you kill me. I wasn't going to ask him that. I didn't want to scare you, but I was going to ask him if we should be concerned about PTSD."

"Oh." My eyes widened as far as they could go.

"I don't want you to be fearful of riding the subway." As soon as he said it, I felt nauseous. I buckled over and held my stomach. He walked me back to the bed.

"I don't want to see anybody about that. I was in so much therapy after my mom died. I'll work it out in my head. I just don't want to think about it right now."

"Okay," he whispered and then kissed my forehead.

"Did they catch the guy?"

"They got him. He confessed. You don't have to worry about him."

"I thought he was gonna shoot me."

"You remember now?"

"A little bit." Bits and pieces had been coming back to me.

We slept the rest of the day away in my hospital bed. When I woke the next morning, Jamie was standing near the window, watching me. He was clean-shaven and wearing different clothes. He held a bag out as he walked toward me. "Beth brought some things for you to wear home."

"You guys left my fashion options up to Beth? She wears basketball shorts every day of her life."

His green eyes looked clearer and his dimple seemed deeper on his shaven face as he grinned at me. "I'm sure it will be fine."

Beth had packed exactly what I wore to the gay club that night she had said I looked hot.

Jamie closed the curtain and then took a seat near my bed. "Are you going to watch me change?" I asked. He wiggled his eyebrows at me. "Come on, let's leave something to be explored."

"I have seen, explored, and probably licked every inch of you."

"True, but seriously." I looked down at my unshaven legs. "How long have I even been in here?"

"One week exactly," he said. I was still staring, waiting for him to turn around.

"Okay, fine." He stood up and walked toward the window to look out. "What should we do today, Katy?"

I slipped my jeans on easily and noticed there were about three inches of space between my jeans and waist. "Beth didn't grab me a belt?"

He turned and walked toward me, studying my midsection. I was still wearing only my bra and jeans. He looked heartbroken. "You're so thin. Christ, you need to eat." He put his hands on my hips and ducked his head to kiss the swell of my breast. "Katy, please tell me you didn't lose this weight because of me."

Swallowing back the lump in my throat, I reached for my T-shirt and sweater. "I've had a rough year, Jamie. I only want to look forward to the future now. I don't want to dwell on the past."

"Well, the first thing we're going to do is get you something good to eat."

"Do you like grilled cheese and tomato soup?" I asked. He laughed and then kissed me deeply for the first time since I had been in the hospital. His arms tightened around my body, pulling me up off the ground. Our tongues twisted and slowed just before he pulled away.

"It's my favorite."

"Okay, I know this place, it's right on the lake. We can take the red . . . the Red Line." My heart started racing.

He tilted his head to the side and looked at me with pity. "We can take a cab. It's probably better anyway. I shouldn't have you out too long. We'll eat and then get you home and settled in."

"What about you? How is the diabetes?"

"Totally under control."

"The two of us are quite a pair. Tonight I'll give you an insulin shot while you dab Neosporin on my stitches."

He kissed my nose. "Sounds like a date. You ready?"

"Yes, let's do this." It was a declaration of more than just my readiness to leave the hospital. It was the beginning of our attempt at a committed relationship. I'm not sure either one of us knew how to do that properly.

When we left the hospital, there was a town car waiting. "What's that?" I asked.

"I thought a cab might be too bumpy."

"Oh no, Jamie. That's too much money."

He turned and braced my shoulders. "Kate, I probably will never have to worry about money, and I don't think you will, either. I don't spend it on frivolous things. You have a major head injury and I don't want you jolted around in a cab."

I crossed my eyes at him and laughed. "Do you think my brain is gonna be okay?"

He pulled me toward the car. "Come on, silly girl."

In the town car he ran his hand up and down my leg nervously. "I don't think this is such a good idea. I should just get you home."

"I'm not fragile."

"Yes, you are. Right now, you are. We can get takeout and go back to your apartment."

"Are you going to spoon-feed me, too?"

He turned abruptly. His eyes focused on my lips. Smiling he said, "Maybe," and then he leaned in and tugged on my bottom lip with his teeth. "I love your mouth, even when you're being a smart-mouth."

"Well, now that I think about it, your plan might not be so bad. After all, you can't very well lick food off my body in a public place."

"Good point, although I'd be willing to challenge that argument. Just not today."

I waited in the car while Jamie went into the restaurant and picked up our food. He practically ran back out to the car and slid in, scanning me up and down.

"Are you okay?"

"Yes, it's been five minutes."

He gave my address to the driver as if he had said it a million times.

"That was pretty good, Jamie."

"I have one of those memories."

"What do you mean?"

He glanced up to the ceiling of the car, looking almost self-conscious, and then shrugged. "Nothing."

"Oh, the genius thing? What, you have a photographic memory?"

"Something like that."

"Tell me. I want to know everything about you."

"Okay, well this sounds scary, but I'm what's called a mnemonist. I have a mnemonic memory."

"Sounds like demon possession."

"Yeah, it feels like it sometimes."

"What does it mean?"

"It means I can remember long lists of numbers or names. I also have an eidetic memory. That's kind of like a photographic memory."

"That must be amazing. No wonder you were able to breeze through school."

"It's a blessing and a curse. Imagine remembering every laugh line on your dead mother's face."

I sucked in a sharp breath. "I'm so sorry. I never would have thought about it that way." I paused, trying to read his expression. "It could be the other way around. I wish I could remember what my mother looked like. It seems like the only memory I have of her face is from a photograph."

"I think it would be easier that way."

"Is that what you think?" I snapped.

He didn't look over at me. He just reached for my hand, brought it to his mouth, and kissed it. Staring straight ahead, he said, "I'm sorry. That was insensitive."

We were in the lobby of my apartment building within an hour of leaving the hospital, but Jamie was freaking out still.

"Shall I carry you?"

"Are you kidding me? There's nothing wrong with my legs."

"I don't want you to overdo it." His arm was around my waist, practically lifting me off the ground. I wrapped my arm around his neck and held on.

"You said that already. I promise, I'm fine. I got bonked on the head a little. It's not a big deal."

"Katy, don't minimize it." He lowered his voice. "Do you know how many hours I sat in that hospital room not knowing if I'd have to watch my angel die?"

"Aww, please don't say that."

When we reached the elevator, I could feel another presence

behind me. We entered and Jamie hit the button for my floor. Then I heard Stephen's voice just as I turned to witness him entering the elevator after us.

"Katy?" He was testing the word. No one besides Jamie had ever called me Katy. He was wearing suit pants and a dress shirt, no tie. His messenger bag was slung over his shoulder. He must've been coming home from work. "Stephen?"

The expression in his eyes turned warm. I noticed that Jamie stood a little taller and angled his body in front of me.

"I heard what happened to you." I nodded. "I'm really sorry, I know how much you loved the subway." He looked toward Jamie apprehensively and said, "Can I hug her?"

Jamie arched his eyebrows. "That's up to her."

I reached my arms out and gave Stephen a hug. He held me with true sincerity and said, "I'm really sorry." It brought tears to my eyes. I knew he was sorry for more than just my injury.

When the elevator doors opened on his floor, I smiled and said, "Good-bye, Stephen."

"Bye," he said to the floor and walked out.

I leaned back against Jamie. He wrapped his arms around me from behind.

"That was my ex."

"I know."

"You remembered?"

"I remember everything."

"Except how much insulin you've given yourself."

"I'll admit, that was very unlike me. I was distracted that night by your transcendent beauty."

"Oh, stop," I said, and then sniffled. He turned me and bent down to look me in the face. "Are you all right? Was it hard to see Stephen?"

"No, that was good, actually. It's amazing how nice people can be when they hear you've been in a coma."

When we reached my floor, I stepped out and noticed Dylan and Ashley standing near my apartment door. He held his arms out. "Welcoming committee!"

"Thank you." I laughed.

"We don't want to bother you guys while you get settled in, we just wanted to give you a hug and say welcome home." They both hugged me at the same time.

"You two are sweet."

My apartment looked untouched. I scurried around, embarrassed, trying to clean up, open the blinds, and air the place out. Jamie set the food on the counter and watched me until I stopped. "What?"

"Your place is nice."

"I'm sure you don't think that. It's eight hundred square feet of uninspired space."

My apartment was a simple U-shape. The living room and kitchen were open to each other, and the windows faced the street. A short, skinny hallway led to my decent-size bedroom and bathroom, which had one window facing the courtyard at the back of my building. I joked that it had been finely decorated by the wonders of IKEA and Target, and Jamie laughed.

I watched him slowly take it in. He picked up a framed photo of my mother that was sitting on a small end table. "Beautiful," he murmured.

"She was."

Jamie was a presence in my small apartment. He stood near the counter, taking the food containers from the bags and opening them up. When I approached him, he removed his jacket to reveal a plain white T-shirt. I ran my hands up his forearms and studied his strange tattoos. They were interwoven in a pale reddish ink. "Did you get all of these in Africa?" He nodded. I brought his hands to my mouth and kissed them. He gently pulled me up to kiss his mouth. His hand went to the back of my neck, just below my injury. I winced. He quickly pulled away.

"See, we can't do that," he said.

"I'm fine."

"It was too much. I could hurt you."

"I'm okay." I grabbed the food and carried it to the small square table at the edge of my kitchen where it met the living room. "What would you like to drink?"

"I'll get it," he said. "You sit down and eat."

"I'll have a beer," I announced.

"I don't think so, lush. You're not allowed to drink on your medication." I was taking a few different medications for the swelling and pain. "In fact, I think it's time for one of your pills."

We ate practically in silence. I was starving and Jamie just sat there and watched me like a hawk, searching for any indication that I wasn't perfectly comfortable. I took my medication and within half an hour I was feeling very groggy and ready for a nap. He walked me to my bedroom and motioned for me to sit at the edge of my bed. He removed my shoes and placed a soft kiss on the tops of both feet. He reached for my hands and lifted me to a standing position and then unbuttoned my jeans.

"I can undress myself. Shouldn't you check your blood sugar?"

"I'm fine." He pinched my chin with his thumb and fore-finger and lifted my face until we were gazing into each other's eyes. "I like undressing you." He left me in panties and my T-shirt and then tucked me into bed.

"Aren't you getting in here with me?"

"I would love to, but I think you need to get your rest. I have a few things to take care of. I need to call Susan and get my stuff from the hotel. Dylan said he would come and watch you so I could do that."

"I don't need a babysitter."

"Well, I would feel better with someone here."

Check Your Sources

We spent the next week figuring out how to exist in such a small place together when Jamie wouldn't allow me to do anything except lay around, read or watch TV. We had our first fight over whether or not I was allowed to bend down and shave my own legs . . . seriously.

"I can do it for you. I'm very good with a razor."

"You're insane. You're not shaving my legs."

"I don't think you should dip your head down, it might make you dizzy in the shower."

"You need to back off a little." We were standing inches apart, face-to-face near the bathroom door. He towered over me, making me feel like a child.

"No, I won't!" He said in a determined voice. "That's what I did before, and you ended up almost bleeding out on a fucking subway."

"This is not the same thing. Nothing is going to happen to me. You're smothering me."

"I'm going for a run. Please wait to take a shower." He lifted the bottom of his white T-shirt to draw his earbud wires up through the neck. He was wearing gray sweats and trainers. Jamie could pull off sweats—he had one of those low angled V-cut stomachs. The sweats hung just below where the side indentations began. My mouth dropped open. I thought about slipping my finger in and tugging the waistband of his sweats down. I was practically drooling, even though I was totally pissed at him. I looked up to find him glaring at me, with a thick sheen of moisture near his sideburns.

"You're sweating already, Jamie. Have you checked your blood sugar?"

"I don't need you to keep reminding me," he barked.

"You've been doing the same thing to me! How do you think I feel?"

He walked over to the entry table where his insulin pen was. He grabbed it and swiftly jabbed himself in the side without pinching his flesh. "There, happy now?"

"You shouldn't do that without metering."

"I'm fine! I've been living with this most of my life. What happened to you is different. It was a trauma; you were attacked."

"I know what it was."

"Then why can't you understand why I'm worried?"

"Is this our first fight?"

He paused in front of the door and took a deep breath. In a low voice he said, "Please, Kate. Please wait until I get back to take a shower."

"Only if you'll join me."

A tiny smile touched the corners of his mouth. "Only if I can shave your legs."

"Fine." I rolled my eyes.

That night I let Jamie shave my legs in the shower. It was intensely erotic, or at least he made it seem that way. *Damn tease.*

He still wouldn't go any further than kissing me in bed. He showed great restraint; I'll give him that, but the caretaker act was getting old.

At my follow-up appointment, Dr. Coco gave me permission to resume normal activities. I made him write it down so that I could wave it in Jamie's face every time he tried to do something for me or every time he tried to prevent me from doing something normal. Every day since I was home, Jamie asked me if I wanted to try and ride the subway. The answer was always no.

We spent one Saturday cuddled up on a bench, sipping hot cocoa at Millennium Park.

"Christmas is in four days. Can you believe it?"

"No, it's so soon. Are you going to go back to Napa for the holidays?"

His jaw clenched. "Why would I do that?"

"Well, I don't know, you have Susan and Guillermo there."

"They have families of their own."

"Don't you have things to take care of at the winery? And what about your organization in Africa?"

"The winery and organization run themselves. I do a lot when I'm there, but it runs smoothly when I'm not. My first priority is you. So what are we doing for Christmas? Should we get a tree and decorate?"

"That would be fun. I haven't done that since I lived with Rose."

He squeezed my hand. "What do you want for Christmas?"

"I want you. I want to make love. I don't want you thinking about my head injury while we're kissing. Do you think you can manage that?"

Smiling, he reached over and fluffed the back of my hair.

"I'll see what I can do, even though you still have this silly hair to remind me."

I punched him in the arm. "Jerk."

The next day, Jamie let me go shopping with Beth. He made me go through a checklist before I left, asking me a hundred questions to make sure I was up for a long day away from home.

"You're not gonna spy on me while I'm shopping, are you?"

"I might. If you feel the slightest bit dizzy or nauseous, call me." Jamie had started to use a cell phone again, but he never texted on it. I knew why. "What's the plan for tonight when you get home?"

"I want to write a little, but my computer has a glitch. It keeps crashing, and I'm worried I'll lose work. I have another older laptop in the closet. I might try and get that one working."

"Okay, and what about dinner? Do you want to stay in or go out?"

"Let's stay in." I walked up to him and slipped my hand down the front of his sweats. I grabbed him and squeezed. He gasped. "Maybe we can go past first base?"

"I think I can arrange that," he said.

The doorbell rang. Jamie quickly darted off to my bedroom. I swung the door open to a smiling Beth.

"Let's shop till we drop."

"You're being sarcastic?"

"Yeah, I hate shopping. Jamie practically begged on his knees for me to go with you."

"You mean he asked you?" She shook her head up and down dramatically. "Jamie, you're in trouble!" I shouted.

"Have fun, ladies!" he yelled back. I grabbed my new purse off the table.

"I need to go by the bank first; I haven't gotten my cards back. Do you mind?"

Before Beth could answer, Jamie shouted again from the other room, "I put a credit card in your purse."

"Hold on one sec," I said to Beth.

I stalked off to my bathroom and found Jamie standing completely naked in front of my sink, brushing his teeth.

I marched up to him. "You!" He spit toothpaste into the sink and turned toward me, exposing himself. He grinned arrogantly.

"Yes, dear, what is it? Have I upset you?"

"I have my own money . . . and you have toothpaste on your lip."

He grabbed both my wrists, held my arms down, and bent so that we were face-to-face. "Can you get it for me?" I squirmed and tried to break my arms away, but he held them firmly.

I leaned in and sucked all the toothpaste off his lip, then I bit him. He pulled away and released my hands. "Ouch, feisty little thing."

"That's what you get. Hey, seriously though, I don't want to buy gifts for you with your money."

"It's our money. You're gonna marry me, right?" He smirked.

"Jamie, I said I thought we needed some time to get to know each other."

"Okay, let's get to know each other tonight." He pressed his body to mine. I felt him hard against me. I got lost in his kiss and then I heard Beth whistling "(Sittin' on) The Dock of the Bay" in the other room.

"I have to go."

"I'll miss you, beautiful," he said near my ear, his voice so smooth and masculine it sent shivers down my spine.

I spent the whole day shopping with Beth. After hours of debate, I finally decided to buy myself lingerie to wear for Jamie. I figured it was the best I could do for a billionaire who had everything he wanted. I got back to the apartment in the afternoon and went straight into my bedroom for a nap. Jamie made sure to strip me down and tuck me in first.

I woke about an hour later, threw on one of his T-shirts, and headed for the kitchen for a glass of water. He was sitting at my square table, shirtless, but he had his black baseball cap on backward. There were computer parts and tools all over the table and floor. He was typing frantically on my laptop. There was something childlike about the way he sat poised and eager as he typed. Jamie was in such a deep concentration that he didn't even notice that I had walked into the room. For a few seconds I stood there and took in a sight I never thought I'd see: Jamie sitting at a computer. He avoided technology as much as possible, and although I knew he had it in him, I didn't know if I would ever witness it, and truthfully I couldn't picture it. He was a far cry from the pale, skinny computer geek he once was. Sitting on the very front edge of the chair, he had his legs spread wide and he was tapping his right bare heel on the ground. The backward baseball hat seemed like a teenage boy's thinking cap. I looked around and noticed in the corner of the living room a small Christmas tree with one string of blinking colorful lights—nothing extravagant, just a little festive touch. I thought of Jamie putting the tree up by himself. He was a lot like me, used to doing things on his own.

When I cleared my throat, he practically jumped out of his seat. "Sorry I startled you."

"It's fine," he said as he stood up and walked toward me.

"What are you doing with all that stuff?"

"Don't worry, I backed up your work."

"I'm not worried, I'm just wondering what you're doing."

He clapped his hands together once and smiled from ear to

ear. "Well, I got kind of excited. I fixed both laptops to run your writing program, but I also wrote some code for a new program that will automatically back up whatever you have written to an online server. That way you won't have to rely on the hardware as much. Don't worry, it's a totally secure server; I have a knack for that sort of thing."

"You wrote code?" I said the last word like I was a kindergartener sounding it out.

He tapped his index finger to his temple. "It's like riding a bike."

"I hardly think so, and I thought you didn't like doing that kind of stuff anymore."

"I wanted to do this for you." He pulled me to his chest. "I won't lie, I kind of enjoyed it."

"Well, thank you." I leaned up on my toes to kiss him. "I never thought writing code could be so sexy."

"Before I get distracted by you, you got a phone call while you were out. A man named Paul Sullivan. He was asking if you knew the whereabouts of Ann Corbin."

When I heard her name, I gasped, my hand flying up to my heart. I was stunned into silence.

"That's your mother, I assume?"

"Yes," I said, struggling to breathe.

"Come here, baby." He tightened his grip on me. "What is it?"

"I just haven't heard her name spoken in so long. Did he leave a number?"

"He left his number. Do you want me to call him for you?"

"No, I want to talk to him. Most people who knew my mother were at her funeral." I glanced at the clock. It was seven p.m. "I'll call him tomorrow."

After I collected myself, I begged Jamie to let me make dinner. He agreed to be my ass-grabbing sous chef while I prepared homemade lasagna. He grated the cheese and continually accosted me until I finally kicked him out. He went back to the table and finished what he had been doing with my computer. Every once in a while I'd catch him stealing glances at me. He'd smile serenely like he was imagining the rest of his life. Jamie was completely happy and content in my dinky, eight-hundred-square-foot apartment. His only complaint was that it wasn't energy-efficient. Within the short time he had been there, he'd changed all of the lightbulbs and faucets and was working on a way to install solar panels on the roof.

We sat on the living room floor and ate our dinner on the coffee table and then moved to the couch, where we fell asleep while watching the entire second season of *Breaking Bad* on Netflix. I woke up several hours later. Jamie was still upright, but his head was resting on the back of the couch. He was sound asleep. My head was in his lap with his hands tangled in my hair. I didn't want to move but I knew he would be uncomfortable like that all night. I sat up slowly, leaned in, and trailed light kisses up his neck. He stirred.

"Hi, baby," I whispered. "Let's go to bed."

"Mmm. Let's stay here for a bit," he said as he pulled me to straddle him.

He lifted my shirt over my head, and with complete ease unclasped my bra and tossed it aside. His mouth was at my breast in an instant. He kissed me gently and took care to hold me close to him, with one hand bracing the back of my neck. I moaned and let my head fall back, giving myself to him as his mouth moved achingly slowly up my body. He kissed and sucked and tugged at my earlobe and then sat back and took a deep breath. I unbuckled his jeans and lifted myself up enough for him to shimmy out of them. I could tell he was being cautious. I reached for the waistband of my black lace panties but he stopped my hands.

"Oh, come on!"

He laughed and shook his head. "No. These are nice. I just think we should leave them on," he said as his fingers stroked me through the fabric. "Mmm, warm."

"I'm wet! Now fucking kiss me." I was practically writhing on top of him when his lips crushed against mine again. Our mouths were glued together, tongues twisting and caressing. His hands continued roaming, but I could feel him harder and harder against me as I moved. He finally pushed the fabric aside and slid his fingers in. I pressed myself deeper against his hand.

"Don't stop, Jamie. I want you, please."

"You are so sexy." He removed his hand, and without caution, entered me, slamming my hips down until I was filled completely with him.

I cried out, arching my back, letting the feeling of him inside of me take over. It had been a while, and the lace fabric between us, although pushed aside, created the perfect amount of friction. We moved seamlessly together. He countered each one of my motions with perfect ease and resistance. I moved harder and faster on top of him. The whole time we were kissing and watching each other until we neared the end. He lifted his head up and closed his eyes and I did the same just as I felt the pulsing ache, then the electricity between my ears and down my spine.

"Katy . . . god Katy, I love you."

Goddammit, if that didn't send me completely over the edge, Jamie brought it all home when he leaned forward and kissed each breast with complete control and determination. The aftershocks were still blasting through me as he tightened his hold and nuzzled into my chest. I wrapped my arms around his head and neck and held him to my body as tightly as I could.

We stayed that way for what felt like days. I imagined the time-lapse version of those moments we sat embracing each other on the couch after we made love, still connected and still overrun with heat. The sun would rush up and blast us through the blinds and then sink down again, casting strange shadows on the walls, but we would be the same, tangled in each other. In the darkness, our connected bodies would burn bright enough to fill the room with a warm glow.

He kissed my mouth and then stood and carried me to the bedroom. We spent an hour lying in bed and talking.

"So you believe in God?" I asked.

"I believe something is out there."

"Like what, aliens?"

"Yes, aliens. That's exactly what I was thinking," he said sarcastically. I was lying on my side in the crook of his arm. He was sweeping his hand up and down against the skin on my back. "What do you think, silly girl?"

"I hope there is something more for the sake of everyone I've loved and lost."

"I feel the same way. What do you think about family?"

"I wish I had one."

"Me, too. Let's make one." It suddenly hit me what Jamie was asking.

"I'm scared."

"Of what?"

"Screwing up my kids. I don't even know what kind of person my father was."

"Well, I know exactly what kind of people my biological

parents are, and I have no concerns that their kind of slime has been passed on to me."

I cupped his face and kissed him. "I don't either, Jamie."

"I believe that even though we've lost so many of our loved ones, we still have family around. They may not be blood related, but the people I considered my real parents were not blood related, either, and I don't see them as anything less than family to me. I have Susan and Guillermo and Chelsea, and you have Jerry and Beth and Dylan, and we fucking have each other, Kate." I nodded hesitantly. "Are you scared to do this with me?"

I shrugged. He grabbed my face and looked me right in the eyes. "How close am I to losing you?"

"What would it take for you to want to lose me, for you to want to leave?"

"It would take a fucking lot to drag me away from you. Don't you see that?"

"Sometimes I feel like I'm broken or damaged."

"I see this kind of splendor and innocent childlike wonder when I watch you. You're always so curious about the world but terrified to be a part of it. You're not broken just like I'm not cursed. I know that now."

"I love you. Isn't that enough?"

He scowled like it pained him to hear my words. "For now," he murmured and then shut his eyes and turned away from me.

The next morning was Christmas Eve. After three cups of coffee, I was a jittering fool, so it might have been a bad decision to call Paul Sullivan back, but I did.

"Hello."

"Thi—thi—this is Kate Corbin returning your call." I couldn't help but feel nervous. This guy knew my mother, but I didn't know him.

"Hello, Kate. I was trying to find the whereabouts of Ann Corbin. I was going down a list of Corbins in the city, calling each one, and landed on you."

"Ann was my mother," I said quickly. "She died in 1994."

"Oh." He sounded stunned. "I'm so sorry."

"Did you know my mother?"

"Briefly. In the Eighties."

"How brief?"

"We dated right up until she met Samuel." *Who the fuck was Samuel? Was he my dad? Oh god.* "Kate, are you there?"

"Can I meet you? I mean, can we meet for coffee or something? I don't know who Samuel is. My mother never spoke of him." Jamie was watching me from the kitchen with concern. He stood, eyes wide, with the coffeepot suspended in the air. I held my hand over my heart in some futile attempt to physically slow the rapid beats down.

"Yes, we can meet. Are you free this afternoon?"

"Yes."

"Okay, how about the Starbucks on State at three o'clock?"

"Perfect, see you then." When I hung up, Jamie was at my side in a second.

"What did he say?"

"He just said he knew my mom and that they dated until she met Samuel. I never heard that name from Rose or my mom."

He wrapped his arms around me and brought me to his chest. "Maybe this will be good for you. Maybe you'll get to know more about your mother."

"I asked my mom about my father once. It upset her so much she could barely speak. I figured he was a deadbeat or something, but maybe Paul will be able to fill in some of the blanks. Rose always said if my mom wanted me to know, she would have told me. That makes me think my father, whoever he is, is a very bad person."

"You don't know that, and you don't know what your mother's reasons were."

"You're right, but I wonder if I'm going against her by digging into this. I guess she's gone, and it doesn't matter now. But still . . ." I leaned up on my tippy-toes and pecked his lips. "I'm going to do some laundry. Do you want to get lunch before we meet Paul?"

"I can go with you?"

"Of course." I slid my hand down the back of his flannel pj's and squeezed his butt. "Wanna do it in the shower to take my mind off of things?"

He scooped me up and carried me to the bathroom before stripping my clothes off in record time. He turned the shower on, took a step back, and scanned me from head to toe. I pulled his pants down as I knelt in front of him. He shivered and then clutched the back of my head.

"Baby, you don't have to do that," he said and then moaned. After he was thoroughly turned on, he lifted me up and kissed me while he backed me into the shower. "Turn around, sexy," he said. When I turned my back to him, he instantly grabbed my hands and pressed them onto the tiles above my head. He leaned in and whispered, "I love you," into my ear. I parted my legs and gasped when he pushed into me forcefully.

"You okay?"

"God, yes, just go." He slid his hands down my arms, reached around with one hand, and began circling the sensitive skin above where we were connected. He gripped my neck hard with his other hand and continued his strong thrusts until we were both breathing loudly and moaning. I threw my head back, and his mouth instantly went to my neck and sucked and kissed and tugged. Then he gently bit my earlobe, and I fell apart, shouting, "I love you, too!"

After a lengthy tryst in the shower, I joked with Jamie about how much water his environmentally conscious ass wasted while he worked me over. He laughed and then tried to lick the water droplets off my body.

"See, the water isn't totally wasted."

I dressed quickly while Jamie spread out on my bed in just a towel.

"I'm gonna get used to having you in my bed all the time."

"So."

I just looked back and shook my head at him. After collecting my laundry and some of Jamie's, I headed for the door.

"I can do that," he said. He had dropped his towel and was standing naked by my dresser, about to give himself a shot. He pinched the skin and jabbed the needle in.

"I've got it. You've been doing my laundry for weeks. I can do it now."

"It's Christmas Eve. You shouldn't be doing laundry on Christmas Eve."

"It's just one load. I'll throw it in and be back in a sec."

The washers in the basement laundry room were full. Irritated, I turned on my heel and ran right into Dylan coming toward me.

"Hey, chica."

"Hi." I set my basket down and gave him a hug.

He braced my shoulders, pulled away, and looked me up and down. "You're glowin', lady. Did you have a good morning?"

My irritation vanished. "Sounds like you're getting familiar with this type of look?"

"Well, yes, I won't lie. Ashley has been glowing nonstop for the last couple of weeks."

"Are you careful with her?"

"Yes, we are."

I smiled. "Good boy. What are your plans with her?"

"She really wants to go to Berkeley next year, so I'm gonna try and get into the music program at the University of San Francisco."

"That's wonderful, Dylan."

"And I'll be close to you guys."

"What do you mean?"

"I thought you were going to Napa?"

"Why would you think that?"

"Kate, you told me yourself."

"I did? When?"

He crossed his arms over his chest and looked up to the ceiling curiously. "Do you not remember anything before you were attacked?"

"I remember stuff, I just don't remember that day very well."

"Jamie sent you a letter asking you to marry him."

"I knew that."

"Well, don't you remember what you told me?"

Searching my mind, I shook my head slowly. "No, I don't remember. What do you remember?"

"I remember your exact fucking words."

"What, tell me?" I poked him in the chest with my index finger.

"You said you were gonna quit the *Crier*, go out to Napa, finish your book, and say absolutely one hundred percent yes to Jamie. I'll never forget the way you looked that day, all bright-eyed and glowing, kind of like you are now."

"Holy shit, I did say that, didn't I?"

"Yep."

But did I still want that?

. . .

Jamie hailed a cab at the front of my building, which took us
to a Vietnamese restaurant on State Street. It was a perfect day
for *pho*. It was in the low thirties but not snowing—just windy
and very cold—so the warm soup in a super intimate setting
was nice. I didn't want to talk about what I would ask Paul. I
just wanted to have a nice lunch and enjoy my time with Jamie.

I stared at him from across the table. He wore a black T-
shirt and black jacket with dark jeans and combat boots. His
hair, although much shorter, still revealed streaks of blond. It was
mussed in a sexy way on top. For some reason, when he was
completely clean-shaven, it made his eyes look greener and the
dimple on his left cheek deeper. His lips were always pale pink
and healthy looking. I watched him slurp up the noodles in his
soup like a little boy. Jamie was, by far, the most unpretentious
billionaire in the world. He lived for the moment. He loved his
life and just wanted to share it . . . with me.

"Jamie?" I said into my soup.

I felt him look up. "Yes, baby?"

"Thank you for everything you've done for me."

"You don't need to thank me."

"I haven't said this, but I'm truly sorry about the article and
jumping to conclusions. I've been running away from making
connections with people most of my life, but I'm finished with
that. I want to go back to Napa with you. I want to try it."

He reached over the table and took my hands in his. "I
would love that."

We walked several blocks in the freezing cold. I stayed tucked against Jamie's side until we reached Starbucks. It hit me as soon as I walked in that I didn't know what Paul looked like or how I would find him, but I didn't have to. He found me almost immediately.

"Kate?"

I turned to see a handsome man, probably in his late forties, much younger than I imagined. He had salt-and-pepper hair, brown eyes, and a thin, fit build. There was something very familiar about him. He was dressed nicely in a sweater and pants, the perfect picture of a distinguished gentleman.

"Paul." I stuck my hand out but he hugged me instead.

"I could have spotted you a million miles away. You're as striking and beautiful as your mother was."

"Thank you," I said, taken aback.

"I'm Jamie, Kate's fiancé." Jamie stuck out his hand and Paul shook it.

"Nice to meet you. Shall we have a seat?" Paul gestured to a table in the corner.

"I'll get us coffees," Jamie said.

I sat across from Paul and scanned his features. "So you dated my mother?"

"Yes, and I know what you're thinking."

"Oh?"

"I was much younger than her. In my twenties. She was close to forty."

"Actually, I was thinking that you look very familiar to me."

"Well, I'm a writer. Maybe you've read one of my novels?"

"Yes, that's it!" It hit me instantly. The man I was sitting across from was the award-winning, bestselling author Paul Sullivan. "What an honor to meet you. I'm a writer as well. I write for the *Crier*."

"Oh yes, I'm familiar with that paper. That's wonderful, but honestly, I'm not surprised. Your mother was a huge fan of the written word."

"What happened between you and my mother?"

He leaned back in his chair and smiled at the memory. "She was a teller at my bank. She was so uniquely beautiful. I would find reasons to go in and see her. She agreed to have lunch with me one day and we started dating from there." He paused and his lips flattened. Looking down at the table in a daze, he said, "I was in love with her." The age difference didn't shock me because my mother always seemed young at heart. What surprised me more was that I'd never heard of this man who had been so madly in love with her.

"So what happened?"

"She was resistant to starting a serious relationship with someone so much younger. She said she couldn't have kids, but apparently she could because she did. With Samuel, I assume?"

"I have no idea who Samuel is."

He squinted and shook his head. "Well, that's why she ended our relationship. She met Samuel. He was her age. She said he was a better match for her. They were engaged within weeks of meeting, and she told me she couldn't see me anymore. The last day I saw her, she showed me her ring." Jamie sat down at that point and took my hand in his. Paul looked a little choked up. "She cried and apologized over and over again. I left her there, crying on a lakefront trail. That was the last time I saw her, but I never stopped thinking about her. I don't think I ever will."

"Wow," I said as tears ran down my cheeks.

"I'm sorry, sweetheart. This must be very hard for you to hear."

"I want to know. I need to know as much as I can. I don't know who my father is. She never told me." My voice was shaky. Jamie remained silent.

"Samuel Morrison. I would start there."

"What about you? Do you have a family?"

The mood seemed to lighten. Paul chuckled. "Yes, I met my wife shortly after I dated your mother. We have five children, two grandchildren, and another one on the way. I have a very big family that I love, but like I said, I never stopped thinking about Ann, and I was curious. That's why I called."

I couldn't believe my mother was a heartbreaker. Why would she ever dump this guy?

We all stood up at the same time. "Thank you for meeting me, Paul. I feel like I have a place to start searching."

"You're welcome. I'm sorry you had to lose your mother so young."

I hugged him and then he shook Jamie's hand before we all walked out into the brisk air.

We walked three blocks before it started raining. I grabbed Jamie's hand and pulled him up the stairs to the nearest L station.

"Are you sure, Kate? I can get us a cab."

"No. I'm doing this. I'm changing this memory." Somehow the meeting with Paul had reinvigorated me.

The train stopped in front of us as we stood shaking on the platform. We were soaking wet and freezing. I pulled him in through the doors by his jacket, pushed him up against a pole, and pressed my mouth to his, kissing him urgently. He cupped my face and kissed me back with so much intensity I thought we'd combust. When we pulled apart, he held my face and said, "This is why I love you. You're amazing."

"This is how I want to remember the L. If we move away and I never come back here again, this is how I will remember it, kissing you sopping wet." I laughed. He kissed me again and then we held each other until it was time to get off.

Back at my apartment, it took Jamie exactly three minutes to Google Samuel Morrison. He lived in the city, less than two miles from me. The thought that my possible father lived two miles from me and didn't even care tortured me and made me not want to seek him out, but Jamie insisted I call. I knew he was right. It would eat away at me if I didn't at least try to find my real father.

After a few rings, he picked up, and my heart started beating wildly. I had no idea what to expect.

"Hello?"

"May I speak with Samuel Morrison?"

"Speaking." I paused, swallowing a huge lump in my throat. "Hello?" he said again.

"My name is Kate Corbin. I'm Ann Corbin's daughter." Jamie nodded at me, encouraging me to go on. "My mother passed away when I was eight. I never knew who my father was, but now I have reason to believe it's you."

His voice became very low and serious. "I'm sorry for your loss. I did know your mother. I was engaged to her, in fact, but I can assure you that I'm not your father."

"How do you know that?"

"Because I was never with your mother intimately. She was pregnant when I met her. I didn't know until we were about to be married. She wanted to keep you, but I couldn't live with the thought of raising another man's child, so we broke it off." I held the phone to my ear, speechless. "Kate?"

"What do you mean?"

"I'm not a bad person. I cared for her. In fact, I stayed in touch with her through the pregnancy. She went looking for your father when she was close to having you, but he had moved on. I don't think she ever told him. She said that she could do it on her own. I believed her. She was a strong woman."

Everything was starting to come together, and the truth was finally within my grasp.

"Is my father Paul Sullivan?"

"Yes, I believe he is."

My biological father was the handsome man I had met at Starbucks just an hour before. The beloved, award-winning, bestselling author. I looked up and could see that Jamie was just as shocked as I was. His eyes were huge, and then he looked at me curiously before smiling from ear to ear.

"Thank you, Mr. Morrison. I have to go. Good-bye."

As soon as I ended the call, Jamie wrapped me up. "Oh my god, baby. Your dad is *the* Paul Sullivan."

"But he doesn't know. What if he doesn't want me?"

"We just call him and tell him the story and see what he says. Now that I think about it, there was a resemblance. His ears stuck out just like yours," he said, trying to lighten the mood.

"My ears don't stick out, jerk."

"They do, just a little. It's actually pretty cute." He picked up the phone and handed it to me. "Well . . . time to call Paul."

"I can't, Jamie—I'm scared."

"You've been through a lot, baby. Come here." He took me into his arms and held me while he spoke softly in my ear. "You're one of the bravest people I know. You can do this. I know he'll want you in his life. How could he not?" He gently pushed me away from him and looked down at me, bracing my shoulders. "You're amazing."

"Okay, I'll do it." Jamie handed me the phone. I dialed the number and waited with my stomach in knots for an answer. "Hello?"

"Hi Paul, it's Kate. I have something to tell you . . ."

The Situation

There are moments when clear images finally begin to emerge within the abstract painting of your life. For me, it was the moment I picked up the phone to call Paul. I saw myself in Chicago and Napa surrounded by Jamie, Beth, Jerry, and Dylan—the people who had been with me through my darkest hours—and I realized that all I ever wanted and yearned for was already within my grasp. I wanted a career I could feel passionate about. I had my novel. I wanted love and lust and everything that comes with it. I had Jamie. I wanted to fight hard, love hard, and live hard. But more than anything, I wanted a family to share my life with. I had that, too, even if they weren't my blood. Everything I wanted already existed within my life. The death of my mother and Rose, my constant reinterpretations of my dream about Rose, and my relationship with Just Bob had paralyzed me in a place of fear and isolation. I had believed I was all I had and all I needed. It was easier that way. But Jamie was right. I was scared to live, to be happy, to take what I deserved.

Once my entire life was laid out for me during that critical moment of clarity, I was immediately grateful for all the traumatic and painful experiences. If I hadn't lived in the fucking darkness, I never would have seen the light. Now I was finally facing that light, fearless, ready to walk into it and take my happiness.

"Paul . . . I think you might be my father. Actually, I know you are, and I wanted to tell you that if you're open to it and comfortable, I'd like to get to know you."

I could sense Paul's emotion over the phone. "I was just going to call you, Kate." His voice cracked. I was trembling and Jamie was watching me cautiously. "On my way back home after meeting you, it struck me that you had never heard about Samuel. There would have been no reason for your mother to hide him from you. I got this feeling . . . I thought about the timing and your age. You look just like your mom, you know, but there's something in your smile that I see in my youngest daughter. Even more obvious, you, my dear, were blessed with the Sullivan ears."

"My boyfriend said the same thing," I said, laughing and crying at the same time. Jamie mouthed the word *fiancé* at me. I walked over and sat on his lap. He kissed my back and rubbed my shoulders while I continued talking to Paul. My father.

"When I got home, I told my wife, Elaine, that I had a feeling. I told her the story. She's very excited to meet you." There was a long pause. He cleared his throat and went on. "I am so sorry that I wasn't in your life sooner, Kate, but I promise you, I will do everything I can to make up for lost time."

It's fair to say that by that point I was hysterical. All I could blubber was, "I'm a writer, too."

"I know. I looked you up . . ." His voice was shaky, and he was crying with me. "I'm . . . I'm very proud of you. None of my other kids . . . I'm just so happy. Please come and have

Christmas dinner with us tomorrow? You can meet your brothers and sisters."

"Tell me about them."

He took a deep breath. "Well, you have a sister, Olivia, who is twenty-five. She has twin boys that are a year old. You're an aunt."

I laughed giddily through tears. "Go on."

"Your brother Aiden is twenty-three. He's engaged to Lauralie, who's pregnant. A little young, we know, but they're in love. And then Gavin is twenty-one. He goes to college in Los Angeles at USC, but he's here for the holidays. Blake is twenty, and he's still finding himself," he said, in an amused tone. "And finally, there's Skylar, the youngest. She's seventeen and still in high school. She's the free spirit—a very gifted pianist."

"Wow. I'm speechless. I've lived all my life thinking I had no family."

"Well, you have a big family, and I know they will welcome the addition. What do you say? Come and meet everyone?"

"Yes, I definitely will."

"See you tomorrow, sweetheart. I can't wait to get to know you."

"Likewise," I said in a low voice and then hung up. I turned around and straddled Jamie in the chair and then buried my face in his neck and sobbed. "Happy tears?" he asked.

"The happiest. Will you go with me?"

"Of course."

We slid into bed, naked and freezing, but within moments we were warm, wrapped up in each other, and dozing off to sleep. I woke up Christmas morning to the smell of breakfast. Jamie was making pancakes and singing to the Black Keys pumping through the iPod dock.

When I came into his view, he shouted, "Merry Christmas, lover" over the loud music. He was shirtless, wearing nothing but his plaid flannel pajamas. I was wearing the slinky black Victoria's Secret purchase I'd made with Beth. I walked around the counter so he could see me from head to toe. His mouth dropped open.

"Oh my god. Screw breakfast." When he lifted me from my waist, I wrapped my legs around him. He slammed me against the dining room wall and attacked my mouth just as the lead singer of the Black Keys shouted, "I got mine!" *Best sex song EVER!* I thought.

After Jamie took me against the wall, we ate our partially burnt breakfast and then showered and got dressed.

"Jamie?"

"Yeah."

"I feel terrible. I didn't get you anything."

"You mean that thing you were wearing earlier wasn't for me?"

I laughed. "Well, yes, I guess so."

"I have a photographic memory, remember? That little number will be the gift that keeps on giving. Trust me."

He was standing at my dresser injecting his insulin pen. When he turned around, he had a small box in his hands. "This is for you, but you can't open it until later." I made a grumpy face. "Oh, is Katy curious?"

"No, I can handle a little suspense."

We decided we would go through the city looking for the holiday train before we headed to my father's house, which was located in a little suburb just outside Chicago.

As we headed out the lobby of my building, I noticed a sign above the exit door was misspelled. It said: MARRY CHRISTMAS.

I laughed to myself. Two blocks away, another sign sitting in the coffee shop window said: MARRY CHRISTMAS.

"Do you see that?" I pointed the sign out to Jamie.

"What?"

"It's spelled wrong."

"Oh, hmm. Idiots." He chuckled and pulled me along by the hand. As we approached the L station nearest to my apartment, I spotted Darlene. She was wrapped in a blanket, sitting on a piece of cardboard. When I got close to her, she said, "Hey, you, girl. Say yes!" I looked up at Jamie. He shrugged and then looked up to the sky curiously.

"Merry Christmas, Darlene." I handed her a ten-dollar bill. "Stay warm."

"Thank you," she said.

We continued walking. I stopped abruptly about a half a block down and turned to Jamie. "What are you up to? Huh?"

"Who, me?" he said in mock surprise. "Let's go, we gotta hurry." He yanked me along.

"Why do we have to hurry?"

"We just do."

"When we got to the platform of the station, it began to snow. "I planned this," Jamie said.

And then lo and behold, the goddamned holiday train pulled up. "You arranged this?"

He pulled me toward Santa's car. "No, silly girl, there's a schedule."

"You're kidding? All these years?!"

Just as we reached Santa, Jamie stopped and looked me in the eye and said, "Merry Christmas, angel."

Then Santa chimed in, "Ho ho ho, marry him!"

Jamie pointed a thumb back toward Santa as he stood in

front of me. "That, I planned," he said. Then he dropped to his knee, pulled the box out, and opened it, revealing a modest pink stone on a platinum band. "Sorry, honey, no blood diamonds for you." I shook my head and laughed. "Marry me?"

"Jamie Lawson . . . is that how you ask nicely?"

"Katherine Corbin, will you please marry me and be my wife and wear that black silky thing at least twice a week for the rest of our lives?"

I dropped to my knees, gripped his face, and kissed him. "Absolutely, one hundred percent yes. And that was a way better proposal than a note."

People all around us on the platform began clapping and cheering. Even Santa was jollier than usual. Jamie put the ring on my finger and then we stood together and rushed onto the train car. Powdered in snow, we kissed the moment the doors closed and made a silent promise that we would do that every time we got on the L. It was our new beautiful memory.

. . .

We rented a car and headed north. Paul Sullivan, my father, lived in a gorgeous, two-story colonial house in the village of Wilmette, a tranquil little suburb north of Chicago. The treelined street and large snow-covered homes were pictur-esque, an ideal place to grow up. I felt a pang of sadness as we pulled down the long driveway. I wondered if it was resentment toward my mother or just pure envy that all of my father's other kids got to grow up here while I was living in a one-bedroom, stuffy apartment with a depressed Rose. I thought about the many nights I'd slept on the pullout sofa, wishing I had my own room. Still, I couldn't forget that Rose had loved me like a mother.

Before we got out of the car, Jamie looked over at me with concern. "Are you okay? You seem somewhere else."

"I'm here, I assure you. I'm here. This hurts a little. I can't figure out why my mother didn't want me to know."

He took my hand and kissed the back of it. "You may never know the reason, and I can tell you from experience that you have to let it go. When my biological parents tried to extort money from me, they told lie after lie. They tried to take me down—their own flesh and blood— when all I wanted was to do good for people. For months, I just kept wondering why. Finally, my adoptive mother told me I needed to stop searching for that answer and move forward. When the trial was over, I promised myself I would never ask why again. Look at this, Kate. See all of these cars?" The driveway and street were spilling over with cars jammed into every spot around the big white house. "This is what you get now. This is amazing. Don't think about the past ever again."

Although he tried very hard to hide it, Jamie was emotional. I couldn't take what I had for granted knowing Jamie had lost most of his family. "Does it still hurt?" I asked.

"There used to be this hole, this void that I thought could never be filled, but it's healing and filling up . . . ever since I met you."

"And now you have all this, too." I gestured toward the cars and smiled.

Meeting my new family was a blur of faces and names. My new siblings and stepmother were more than welcoming. I got to hold my baby nephew and hear my youngest sister, Skylar, play the piano beautifully. Jamie fit right in to the warmth. I stole glances at him often while we were at my father's, and he always returned them with a smile.

On our way back into the city, we talked about our plan. "I feel like I don't want to leave now, but I know you need to be in Napa."

"We don't have to choose, Kate. We can live in both places. That's the beauty of being a writer."

"What about you?"

"I've always been all over the place. I like it that way."

"Really?"

"Yes, of course. Do you want to keep your apartment?"

"I don't care about my apartment. I just want to be able to come here once in a while."

"I think we can arrange that."

Segue

In the week following Christmas, I spent most of my time packing and writing while Jamie made travel plans for us to go back to Napa after New Year's. We decided that we'd have our wedding at the winery in the spring, barring any unforeseen circumstances. Jamie said there would be no unforeseen anything, and that I needed to stop believing things were too good to be true. He spent a lot of time reassuring me that everything would be okay.

Late in the week one morning, I heard him tinkering in the kitchen.

"What are you doing?" He was dressed, ready, and waiting for me to get up.

He set a chocolate croissant and a latte from Starbucks in front of me. "Morning, baby. I was so excited, I couldn't sleep."

I sat down at the table surrounded by boxes. "Excited about what?"

"I can't tell you." He was amped. "I just have to show you, but we can't go until nine."

I bit into the pastry. "Aren't those the best?" he said.

"Did you eat one?"

"Yeah." By that point he was at the counter checking his blood sugar with the meter. "Holy shit," he said and then reached for his insulin pen. He gave himself a shot and then sat down next to me at the table. He still seemed a little hyper, but then I brought him down as soon as I opened my mouth.

"Are you worried that your children will get it?"

"Our children?"

"Yes."

"Are you worried, Kate?"

"You're the one living with it. Should I be worried?"

"If, God forbid, one of our children gets it, then I would be able to help them learn to live a pretty normal life. Despite the fact that neither one of my parents had it, they were still able to help me live the healthiest possible lifestyle. But, if that scares you too much, then we can adopt. I think we should anyway. I want a big family."

"I think I do, too, and I won't be scared if you're not. I trust you."

"Okay." He leaned over and kissed my nose. "Now what's the plan for tonight?"

"I told Dylan and Ashley if you were up for it that we'd meet them on the roof at midnight and drink champagne and bang pots and pans or whatever."

"Sounds perfect."

After I showered and got ready, we grabbed a cab and headed into the upscale Gold Coast neighborhood. We stopped in front of a building that I'm pretty sure was owned by Oprah. Jamie led me through the lobby toward the elevator. He inserted a key and pressed the button for the penthouse. We entered a vacant foyer and walked down a hall until we were standing in a large loft-style room with floor-to-ceiling windows overlooking Lake Michigan. The floors were a warm and inviting hardwood. Even though the space was empty, something about it felt like home. Maybe it was that I could see so much of my beloved city, or maybe it was because I was standing there with Jamie.

"So you want to buy this place?"

"Want to buy?"

"Yeah."

"No."

"What, then?"

He just stared at me with his hands shoved deep in his pockets. He shrugged and then rocked back a few times on his heels.

I squinted, scowling at him. "You! You already bought it?"

"Bingo." He smirked, and oh, that goddamned dimple.

"For me?" I shrieked.

"Uh-huh. Well, for us, silly girl."

"Oh my god, how much did this cost?"

His lips flattened. "Not very much, and anyway, I need the write-off."

"Not very much by whose standard?"

"Katy, stop, seriously. There's an amazing loft that will be the perfect place for you to read and write. Come see." I followed him through an insanely clean and ultramodern gourmet kitchen to an open staircase and loft lined with bookshelves. There was a large window in the loft with the same gorgeous view looking out onto the lake. I was mesmerized; I couldn't take my eyes off the water. The white outline from the snow and ice piled on the shore reflected so brightly, I had to squint. It was uncharacteristically sunny for that time of year. I imagined the snow melting and breaking away into the glimmering, still water.

"It's beautiful." I turned to see him watching me.

"It is now," he said.

I smiled all the way to my ears. "Should we christen it?"

He stalked over to me, braced my neck, kissed me thoroughly, and then murmured, "Katy, you dirty girl," right into my ear.

I grabbed his butt. "Well?"

He pulled back and took a loud, deep breath. "I'm sorry, baby. I need to eat. I'm feeling a little weak." Jamie never complained about his diabetes, and because of that I wasn't that aware of its impact on our lives. He was determined not to use an insulin pump, so I knew he was cautious. Exerting himself would make his blood sugar even lower.

I ran my fingers through the hair at the back of his neck and gazed into his eyes. He held me around the waist. I cocked my head to the side and stared dreamily at him.

"What?" he asked.

"I have a Balance bar in my purse. Do you want it?" He smiled kindly and nodded. "I love you, Jamie. Thank you for this. It's the nicest thing anyone has ever done for me."

"I love you, too."

We started moving very gradually in a circle, still embracing each other, slow dancing to the sound of our beating hearts.

Remember playing hide-and-seek as a kid? You would run full speed away from the one who was "it." Every time you played, you thought you'd found the best hiding place. You would sit, shaking with anticipation because even though the object of the game was the opposite, all you really wanted was to be found. You wanted to be found by the one who was "it." For months, I had been hiding. I had run so far and hidden so well, I thought no one would find me, but then he did.

I had been only half awake until Jamie came into my life. I know now that it's true, what they say: love cannot be taken out of you because it changes you. I woke up when I met Jamie. The world became louder, crazier, more exciting, and more achingly beautiful.

"Do you think it will always be like this?"

"I think there will be times when we'll have to work at it." He paused. "I'm willing to do that until the day I die if it means I get to hold you like this."

. . .

On our way back to my apartment, I gave Jamie a good laugh when he asked if I was going to give him the New Year's Eve kiss he'd always wanted.

"Well, I'm not gonna be kissing Dylan, not that he's a bad kisser."

"How would you know?" He seemed shocked but was still smiling.

"One day, Dylan and I went down to the basement laundry room and walked in on Stephen making out with some girl. This was in my 'woe is me' phase, mind you. Anyway, Dylan felt sorry for me so he pressed me against the wall and kissed me in front of the bimbo and Stephen. He put on a pretty good show."

Jamie was clutching his heart, laughing hysterically. "You're kidding."

"No, I swear to God."

He shook his head. "What a good guy."

"Totally."

"But he better keep his hands off you."

"I don't think you have to worry about that."

Later that night, after kissing Jamie on the roof and toasting to the New Year with Dylan and Ashley, we were in bed by 12:10 on the dot. I woke up a few hours later to find Jamie gone from our bed. I discovered him in the living room, swaying and disoriented.

"Jamie, are you looking for your meter?"

For a second, when he looked up, it seemed like he didn't recognize me, and then finally he spoke. He sounded like a frightened child. "Katy?"

I went to him and pulled him to sit on the couch. "Yes, baby, I'm here."

"I feel nauseous."

"Let me find your meter." I got up and immediately found it on the counter. I rushed to him and nervously fumbled with the lancets for a few seconds until I finally pricked his finger and put the blood onto the meter tab. The screen read twenty. "You're very low, baby. Hold on." I ran into the kitchen and poured orange juice into a cup and then took it to him. He seemed extremely weak as he reached for it.

"I'm okay, Katy."

"You need to eat." I went to the kitchen and threw graham crackers, nuts, a cereal bar, a banana and some cheese on a plate. It took me less than thirty seconds. I ran it over to him and could tell he was already a bit more lucid.

He laughed. "What's all this?"

"I didn't know what you would feel like."

"You are such a sweetheart."

"Did this ever happen to you when you were alone?"

"If I felt low at night, it would wake me up. I would keep the meter by my bed. I think it must have been the combination of the long day and then the champagne. I'm glad I was here with you."

"Me too."

After he ate and we checked his blood sugar again, he fell asleep on the couch with his head in my lap. I sat there for part of the night, unable to sleep. I thought about Jamie and I together, going to Napa, getting married, starting a family, and coming back to Chicago every now and then. It started to become impossible to imagine my life without him. The ending to my book was the beginning of my life. It was the story of us, and how we came to be. What started out as a journey for one girl who kept herself hidden in the darkness became the story of two souls connected and growing together in the light. I couldn't imagine exactly what the future looked like for us or where in the world we would be, but I knew that none of it mattered because we were becoming a part of each other. There was no other place but where we were, as long as we were together.

In the morning, Jamie asked me about birth control. We hadn't talked about it, and I assumed he was leaving it up to me. I had an idea of where Jamie stood on the matter.

"I haven't been using any. Should I?"

"No," was all I said. He squinted his eyes curiously, and he flashed me a small, tight smile before looking back down at his magazine.

Jamie rented a car and decided we would road-trip it back to Napa since I would be taking some of my belongings. We moved everything else from my place to the new gorgeous apartment Jamie bought, and then we left Chicago. We hoped that we would see everyone at our wedding in the spring.

We got to know each other in every possible way as we drove to southern California before heading up to Napa. We stayed in a cute boutique hotel in downtown San Diego overlooking the gorgeous bay near the East Village. We stopped into a restaurant called the Cowboy Star. Jamie went off to the restroom while I took a seat at the bar. I ordered a martini called a Mae West from their cocktail menu, and then a few moments later I heard Jamie behind me ask for a glass of the Lawson Pinot. I turned around and smiled. "Good choice, sailor."

He sat on the stool next to me and held his hand out. "I'm Jamie."

"Kate," I said, as I shook his hand.

"It's nice to meet you." He bowed his head very slightly.

"That's a very sexy wine you ordered."

"Agreed. I know a little bit about it. I'm R. J. Lawson."

"Get outta here." I socked him in the arm.

He laughed. "It's no lie."

"But you said your name was . . ."

"Jamie. That's right. That's what my friends call me."

"Jamie, huh? So we're friends?"

"I'd like to be." His gaze fell to my mouth.

I took a sip of my martini and worked very hard not to crack a smile. "Well, I'm Kate Corbin. I used to be a reporter for a newspaper, and I would have killed for an exclusive with you."

"Sounds quite violent of you, Kate, but what the hell, I'm exclusively yours . . . Ask away."

"I said I *used* to be a reporter."

"Oh . . . I see. What do you do now?"

"I'm writing a book, actually, and I could use some inspiration."

"How can I be of service to you?"

"Why don't you tell me something about yourself that I won't find on Wikipedia. Like, what's next for you?"

"What's next for me? Hmm . . . Just one thing?"

"Yeah, why not."

"Okay, I'm hoping that by some serendipitous miracle I will end up in bed with an angel tonight."

Looking sharply at him, I shook my head. "Seems impossible, and anyway, what fun is that? Angels are so pure."

"Okay, maybe a mildly naughty angel."

"What will you do with her?"

He arched his eyebrows, leaned in, and whispered, "Would you like a preview of what I would do to her?"

"Yes!" I practically shouted at him. My heart was racing, and I could feel the beginning of that pulsing ache between my legs.

He shook his head back and forth very slowly. "No, we only just met. I think we should take it slow."

"What?" My voice got really high.

"Yeah, I mean, telling you, a complete stranger, a reporter no less, my innermost thoughts and feeling . . . I don't know, it just seems a little reckless."

"Is that how you want to play it?" I said before downing my entire martini in two gulps. He didn't respond. He just watched me as I looked at the time on my phone and then reached into my purse and grabbed a ten-dollar bill. I threw it on the bar, waved to the bartender, and hopped off my stool.

"What are you doing?"

"I'm calling it a night. I hope you find your angel." I winked at him.

He followed me all the way back to the hotel and then stepped in front of me to open the large glass door.

"Ma'am."

"Sir, are you following me?"

He walked beside me toward the elevator. "I'm stalking you," he said matter-of-factly. "I'm going to stalk you for the rest of my life."

We stepped in and the doors closed. "Sounds terrifying."

He pushed me against the wall and tried to kiss me, but I

dodged his face back and forth. We started laughing. "For the love of god, let me kiss you."

"I don't kiss on the first date."

"You had sex with me eighteen different ways on our first date."

The elevator doors opened and I hurried out. "That wasn't really our first date."

"Okay, how about this, you stripped down and went skinny-dipping with me five hours after you met me."

"What are you trying to say?"

"I'm charming."

"You have an ego," I said as I slipped the key card into the door and pushed it open.

"I like it when you're a tease."

I flipped on the lights as the door closed behind Jamie. I threw my purse and coat on a chair and put my hand on my hip. "Okay, then I'll be a tease more often."

"I'm lying, I don't really like it when you're a tease. Now, get naked," he said as he tore his clothes off.

I obliged.

We were still naked in the morning, with the covers pulled all the way up to our necks. We were lying on our sides, facing each other and smiling like two lovesick kids. "You know what I find entertaining?"

"Tell me."

He scowled and then spoke in a deep, steely voice. "Watching you squirm." He laughed maniacally and then sunk beneath the sheets.

"You will not tickle me!" I protested.

He turned me forcefully so that I was lying flat on my stomach, and then he bit my butt.

"Ouch!"

From under the covers, I heard him mumble, "Oh sorry, baby." He tore the sheets away and then grabbed my arms and forced them above my head. The light from the window was blaring across the bed. He didn't move for several seconds, he just hovered, holding my hands tight. My face was resting sideways on the pillow so I could just barely see him in my peripheral vision. "Am I hurting you?"

"No, but what are you doing?"

"Looking at you."

"Looking at my ass?"

"All of you. Your shoulders and your hair sweeping across your back. I'm looking at your breast pressed against the bed." He paused. "I'm going to lick that soon, just so you know."

I giggled into the pillow. "I'm starting to feel a little vulnerable and self-conscious here."

"Why? You're beautiful, Kate. You have a beautiful body," he said seriously, and then laughed. "And a really nice ass." He bit my butt again.

"Stop! You're making me crazy."

"Am I? I'm just looking at you, at what's mine."

"Listen, sailor, you don't own me. I'm not yours."

"You're right, I don't own you." He bent, still hovering, but his mouth came close to my ear. "I never want to own you, but you are mine. You're mine to love as long as you'll let me." He released my arms and then turned me onto my back. Smiling, he said, "Can I kiss you now?"

He didn't wait for me to answer.

. . .

It was sunny the day we reached the winery. We were greeted by Susan and Guillermo and a very excited Chelsea. I learned

that Susan had already begun planning the wedding and making travel arrangements for my family and friends in Chicago.
She really was like a mother to Jamie, someone I felt would
always be a large part of our lives. Her children were grown, and
although she often laid on a thick layer of tough love, I knew
underneath it she was a soft, loving, and warm person who put
a lot of value on family.

We settled into our life in the barn. Jamie said we should
stop calling it the barn and start calling it our home. I loved
him for that spirit. He built me a writing loft inside of it with a
window that looked out onto the vineyard. I spent most of my
days up there writing, and sometimes I would look out and feel
like my life couldn't possibly be real. I would sit up there and
watch Jamie interacting with the other workers or operating
some huge machine or just standing out among the sea of vines,
staring up at the sky and marveling at his own life, the same way
I did.

Just Bob had sent me on a bit of a journey that year, and I
didn't blame him for making me think I should be closed off
to love. I thanked him for showing me the contrast. It's hard to
know how green the grass is if you've never been on the other
side of the fence. That's the whole point, right? Sometimes I
think that if I were preaching on the L to me from a year ago, I
would simply say, "Live your fucking life, Kate, and let yourself
be open to love." But then I realize that's not the kind of advice
people understand and take. Everyone thinks they're living their
life.

This is what I would really say: "Leave your life. Leave everyone you love, every care, every stress, every commitment. Live
alone. Understand what it feels like to know that if you go into
cardiac arrest, choke on a piece of hot dog, or get electrocuted,

no one will find you. You'll rot. No one will mourn you. Imagine this feeling haunting your thoughts for the rest of your life. You'll wither and vanish, and some stranger will take care of your things and your burial, and you may not even get a placard. Imagine that, live it, and let yourself believe that you should be alone, and then go back to the people who love you." That is what I would preach. That is the challenge I would present. Gratitude is the quality of being thankful and the readiness to show appreciation in return. On my journey, I learned what it felt like to live. To live is to be grateful.

. . .

The sky was cloudless and more beautiful than usual on the day of our wedding. Jamie looked gorgeous in a black vest over a white dress shirt. I watched him standing under an iron arch, waiting for the ceremony to begin. I was hidden behind the massive tent set up for our reception, but could see through an opening that the seats on both sides of the aisle were filling up. We didn't have a wedding party, but we had invited all of the greatest people we knew. Susan, Guillermo, Chef Mark, and their families were there. On my side were all my new siblings and their significant others. Even my newly acquired grandparents and stepmother were there. I spotted Jerry and Beth and smiled really wide when I saw Dylan and Ashley take a seat.

I watched Jamie for several moments. Sometimes you can learn even more about someone by watching them from afar. His shirtsleeves were rolled up and his hair was tousled messily. He was absolutely adorable, smiling at all of the guests. I could see the excitement coursing through him, and I could tell that he was touched by how many guests had come all that way to California for us.

The ceremony was to be a casual affair at dusk, that magical hour when the sun tucks itself behind the hills but the sky still glows steadily. I left my hair down in soft waves against my back. My veil was attached to a wreath made of wildflowers, and my bouquet was a bunched-up cluster of daisies and poppies. I wore a vintage white lace and satin dress and very natural makeup. I wanted to marry Jamie purely, as we were, the way we saw each other.

"There are a few things I need to say before I walk you down that aisle."

I turned to see Paul, my father, looking dashing as ever in his black suit. "Hi, Dad."

"Hi, sweetheart. First of all, Jamie is a lucky man. You're beautiful and smart and you deserve to be cherished for the rest of your life. If you don't think with a hundred percent certainty that Jamie will be able to do that, then I will bust you out of here in ten seconds flat. Just say the words. There's still time," he said in the most pragmatic tone.

We both laughed. "I'm sure, Dad."

"Okay, fine. The next thing is that if you don't know with one hundred percent certainty that you will be head-over-heels in love with Jamie forever and a day, then I will do the same—I will bust you out of here. That's my job, if the need arises."

"You won't need to do that. I know what Jamie and I have."

He nodded. "Okay, now, as for you and me, I want to make a promise to you that I will be here for you, no matter what, until the day I die. Even though you met your husband before your father, it doesn't mean that you're not still my baby, and I would do anything to protect you."

"I know," I said and then kissed him on the cheek.

"You have to promise me something."

"Yes."

"When you finish polishing that manuscript, you'll send it to me first."

"I promise."

"Good, now we have a wedding to attend." He stuck his elbow out to me, and without hesitation I took his arm. I watched Jamie the moment I turned the corner. There was a magical light in his eye as I came walking down the aisle. He watched me with wonder and amazement until I reached him, and then he smiled at me so beautifully it made my legs shaky. There were no words, just a knowing exchange from my father to Jamie, two cordial smiles and a handshake.

He took my hand in his as we turned to face the officiant. Under his breath, Jamie said, "You're even more beautiful than I imagined. How is that possible?"

It took everything in me not to lean up and kiss him. Instead, I squeezed his arm and quietly said, "Thank you."

Our ceremony was like being in a bubble. I knew our loved ones were watching, but we were able to tune out the world and take each other in. I could tell when we read each other our vows that Jamie felt the same way, like we were the only people in the world.

"Katy, my angel. Since the day I met you, I've been falling in love with you, and I vow to never stop. There is nowhere else in the world I would rather be than by your side. Nowhere but here do I feel as whole and most genuinely me. I promise I will do the best by you and our children." He swallowed and his eyes began to water. "I promise that these hands will hold you with passion and thoughtfulness and warmth and respect every day for the rest of my life." I had never seen a man look so equally strong and sensitive. My lip began to quiver and my eyes filled with tears. He squeezed my hands, encouraging me to say my vows.

"Jamie, you are my light. When I found you I could finally see the leaves on the trees and the intricate details in fabric. I could finally hear the birds calling to each other. I finally felt alive. I woke up when I met you, and you've given me more than you can imagine. I promise to never take the love that exists within us for granted. I will stand by you no matter what, and I will be grateful. I will give you everything that I have inside of me for all the days of my life."

Without permission, we kissed. There were a few moments in that kiss where I lost track of where we were. His lips were so gentle but determined. When he finally broke away, he said, "I love you," as if it were the first time he had said it.

I smiled. "I love you, too." In that moment, I finally became aware of the guests as they started to clap. My sister Skylar hit the first note on the piano, which cued us to walk back down the aisle and toward the tent. We walked hand in hand, saying hi to everyone and smiling. There was thrilling energy running between me and Jamie.

Our reception was intimate and romantic. The tent was lined with white lights. Each of the long farmhouse tables had sunflowers and other wildflowers in vases running down the center. The food was impeccable, of course, thanks to Chef Mark, who had hired the best. I left the entertainment up to Jamie, so I was a little surprised that I didn't see a DJ set up. Skylar played to us through dinner, and then just before it was time to cut the cake, I turned to Jamie. "What's the entertainment?"

With no trace of humor, he said, "Karaoke, of course."

"You're kidding?" I was actually a little peeved.

"I am kidding. I wouldn't do that to you. The entertainment is my wedding gift, and it's a surprise." He smirked.

"Oh, I'll give you your gift later." I winked.

"You better. We have to consummate this marriage, you know."

"Oh, I think we've covered that."

He frowned. "You mean we're not going to . . . on our wedding night?"

"We can, but that's not my gift to you."

"You're gonna make me crazy thinking about it."

After we cut the cake, I noticed someone began setting up instruments on a little stage at the end of the tent.

Two people took the stage, and as I got closer I recognized that it was Mia and Will Ryan, a musician couple that I had been following for a few years. They had their two young sons sitting at the front of the stage, their little legs dangling over the edge. One held a tambourine and the other had some sort of shaker. Will spoke into the microphone.

"Good evening. My family and I are honored to be a part of this day." He spoke confidently and clearly as he made eye contact with Jamie and me. Mia gazed over at him with the most tranquil and loving smile. "To exist in each other's souls so strongly that you are bound without a physical tie is the greatest mark of love, and Jamie and Kate are lucky enough to be blessed with it." He held up a champagne glass, as did the rest of the guests. "May your heaven be here on earth with each other always. To Jamie and Kate!"

The whole group yelled, "To Jamie and Kate!" and clinked their glasses along with us. We kissed and then Mia took to the piano and Will picked up his guitar and they immediately went into an original upbeat song. Someone else played the bongos and another musician played the stand-up bass. The little boys played their instruments at the front of the stage as if they had done it a million times. It was a true family affair. Jamie took me in his arms, spun me around, dipped me, and then kissed me very seriously.

"What do you think?" he said after catching his breath.

"I am truly amazed. What did you have to pay to get them here?"

"They were on the West Coast and needed very little convincing. They're genuinely good people."

"Well, this is amazing."

He stared down at me, mesmerized. "I like this," he said, pointing to the wreath that held my veil. "Truly, my angel, aren't you?"

"I'll be whatever you want me to be, Jamie Lawson. I am so in love with you."

After Mia and Will wrapped up their set, we said our good-byes to them and then to the rest of the guests. Jamie seemed very eager to get back to our little house in the barn.

We walked hand in hand through the dark vineyard until we reached the single light outside the door to our home.

"Here we go," he said as he swooped me up in his arms. Once inside, he kissed me near our bed, a very tender and loving kiss. He took my veil off and set it aside while he kicked his own shoes off. He unzipped my dress slowly and cautiously. I wore a white silk and lace slip underneath. "Wow, this is even better than the black." I helped him remove his clothes and then I marveled at Jamie in all of his naked glory. There was one warm, soft light silhouetting him and shining on me. I traced his broad shoulders and defined arms. He kissed me on the mouth and traveled down until he was kissing me through the silk, down my side to my hip.

"Jamie?" I said quietly.

He was on his knees at that point as I stood in front of him.

His hands traveled up the back of my legs and slowly pulled my lace panties down. Between kisses through the silk, he said, "Yes, what is it?"

"I want to tell you about your gift."

He still had not looked up at me. He pushed me to sit on the edge of the bed and then began kissing a trail up my inner thigh. "Okay, tell me, baby," he whispered.

"You're going to be a father."

He stopped kissing and looked up at me. There was so much love in his expression. I wished that I could bottle it. "Really?" Tears quickly filled his eyes.

I smiled and began crying myself. "Yes. We're going to have a baby."

He stood up, reached for the hem of my slip, and pulled it over my head, then he moved us up onto the bed together. He kissed everywhere and then stopped near my stomach and spoke quietly. "I loved you before you existed, and I'll love you after I'm gone." I felt a tear hit my belly. He kissed it away and then looked up at me. "Thank you. I'm the happiest I've ever been."

"Me, too," I whispered.

Epilogue

Jamie

Whispers, that's what she calls them. They're signs, small sounds, or little reminders, letting you know that there's something bigger than us out there. That there's a force working hard to make things right in the universe. That's what she says, anyway. The whispers came to her in a dream. She believed that her fate was predetermined and that she had to follow these whispers or listen to what some grand power told her to do.

I've never said it to her, but I know the dream was a manifestation of something that was alive in Katy from the beginning. It came from her. It's the desire we all have in us to love and be loved. It's what lets us get our hearts broken over and over again. Maybe the force she talks about is a collective energy put out by the whole of humanity that simply says: love each other, fight for each other, take care of each other. I know I fought it out of fear, just like her. I needed to feel a force so strong that I couldn't fight back. The pull toward her was like our own world existed around us, spinning so hard that the gravity forced us to the center, to each other, into each other's arms, into each other's souls.

Katy exists in my soul now, and she can't be taken out. If there were whispers happening in my life, then they were loud and clear. Mine were shouts that came barreling at me in a tiny Toyota rental car. It crashed into me with the force of a thousand suns and never stopped crashing, over and over again. She still hasn't stopped crashing into me.

I know that now, as I watch her from across a field of vines. She takes my breath away. She's holding our baby girl, Charlotte, looking up to the sky and soaking in the sun. Every day they are both more beautiful than the last. I stand here for several moments, watching her in her white sundress. Charlotte's in white, too, and I realize that heaven does exist on earth. The wind hits the back of my neck, pushing me gently in their direction. She spots me and smiles serenely as she bounces our baby girl. When I reach them, I take Charlotte in my arms. She coos between little belly laughs.

"Someday you're going to break my heart, little girl, do you know that?" Her little smile literally makes my heart skip a beat. "It will all be worth it."

Kate and I know that there's no light without darkness—there's no joy without pain—but we promised each other, through it all, that we would always choose to be here, living in the moment, right by each other's sides. And I believe that's truly what love is.

Susan happily takes Charlotte from my hands and off for a little walk. I follow Kate into our home and catch her by the hand. She turns. I smile brazenly. "I heard a whisper, Kate. It said I need to take you to bed this instant."

She socks me in the arm. "Would you stop with that?"

"I have to listen to the whispers." I bend and throw her over my shoulder and then stalk off to our bed, with her giggling all the way.

Acknowledgments

Endless thanks to my friends and family members who have supported and encouraged me throughout this process, especially my brother, Rich, who has always had my back, even if he was making stupid faces behind it. Thanks and love you, bro.

Mom and Dad, thank you for running the grassroots campaign by taking my books into the bank and sharing the news with the bank tellers, and also for getting the Portuguese community involved. Donna, thank you for your kind words and willingness to read at the drop of a hat.

To my cousin, Debbie: thank you so much for the love, support, and encouragement.

Kristina Radi, for offering all of that fantastic Chicago material. I got such a sense of the city from you. Thank you.

Many thanks to my agent, Christina Hogrebe, who from day one believed in the work.

Angie, thank you for taking the time out of your crazy schedule to be a part of this.

Daralyn Christensen, from my entire heart I am thankful to you for so graciously sharing your story with me. You opened my eyes to diabetes and the experience of living with a diabetic partner. The details you offered helped me to grasp the disease in a way that made it tangible and real and possible for me to present through Kate's eyes.

To Roberta Bohn, for the time you took to answer my questions and for your superb Chicago inside scoops.

To my editor, Jhanteigh Kupihea, who I'm pretty sure has cloned herself at least four times. Your speed, energy, and enthusiasm have to be unmatched. Thank you for your hard work and responsiveness.

To the authors who have offered me so much advice and support, including Authors Off the Shelf, Joanna, Kylie, Kim J., Katy, Kim, Carey, and the goddesses—thank you.

To the D2 crew and the Ramies, you inspire me.

To the readers and bloggers who read and loved *Sweet Thing* and have been on the lookout for my next work, thank you so much. Your enthusiasm has kept me going all these months.

Heather, there are no words to express my gratitude. "Thank you" barely scratches the surface of what I want to say to you, but I'll start there. Thank you for being passionate about this world and for being the best signing assistant EVER! And for being a great friend and all-around awesome person. Love you.

To my boys who remind me every day how much fun it is to daydream and pretend. Thank you for not letting me grow old too fast. Thank you for being my best teachers.

Finally to Anthony, a true Renaissance Man, who can build anything, weld anything, grow anything, do anything while wearing his Converse well. Thank you for making the best coffee and for the eighteen billion other things you do.

Dear Reader,

Thank you so much for reading. I hope you enjoyed *Nowhere but Here* and would consider sharing your thoughts by writing a review on the retailer website. On the last page you can also rate *Nowhere but Here* on Facebook and Twitter. Your feedback is greatly appreciated.

For the latest news, book details, and other information, visit my official website at www .reneecarlino.com or follow me on Twitter @renayz.

Continue reading for a sneak peek at my up-coming novel *After the Rain*.

CHAPTER 1:

Healer

Avelina

Fall 2003

My middle name is Jesus. Actually it's Jesús de los Santos. In Spain, it means Jesus of the Saints; in America, it's just a really strange middle name to grow up with. My parents came to America from Spain in the early eighties so my father could go to work on his cousin's cattle ranch in Central California. To my mom and dad, America meant freedom, education, prosperity, and happiness. I was born here in '87, ten years after my brother Daniel. My mother, being a devout Catholic, continued her family's tradition by giving the daughters religious middle names. I was Avelina Jesús de los Santos Belo, which was quite a mouthful, so on school and medical records my mother shortened it to Avelina Jesús Belo. No pressure there.

Aside from putting up with the occasional jokes from classmates about my middle name, I had an otherwise idyllic childhood living on the ranch and attending the local public schools.

Since before I could remember I was riding horses and moving cattle with my father, brother, and cousins. The work was in my blood and riding horses came to me naturally, unlike making friends or doing other typical girlie things.

We had everything my parents wished for when they came here, until I turned sixteen. That's when my father was diagnosed with lung cancer. He was the first of many whom I loved but wasn't able to mend. There were no healing powers in my hands; I was just a little girl with too many hard lessons to be learned. After he passed, my mother fell apart. His memory haunted her; it made her frail. For months she sat inside the ranch house, in front of the window, looking out for someone to come and rescue her—perhaps my father's spirit, or maybe death.

I resented her for not being stronger, for not seeing how blessed she was. After my father passed, my brother dove into his own life, going to college and starting a family in New York, far away from the ranch. The horses became my friends . . . and family. I started barrel racing in rodeos and competitions to make extra money while I watched my mother wither away in front of my eyes. In my last year of high school, right after I turned eighteen, my brother made the decision to send our mother back to Spain. Daniel promised me it was for her own good and mine. He agreed to take me in so I could finish my last year of high school, which meant moving all the way to New York, living in the city with his pretentious wife, starting at a new school, and being without my horses.

I had no other options; I knew I would have to go some-where, and New York sounded like a better option than Spain at that point. Two weeks before we were supposed to move, fires began raging in Southern California, sending clouds of smoke and haze into our valley, so I took my mother with me to a rodeo in Northern California to escape the dreadful air. We trailered all four of our horses, stopping periodically and letting them graze in the beautiful, untouched land of California's Central Valley. During our drive, she spoke few words to me. She stayed hunched in the passenger seat, gazing out the window. When we traveled west to a small stretch of road where the mountains met the ocean, she sighed and said in her heavily accented English, "You are a healer. You must be. You have a gift. You've brought me home, la belleza." Beautiful, she called me. I looked exactly like her, with brown eyes too big for my head and long, dark, unruly hair.

"I'm not, mama. I'm just a girl and we're still in California," I said to her. She didn't respond—she was too far-gone. Most of the time she was despondent, then there would be the occasional nonsensical observation, and she would go back to quietly mourning my father. She existed in a grief-filled world that was off limits to the living. She existed in the past, and I knew I would never be able to help her, which made it the second time in my short life that I felt utterly powerless.

. . .

Most of that weekend she spent in the cab of our truck or the dingy motel we had rented while I got ready for the competition. I brought her meals and made sure she was okay before I went back to tending to the horses. I was scheduled to race that Saturday afternoon so I spent most of the morning watching the other events, sitting atop the corral just outside of the arena. It was a small rodeo; basically the main arena and two corrals freckled by a few sets of old, wooden bleachers. There wasn't much money in the purses at those rodeos, but it was good practice and it wasn't too far for me to drive.

During the men's team roping finals, one of the horses, saddled and waiting in the corral, sauntered over to me. She nudged my leg and sniffed at my jeans. I let her smell my shoes, and then I pushed back on the front of her face, in the space between her eyes and nose. "Go, get outta here."

As soon as the words left my lips, I heard a brief whistle meant as a call. From across the corral stood a man, his face shadowed by the large brim of his black Stetson. The mare left my side abruptly and trotted over to him. I watched as he climbed into the saddle with grace before giving the horse a subtle foot command to move forward into the arena. His team-roping partner entered from the other side. Just before the steer was released, the man looked over to me and nodded, the kind of nod that means something. It's the quiet cowboy's version of a wolf whistle. I lost my balance on the top of the corral and wobbled just for a moment before smiling back at him.

Instantly, the steer was out of the chute followed by the men, one from each side. They roped the speeding little creature in five-point-five seconds. It was fast, very fast but not fast enough to win. I fully expected to see two sulking cowboys trot back to the gate, but there was only one who passed me looking totally defeated. The other, the man in the black Stetson, was smiling and riding toward me.

As he approached with the reins and lasso in his left hand, he removed his hat with his right. He was so much younger than I expected and he was grinning emphatically. Two deep dimples appeared on the sides of his boyish cheeks. "Hey there, you distracted me," he said, still smiling.

"I'm sorry," I mumbled.

"I'm kidding. I picked me a dragger. We didn't have a chance." His voice was smooth and confident. He was referring to fact that the steer wouldn't lift his hind legs to be roped.

"Good thing, I thought I blew it for you."

"It takes more than a gorgeous woman perched on a fence to throw me off my game," he said, placing his hat back on his head. I never thought of myself as gorgeous or even a woman, for that matter. My heart leapt and bounced inside my chest. He maneuvered his horse through the gate, hopped off, and led her into the corral where she came up to me again. "Bonnie likes you." He laughed. "You're the only one, besides me."

I stepped down and began helping him remove her saddle and bridle. "She's a fine horse."

"She's a baby, a little too eager, but she'll learn." He said it almost to himself.

"Bonnie, huh? Cute name. Are you Clyde?" I asked.

He smiled. "Oh, excuse me, ma'am." He removed his hat again. "Where are my manners? I'm Jake McCrea." He reached his hand out.

"Avelina Belo."

"Beautiful and exotic name. It suits you." The corner of his mouth turned up into a handsome smirk. His eyes were the most vibrant blue. In the sunlight it looked like little electrical currents circled his pupils.

"Thank you," I said but found myself at a loss for more words. His compliment woke some feeling in me I had never had. I was never interested in dating. I never thought of myself as attractive. That tingly feeling girls get long before they're eighteen finally hit me like a million pulses of light striking my chest and moving south.

"What's a girl like you hanging around the corrals for?"

I hesitated. "Like me?"

"Yeah, like you?"

"I'm racing." I pulled my phone from my back pocket and

checked the time. "Oh, shoot. I'm going on in twenty minutes. I gotta warm up my horse and change."

"I can warm up your horse, just point me in the right direction."

"She's the Appaloosa, right over there. The one trying to bite that kid."

He followed my gaze to where Dancer was stretching her neck through the corral slats, trying to bite the arm of a young kid who was leaning back. Jake whistled to call her over, but Dancer ignored him. He glanced over to me with a questioning look.

"Dancer." I said just above a whisper. She pinned her ears before turning and trotting toward me.

"Huh." Jake said, shaking his head. "Never seen that before."

I led her out of the corral to the back of the trailer and began dressing her for the race.

"She has great lines." He smoothed a hand over her spotted flank.

"Most people think she's ugly.

"No, she's beautiful." He was stroking the horse but looking right into my eyes when he said it.

My heartbeat spiked. "You can just take her around a couple of times while I change. She tires fast."

"Okay," he said as he worked to lengthen the stirrup. He lifted himself into the saddle, and Dancer immediately bucked. He sat firm in his seat, clearly a great horseman. Pulling the reins tighter he caused Dancer to trot back a few steps. She swished her tail and then pricked her ears up with irritation. Jake leaned down and spoke to her in a smooth tone. "Easy now. You're not gonna embarrass me in front of this pretty lady, are you?"

"She always takes the third barrel too wide. I can't break her of it, just so you know."

Dancer trotted in place, anxious to run toward the practice barrels. "How can you win if she's always making mistakes?" Jake asked, smiling.

"She's fast enough."

"We'll see." He gave her a tight squeeze with his boot heels and off they went.

I changed quickly into my competition shirt, jeans, and boots, and within five minutes he was back. Dancer was warm, but Jake looked downright worn out.

"You okay, cowboy?" I smiled up at him.

There was a glistening stream of sweat dripping down his sideburns. He jumped off and handed me the reins before removing his hat and brushing his dirty-blond hair back. He let out a huge breath. "Man, she's a mean bitch, full of piss and vinegar, that one. I don't know how you race that horse, skittering around like that. She didn't take the third barrel wide, she practically tossed me over it."

I laughed. "You'll see." I took the reins, hopped up into the saddle and headed toward the arena. "This is no roping horse. She dances on air," I shouted back to him.

He was right; she was a hard horse to handle but not when I rode her. I got to the gate opening just as they called my number. The buzzer rang and we were off. I bent low into her body as Dancer raced toward the first barrel. She rounded it with perfect ease, and then we were off to the second barrel and then the third, which she took just a bit wider than perfect. It was an improvement. I kicked her hard and smacked the end of the reins back and forth against her shoulders. She picked up and flew home to the gate, barely touching her hooves to the ground.

As I glanced toward the time clock, the announcer called my score. I won.

After collecting my prize I headed back to the stable where my truck and trailer were parked. Jake was sitting on the tailgate, laughing as I approached.

"You got something good there, honey?" he asked.

I held up my trophy and shook it in the air. "I won three hundred dollars!"

"Are you telling me you're gonna take me out for a beer to celebrate?"

I swallowed hard as I looked down at him from atop Dancer. I shook my head slightly, and then tried desperately to peel my eyes away from him. He had changed into a clean pair of Wranglers and a white button-down shirt. Still wearing a confident grin, he swung his legs back and forth playfully on the tailgate.

When I jumped down to remove the saddle and bridle, he came around and put his hand over mine. "I was kidding. Not about the beer but about buying. I'd like to take you out for a proper dinner. Can I do that?"

He squeezed my hand, gazing into my eyes, waiting for my answer.

"My mom is at our motel. I'm . . . only eighteen." My voice shook embarrassingly.

"Oh, well, I only just turned twenty-one." He smiled. "I'm far away from my home in Montana, doing the rodeo circuit through California. It's just me and my roping partner, so it gets kind of lonely." I could tell he meant lonely in the genuine sense, not in a sexual way. "Maybe you can bring her along? You both need to eat, right?"

"Okay," I said to Jake McCrea, just three short months before I married him.